RIGHT CROSS

A DAN RENO NOVEL

DAVE STANTON

LaSalle Davis Books

ALSO BY DAVE STANTON

Stateline

Dying for the Highlife

Speed Metal Blues

Dark Ice

Hard Prejudice

The Doomsday Girl

FOR MORE INFORMATION, VISIT DAVE STANTON'S WEBSITE:

DanRenoNovels.com

For Chuck and Trish,
the Duke & Duchess of Campbell

1

It was four in the morning, and I'd spent the last hour awake in bed. I finally gave up on sleep and walked through the darkness to my kitchen table. I sat staring through the large window in the family room, looking out at the snow-covered meadow behind my house. The white fields glowed in the scant moonlight, and farther out the eastern ridge of the Sierra ran in a jagged silhouette against the night sky. Spring had come, but the mornings still dipped into the twenties.

Candi, now my fiancée and three months pregnant, seemed to have no problem sleeping, but recently I'd become a regular nocturnal sojourner to places outside our bedroom. Sometimes I'd even dress and leave the house, to secure the perimeter and pace the predawn streets. Why my sleep was disrupted, I didn't know, but I'd fallen into the habit of embracing a certain narrative during my restless hours in bed. I'd think of evil regimes and the tyrants who ruled unfortunate corners of the earth. I'd review their crimes against humanity, their heinous and sadistic acts against the powerless citizens they subjugated. And then I'd invest myself in elaborate planning to not only bring down these dictatorships, but to exact retribution on the despots, as if this would restore balance in the world.

My fantasies were no doubt perverse in their violence, and also infeasible and hopeless. But on rare occasions, the worst that spew from the fetid bowels of our gene pool get some degree of payback. The best example I knew of was Saddam Hussein, whose genocidal barbarity included chemical gassing. Upon his capture and conviction, Hussein requested his execution be by firing squad, which he considered the most painless and dignified way to exit the world. He was denied this concession—instead, his captors taunted him, then tightened a noose around his neck and dropped him from the gallows. But given that Hussein was responsible for the murder of over half a million people, it hardly seemed adequate.

I closed my eyes and let my head lull forward. If the grim inventions of my mind provided solace and helped me sleep, I'd neither question nor resist the indulgence. After all, my semi-slumberous visions were like passing clouds in the night. In the light of day, my thoughts would turn positive. I'd think about my life with Candi and what fatherhood would mean to me. I'd think about making a living and providing comfort and safety to my family. I'd not dwell upon the trajectory of my career as a private investigator, nor on the criminals who'd died by my hand. Nor would I revisit my father's death by a felon who lacked the intelligence to graduate from high school. My frame of mind was something I could choose, and my choice was to think positively and be happy on a daily basis.

That's what I kept telling myself.

.   .   .

Later that morning, I was parking at the gym off Highway 50 when my cell rang. The screen displayed an anonymous number, and I didn't recognize the area code. Probably a solicitor with a bogus free vacation offer, I thought. I'd been getting a lot of those calls recently, even though I'd submitted my number to the Federal Trade Commission's Do Not Call Registry. I sat behind my wheel, turned the engine off, and accepted the call. I was ready to immediately hang up.

"Yes?"

"Is this Dan Reno Investigations?" The voice was male, with an accent I couldn't quite identify.

I cleared my throat. "Yes, Dan Reno speaking."

"My name is Luis Alvarez. I'm interested in hiring an investigator."

"For what purpose?"

"Are you not a private investigator?"

"My license is up to date, if that's what you're asking."

"I see," he said after a moment. "Okay, I'm looking for my nephew. He's gone missing. Do you handle this sort of thing?"

I stared out my windshield at the pine needles stamped into the snow-pack along the walkway to the gym. "Yes. Would you like to schedule a meeting?"

"As soon as possible, please. Where is your office?"

"Are you in South Lake Tahoe?"

"No. My wife and I are in Reno."

"Well, it's a nice day for a drive. I'm about an hour and fifteen minutes south of Reno."

"Ah, I didn't realize."

"Where are you from, Mr. Alvarez?"

"I live in Miami."

I looked at my watch. "I'm available at one o'clock, if you like."

"Where should I meet you?"

I tapped my steering wheel. Renting office space was not something I'd ever done. My options for client meetings were casinos, restaurants, or bars.

"Zeke's Pit on Highway 50. It's a restaurant on the main drag of South Lake Tahoe."

"I'll find the address."

.   .   .

I didn't contemplate what Luis Alvarez's case might entail as I pounded out eight sets of heavy bench press, followed by curls with a ninety-pound bar and ten sets of seated cable rows. Then I spent half an hour on the heavy bag, perfecting some new kicks I'd learned from the cage fighters I sparred with every Wednesday at Rex's Gym in Carson City.

The two-hour workout drained me physically, but left my head clear, as if the exercise dissolved whatever tension might be lurking in my gray matter. I drove home and turned the shower as hot as I could stand it, then put on fresh jeans, a collared shirt, and my steel-toed work boots, which were stout but flexible enough to allow me to run at a full sprint.

Candi was at work teaching art at the local community college, so the house was empty except for Smokey, the gray fuzz-ball cat Candi had brought home shortly after she moved in. As I put on my black coat, the cat reached up and took hold of my leg, her claws latching onto my jeans. She looked up at me with her green eyes and meowed.

"Okay, Smokes," I said, and poured some food into her bowl. Then I grabbed a pad of paper from the cabinet in the spare bedroom that served as my office and went out to my garage, where my faithful Nissan pickup truck waited.

I'd bought the truck after my previous vehicle, a Nissan sedan, had been destroyed when the brake lines were cut. I was on Highway 80 outside of Truckee when the brakes failed, then I was rammed off the Interstate and down a 250-foot canyon. I survived with minor injuries, but the car was reduced to scrap metal. Out of nostalgic loyalty, and also because the car had been reliable, I replaced it with another Nissan.

I backed out of my garage and drove toward Lake Tahoe Boulevard. The houses in my neighborhood were a Bohemian mix of older log cabins and recently remodeled homes. Some were painted turquoise, yellow, or pink, in contrast to the dark hue of the cabins. All were shadowed by ponderosa pines, but the sun was high and the pavement was streaked with runoff.

A minute later I reached the main drag and turned left. I drove past a discount gas station, an auto parts store, a 7-Eleven, and Whiskey Dick's, the bar closest to my house, about a fifteen-minute walk. A block later I turned into the parking lot for Zeke's Pit. The lot was plowed, but the asphalt was badly rutted. I still owned a small stake in the joint after bailing out the primary owner, Zach Papas, when he was circling the drain at the tail end of a six-month cocaine binge. I made the investment because I didn't want to see

Zeke's funky, ramshackle, Old-West ambiance replaced by whatever commercial vision new ownership might have. Plus, I considered Zach Papas' recipe for Texas brisket, along with his barbecue chicken, a local treasure.

Parked among the dozen or so American-made SUVs and Subarus in front of Zeke's was a Hyundai sedan. The license plate frame advertised a car rental company.

I went through the heavy wooden door into the saloon. The scent of hickory smoke from the open pit in the adjoining dining room was thick. I spotted Luis Alvarez and his wife right away. They were sitting at a cocktail table in front of the bar, facing the door. The room's only other occupants were three day drinkers parked on stools, nursing pitchers of beer. Alvarez and his wife looked at me and waited.

"Dan Reno," I said, extending my hand. Luis Alvarez rose partially from his chair and we shook. His hand was large, almost the size of mine, but it was soft and not calloused.

"Ma'am," I said, nodding at the woman at the table. She nodded back, but did not introduce herself.

"My wife, Claudia," Alvarez said. His accent was definitely Spanish, but the dialect was different than the Mexican version common in California. I sat across from them and said, "What can I do for you?"

"It's about my nephew, Manuel. He was driving here from Miami, and we were supposed to meet him last week. But I can't reach him by phone, and I have no idea what happened to him."

"Where were you supposed to meet him?"

"In Reno."

"I see," I said, studying the man. His torso was thick and muscular, but his face was round and pudgy. His complexion was pitted and much lighter in color than his brown forearms. His hair was black and curly, and a deep scar in the shape of a half-circle, like the letter C, was planted between his eyes, almost like a brand of some sort.

"When exactly were you supposed to meet him?" I asked.

"A week ago today."

"What happens when you call his cell?"

"It goes straight to voice mail, as if the phone is turned off."

Alvarez sat erect, his feet flat on the wooden floor, his hairless forearms resting on the table. The woman he introduced as his wife was staring at me. She was tall and slender, her hair silky black, her eyes small for her face. She wore a blue, padded winter vest over a long-sleeved shirt that clung to her shoulders. The vest obscured her bust, but I could tell her chest was unnaturally heavy for her gracile physique. Her fingernails were cut short, but they had the shine of a professional manicure. I could see lighter bands of pigment on a few of her fingers, as if she usually wore rings but had removed them, except for a small diamond on her left ring finger.

"Why was he driving from Miami to Reno?" I addressed the question to Luis Alvarez, then shifted my eyes to Claudia. Her lips parted and she blinked.

"Manuel is a young man," Alvarez said. "A restless spirit, like many men in their early twenties. He wanted to move west, to live, to work, to seek his fortune."

"Was he driving alone?"

"No, he was with a group of young people," Alvarez said with a sigh. "I did not know them, but one of them owned a small Ford bus. Manuel said they were traveling together, all planning to get jobs out west."

"Do you have any of their names? Any phone numbers?"

"No, unfortunately. Manuel wasn't living with us, and I don't know the names of his friends."

"Were they all male?"

"No, I think it was a man and two women. I'm not sure about it, though."

"Was one his girlfriend?"

"I don't exactly know."

"I see. What kind of work was Manuel doing in Miami?"

"Odd jobs. A variety of things."

"Why were you going to meet him?"

"His parents died when he was young. Claudia and I have been supporting him ever since. I wanted to help him get established, you know."

"I'm sorry about your brother."

Alvarez's brow pinched and he tilted his head. "What?"

"Manuel is your nephew. Your brother was his father, right?"

I saw Claudia's eyes dart, and she moved her hand from the table to her lap.

Alvarez pulled the front of his fleece jacket to better situate the collar around his neck. The jacket was an inexpensive brand sold at grocery stores in the region.

"My brother died a long time ago." He set his jaw and rested his eyes on mine.

"When was the last time you talked to Manuel?"

"It was a week ago today, at two P.M. He called and said he was an hour outside of Reno."

"Do you have any idea what happened to him?" I asked.

"If we did, we'd surely tell you," Claudia Alvarez said. Her voice was soft, and her accent was elegant, as if she came from an upper cultural echelon. But it seemed overdone, and I suspected it may have been an affectation manufactured to hide her true origin.

"Did he know anyone out here?"

"Not that I'm aware. Sir, are you available for hire?" Alvarez said, his eyes flickering, the impatience plain in his voice.

"I am," I said, placing my folder on the table. "This is my work contract. Since you're from out of town, I'll require a retainer."

"What does that mean?"

"Money up front. Two thousand."

Alvarez and his wife exchanged glances, then she moved her hand onto the table, and Luis rested his on top of it, as if to show their mutual commitment.

"It's a lot of money," she said. "But our nephew is very important to us. Please find him for us."

"Yes," Luis added, "But when you do, please don't alert him to your presence. I don't know what he's gotten himself into, but he has a lot of pride, and might be too ashamed to accept our help. Please simply locate him, then immediately call me."

"All right," I said.

.　　.　　.

Ten minutes later the Alvarezes left, after declining my suggestion that they try the dining room for lunch. I moved to the table on the raised stage, looked out the big plate glass window facing the boulevard, and watched them drive away in their rental car. Before they did, I snapped a picture of the license plate.

Once they were gone, I sat in the broad shaft of sunlight pouring in from the window. In my pocket were twenty crisp one hundred dollar bills. Luis Alvarez had insisted on paying in cash. He'd also provided a sheet of paper with a picture of Manuel, a face shot, and shared that Manuel was twenty-two years old, five-foot-nine, about 160 pounds, and spoke passable English. When I asked about hobbies, Alvarez shrugged, and said, "He knows boats."

I opened my notepad to a clean page and set Manuel's picture in front of me. His face was square and his features were small, including his ears. The tone of his skin was darker than that of many black men I knew. I didn't see the slightest family resemblance between him and Luis Alvarez. As for his expression, it was blank. I saw no sign of happiness, despair, insecurity, irreverence, or confidence.

For a moment my eyes settled on the dust motes floating up from the floorboards. Then I pulled up a U.S. map on my phone and tracked the most logical freeway route from Miami to Reno. The shortest distance option was the most southern path, which led through Dallas and Albuquerque and into Las Vegas. From there, Route 95 headed north through Nevada's eastern Mojave Desert and into the higher elevations of the Great Basin Desert, to the small city of Fallon, which was 63 miles due east of Reno. I'd passed through it before, when driving across the desert to Utah.

The other potential route from Miami was 79 miles longer, but Google Maps estimated it was an hour less driving time. It led north through Nashville and Kansas City and across Wyoming, then followed Interstate 80 into Salt Lake City. From there, it was a simple matter of staying on 80, past the Bonneville Salt Flats and into Nevada. The road bisected the Great Basin Desert, passing through Elko, where I'd first met Candi almost three years ago, to Winnemucca, and then to Lovelock, which was 90 miles northeast of Reno.

I put my phone down and considered the most practical starting point for my investigation. Luis Alvarez and his wife Claudia, if those were their real names, and if they were actually married, were not typical clients. For one, they claimed to be from Miami, a place on the opposite side of the country and somewhere I'd never visited. It was also unusual they paid me in cash, on the spot. In today's era of electronic commerce, I didn't know anyone who carried more than a few hundred dollars on their person.

"Anything interesting out there?" a female voice said. I turned from the window and nodded at Liz, who had walked out from behind the bar. I'd met her when I moved from San Jose to Tahoe four years ago. She wore a half-shirt to expose her slim, tanned waist and the silver hoop in her belly button. The nipples on her small breasts were pointy against the material. I'd never known Liz to wear a bra.

"Maybe so," I said.

"Who were those people?"

"Clients."

"From the Dominican Republic?" She folded a towel and began wiping down a table.

"Why would you say that?"

"They were talking in Spanish before you got here. I don't think they knew I could understand them. She mentioned something about the Dominican. The man told the woman to keep quiet and just do as he said. It sounded kind of demeaning."

When I didn't reply, Liz said, "You want a beer or anything?"

"Later," I said, walking out to my truck.

. . .

Back at my house, I sat at the metal army surplus desk in my spare bedroom and ran a people search on Manuel Alvarez. The search engine generated a list of forty-six people with that name. Eleven were deceased, and twenty more were at least fifty years old. Of the remaining fifteen, only two showed Miami addresses. One was thirty-five years old, the other thirty-one. The only twenty-two-year-old had an address in San Diego. I pulled up his details and found a picture. He looked nothing like the picture Luis Alvarez had provided.

I rubbed my fist at the smooth metal where the green paint had faded from the edge of my desk. The subscription people finder service I used was fairly reliable. The only way an individual could avoid a listing was to have no public footprint. That meant no record of owning or renting property, no utility accounts, no loans from banks or mainstream lending institutions, and no history of paying income taxes. While it was possible a man in his early twenties could have stayed off the grid, it was unlikely.

Next I ran a search for Luis Alvarez, and then Claudia Alvarez. When neither name matched any profile in the online database, I shook my head, and considered if I should call the number Luis Alvarez had given me, and tell him to come pick up his two grand.

I pulled the bills from my pocket and set them on my desk. I'd half-expected the man who went by Luis Alvarez to reject my requirement for prepayment. Maybe I'd hoped he would take issue and walk out in a huff with the silky-haired woman. It wouldn't have bothered me if they did, because, at a minimum, I like to know the real names of my clients. If someone has reason to hide their identity, who knows what trouble might lurk behind?

"Beggars and choosers," I mumbled. It wasn't as if I had my pick of jobs. That was the reality of living in a town like South Lake Tahoe. My opportunities for a paycheck tended to be sporadic. If I passed on a job, it could be weeks before another presented itself.

I repressed a sigh and opened the safe hidden in my closet. I tossed the bills in, then returned to my desk and called the number for South Lake Tahoe PD.

"Marcus Grier, please," I said.

"The sheriff's not available at this time. Who's calling?"

"Meg, its Dan Reno."

"Oh. You want me to tell him you called?"

"No, that's all right. I'll try him later."

I hung up and dialed Sheriff Grier's cell phone. He'd told me to only use it for emergencies, and always acted annoyed when I ignored that prerequisite. But our shared history afforded me a certain latitude.

"Yes, Dan?" he said, his voice a low rumble.

"Afternoon, Marcus. I've been hired to find a missing person, a twenty-two-year-old male from Miami named Manuel Alvarez. He was driving here from Miami and was last heard from a week ago, an hour outside of Reno. Have you heard anything?"

"Doesn't ring a bell."

"I'm thinking, maybe he got in a fatal accident."

"Where?"

"I don't know. Somewhere east of Reno."

"Then why don't you call Reno PD?"

"Because they don't like me."

"I can't imagine why."

"You haven't heard anything, huh?"

"Why don't you try your old buddy DeHart in Carson City? You're still on speaking terms with him, aren't you?"

"Somewhat, I guess."

"Good luck," he said.

2

Lieutenant DeHart had once locked me up for two days, hoping I'd implicate myself in a case that left four dead bodies on his beat. I'd waited him out, and although he finally conceded I was innocent of any crime, he made it clear he didn't owe me any favors. I doubted he'd take or return my call unless he had a good reason to do so.

The days were getting longer, and if I left right away I could make it to Fallon by four P.M. That would be the most likely place Manuel Alvarez was when he last spoke to the man who'd hired me. It was a two-hour drive from South Lake Tahoe.

A few minutes later I drove past the high-end resorts and retail store fronts on the California side of the border, then crossed the state line into Nevada. I passed the glittery casinos under a sun high in the spring sky. Between the buildings, the lake looked like a sheet of blue glass. The temperature had risen to sixty for the first time this year, and tourists were on the sidewalks without coats. I steered around the east side of the lake, through the narrow tunnel at Cave Rock, and then sped around the curves until 50 veered east toward Spooner Pass. The alpine landscape receded, the tall evergreens replaced by the sagebrush-dotted brown hills of the high desert. The sky's brightness faded to a pallid blue.

It wasn't until I cleared the sweeping summit and started downhill to the Carson Valley that I remembered to call Candi and leave her a message saying I'd be home late. It wasn't intuitive for me to account for my whereabouts. But it was a habit I needed to develop to maintain my relationship, I reminded myself. Especially since Candi was pregnant.

Years ago, my first marriage had gone up in smoke like dry pine in a bonfire. I never blamed anyone but myself for it. The self-destructive drunk binge I'd embarked on as a salve for my guilt over killing a man was nothing more than an excuse to be selfish and immature, exacerbated by a notion that there was something romantic and noble about boozing myself into oblivion.

Now, whenever I feel the urge to wrap myself around a bottle, I remember what I'd learned during those dark days. The memory serves a purpose. But that doesn't mean I'm without my weak moments.

I came off the grade and turned left onto Carson City's commercial thoroughfare, then headed east. Six miles later I drove past the cathouses in Mound House and Dayton, and then I entered the deserted vastness of The Great Basin Desert. The two-lane highway known as "The Loneliest Road in America" led straight into the horizon, splitting the brown flats, the landscape featureless except for tumbleweed, dry grass, and low, distant ridges.

I drove past the exit for Stagecoach, Nevada, then stopped and used the restroom at the Silver Springs Nugget Casino. Then I sped east for another twenty minutes before slowing at the Fallon city limits. Like many small towns in the sparsely populated West, there was no exit for Fallon; the highway simply became the main drag.

Once I reached the intersection where Route 50 intersected 95 at Taylor Street, I pulled over and parked at a Jack in the Box. If Manuel Alvarez had indeed driven through Fallon, he would have passed through this stop light.

At 4000 feet in elevation, the late afternoon temperature had already started to drop. I put on my coat and walked through the brisk air into the fast food restaurant. The teenage girl behind the counter had short black hair, a ring in her nose, and tattoos on her forearms. When I approached, I caught a faint whiff of reefer.

She looked up at me with eyes surrounded by too much makeup. Her face was pale and when she spoke I could see a small chip in her front tooth.

"May I take your order?"

"Just a coffee," I said, putting my manila file next to the register. "I'm searching for a missing person. Have you ever seen this guy?"

She stopped and stared down at the open folder. "I don't think so."

"Would have been here about a week ago, in the afternoon. Were you working then?"

She put her finger on her chin and rolled her eyes to the ceiling. "I don't remember," she said.

Behind her, a man in a white shirt and necktie walked by. "Excuse me," I said.

"Yes?" He was plump and balding and had a wispy mustache that looked silly on his fleshy face.

"This man is missing, and he may have stopped here a week ago. Does he look familiar?"

"No, sir," he said after a moment.

"You're sure?"

His small eyes met mine. "I can't tell if he's black or Mexican. But I'd remember if I saw him. I'm good with faces."

The girl placed a steaming paper cup in front of me. "Thanks for your help," I said, but when I turned to leave, two men who'd come in after me blocked my way.

"Missing person?" one said. He was in his twenties, and he and his partner both wore one-piece camouflage uniforms.

"Yeah." I held up the single picture I had of Manuel Alvarez. They both studied the photo, and shook their heads.

"Never seen him," one said.

"He's definitely not from the base," the other said.

"The base?"

"The Fallon Naval Air Station. A few miles that way." He pointed out the window.

I nodded. "Thanks, men."

"Yes, sir."

Outside, I looked across the street at a cheap hotel and a chain drug store. Then I got back in my truck and drove west toward Reno. I stopped at six fast food joints and three gas stations before reaching the edge of town. Not a single person recognized the man in the photo I carried.

It was past five P.M., and I figured I'd make one last stop before heading home. I drove back east and turned onto Maine Street, then parked at a red roofed, white stucco building with a flagpole out front. From outside, the Churchill County Sheriff's office looked clean and more modern than I expected for a small town police facility.

Inside though, it had the same dreary and depressing ambience that all cop shops have. This was a place where people came to sort out the aftermath of criminal misconduct. In the case of those who came forcibly, they were usually cuffed and sometimes injured from altercations with law enforcement officers. They were escorted with little ceremony into the bowels of the building, to holding cells with open toilets. To the uninitiated, this was the first sense of what the revocation of their freedom meant.

For those who came to report crimes, they were required to wait in lines and fill out paperwork, and then were spoken to in monotone voices by police representatives who sometimes viewed victims and perpetrators with equal suspicion. These interviews often involved repeated questions from detectives in an effort to catch the victim in inconsistencies or outright lies. More commonly though, the aggrieved were allowed to state their complaints without interruption to officers who were stifling yawns and counting the minutes to quitting time.

Of course, not all police officers are weary and cynical. Those new on the job might view their roles as that of public servants. But after enough experience with the criminal element, an officer either becomes hardened and dispassionate, or they opt for a different career. Such is the nature of a job that requires daily interaction with the worst that humanity has to offer.

As soon as I stepped into the lobby, I heard raised voices and saw a wiry man struggling with two uniformed cops. The man had long, scraggly hair and dirty clothes and looked like he might be homeless. But he had an angry, kinetic gleam in his eyes, and he seemed to easily evade the officers' efforts to cuff him.

"You fat fuckin' shit hog, take your dirty paws off me," the man hissed, spinning and flailing his arms. He twisted away from a pudgy cop, and the back of his fist caught the other cop, a man in his fifties, flush in the nose. It was a solid shot, the smack of bone on flesh loud, and the officer sunk to his knees. In an instant the man grabbed for the pudgy officer's holster. The cop grabbed the assailant's wrist with both hands, straining to keep possession of his weapon. The cop's round face was tomato-red, and he tried to stomp the man's foot, but the man avoided the move and kicked the cop hard in the shin. I saw the policeman's eyes go round with pain, while the older cop was still on his knees, holding his nose, blood seeping from around his fingers.

I was already moving forward when the portly cop yelled, "Help me!" His voice sounded as if he was expending his last reserve of energy.

Both the combatants looked at me as I approached. The crazed man seemed to summon a burst of strength as he pulled on the officer's handgun. Right as I got there, I saw the barrel clear the holster.

Since the man's hands were not free to block a punch, I was at an advantage. But I had to make the strike count, because at any moment he might tear the pistol from the cop's grasp. I could smell an odd stink on the beleaguered cop, as if desperation was seeping out of his fleshy pores.

My first punch was a straight left, aimed at the wiry man's jaw. This is the surest chance at a knockout blow; a hook or uppercut, while generating more power, is less accurate and easier to evade. Best to use the jab.

I executed the blow perfectly, and the man's head snapped back as if on a spring. He should have gone down like a sack of wet manure. But he didn't.

For a moment he stared at me, his eyes wild with fury. I had an instant to consider whether he was just incredibly hard-headed, or whacked out of his mind on angel dust. Probably both, I concluded, as I cocked my hips and threw a right hook. My fist slammed into his face like a sledgehammer. Blood spewed from his nostrils, and he staggered back and collapsed against the wall, then sat staring at me, dumbfounded but plenty conscious.

I stared back, amazed I hadn't knocked him out. I looked at my knuckles and wondered if I'd lost my punch. "The only place you can't hurt him is the head," I muttered.

Arms shaking and sweating profusely, the pudgy officer aimed his gun at the sitting man. The older cop with the busted nose staggered to his feet and drew his weapon. At that moment two more uniforms rushed in from a back entrance.

I picked up my manila folder and stood back while the four cops cuffed the man and pulled him to his feet.

"I'd get him some medical attention," I said.

"I'd kick your ass in a fair fight," the man said, spitting blood in my direction.

• • •

Twenty minutes later I was in an interview room, seated across from the fleshy cop and a person about fifty who wore a wide-brimmed cowboy hat and smelled of chewing tobacco. He hadn't introduced himself by title, but it was clear he was in charge, probably the captain of the Fallon police department.

"I suppose I owe you thanks," he said.

"Your man asked for help. It looked like he needed it."

The pudgy cop sputtered something unintelligible, then straightened in his chair. "True enough," he said.

"You work out of South Lake," the captain said, holding my business card between his fingers. "You got business in Nevada?"

17

"I'm working on a missing person. He may have come through Fallon about a week ago."

The captain's eyes were hidden below his gray brows, but when he spoke the disinterest was plain in his voice. "Lots of folks pass through here."

I pulled the picture of Manuel Alvarez from my pocket.

"He was a passenger in a Ford minibus," I said, pushing the sheet of paper across the table.

"A minibus," he said, staring at the picture.

"Yeah. Supposedly he was with a man and two women, so four people total in the vehicle."

He grunted and rubbed at the stubble on his big chin. Then he said, "Harry, we're good here. Why don't you go make sure Louis is okay?" The cop rose with a grunt and left the room.

"You got a name for this guy?" the captain said, raising his head and eyeing me as if I was complicit in something distasteful, if not outright illegal.

"Manuel Alvarez. He was driving from Miami, headed to Reno."

"That right?"

"That's what I was told."

He jabbed at the picture with a large, grizzled finger. "I'm gonna refer you to Sheriff Swearingen, up the road in Fernley."

"Why?"

The captain removed his hat and ran his hand over his wiry gray hair. "Because that's where a Ford minibus was found."

"Abandoned?"

"Not exactly."

I opened my hands and turned my wrists outward. "What, then?"

"The driver was still at the wheel, a stab wound in his neck. He'd bled out hours before they found him."

·　　·　　·

The sun was low on the horizon by the time I'd driven the fifteen miles northwest to Fernley. At about 20,000, their population was roughly double that of Fallon's, but that didn't make Fernley any more memorable. The inexpensive chain hotels, fast food restaurants, and nondescript buildings on the main drag were devoid of personality, as if a bored city planner deemed that anyone who'd live in this desolate patch of desert wouldn't care.

The man who met me in the lobby of the single-story police station had black hair too long for a cop's. It was combed back behind his ears and errant locks streaked with gray covered the back of his neck. There were deep circles under his eyes and his complexion was dark with five o'clock shadow. He did not wear a hat.

"Lonnie Swearingen," he said. "Fallon told me to expect you."

I handed him my business card, along with Manuel Alvarez's photo. The folds in the paper were wearing thin. "This man may have been in your minibus," I said.

"You've been hired to find him?"

"Right."

"By who?"

"A man claiming to be his uncle. Said his name is Luis Alvarez. But I ran a people search and couldn't find a match."

"Come on back," Swearingen said, and I followed him through a card-activated door and down a hallway to a copy machine. He had a bit of a gut and was noticeably bowlegged, but he moved with the grace of an ex-athlete. He printed a copy, and when I asked him to print me a half-dozen, he did so without comment. Then we turned a corner and entered his office.

He sat at his desk and motioned for me to sit across from him. "We still don't have an ID on the driver," he said, peering at me with dark eyes.

"He was murdered?"

"He didn't stab himself."

"How about prints in the bus?"

"All over the place. But not a single print came up in the federal data-base."

"Any luggage?"

"Nothing."

We fell silent and I stared out his office window at where the small sun was descending behind a brown ridgeline ten miles or so beyond the sagebrush-dotted plains.

"What did the driver look like?" I asked.

"About six feet, medium build, probably around forty. Mexican would be my guess."

"What kind of vehicle was it?" I asked.

Lonnie Swearingen opened his drawer and withdrew a stack of papers. He flipped through them for a moment before stopping. "1999 Ford E450 16-passenger Minibus." He paused, then added, "A big, gas guzzling, bucket of bolts."

"Where is it?"

"In our impound yard."

"Mind if I take a look at it?"

Swearingen grimaced, looked at his watch, then shrugged. "Sure, if we make it quick."

We walked out the front of the building, huddled in our coats against the dry cold. I followed Swearingen to a chain-link, barbwire-topped fence behind the station. I saw the Ford right away. It was one of three vehicles sitting in the dirt lot. Next to it was a wrecked Dodge Charger, its front tires flat, the metal rusting where the paint was flaking from the mangled hood. The other vehicle was a mud coated all-terrain three-wheeler.

The Ford looked like it started as a commercial grade truck, and was repurposed for passenger duty. An enclosure with rows of windows was mounted behind the cab, and its width looked disproportionate to the chassis. To accommodate the weight, the rear axle was a dual tire ensemble, two tires per side. The minibus was white with blue pinstripes, but it was so dirty it could have been mistaken for beige.

Swearingen turned a key and released the padlock on the gate, and we walked to the vehicle. He climbed into the cab, pulled on a lever, and the glass door to the passenger section swung open with a hissing screech. I stepped inside and looked at four rows of seats separated by a middle aisle. A light in the ceiling came on.

"Looking for anything specific?" Swearingen asked.

"Not really. Just trying to picture it."

"Picture what?"

"Manuel Alvarez and three others from Miami, driving this heap across the country."

"You sure they were coming from Miami?" he asked.

"That's what I was told. And the rig has Florida plates."

"First thing we did was run the plates. The vehicle was sold two months ago by a private party in Orlando. The new owner never registered it."

"How about the deceased?"

"We fingerprinted and took pictures of him, and sent it all to the Florida State Police. No record of him, missing or otherwise."

"Well, he's only been dead a week, right?"

"Six days now, since we found him last Thursday morning."

"He wasn't carrying ID?" I asked.

"No wallet or phone. Not even a book of matches."

"Any scars, tattoos, or disfigurements that could help identify him?"

"He was tattooed, but nothing gang-related or unique."

I walked down the aisle, peering at each bench seat, then I ran my hands in the creases between a seat and its back, hoping to find a lost article.

"I already did that," Swearingen said. "Didn't find a thing."

"So, the driver was found dead in the driver's seat?"

"Yeah." We walked to the front of the bus, to a rectangular cutout between the passenger section and the cab.

"I think they pulled over, and one of the passengers reached in through here and stabbed him. The blade sliced his jugular, and then he stabbed him a second time, just for good measure." Swearingen was staring through the opening at the driver's seat, where I could see a large bloodstain.

"How do you know it was a *he*?" I said.

He turned to me, his eyebrows raised over his half-lidded eyes.

"According to the man who hired me, there were four people total coming from Miami," I said. "Two were women."

Swearingen shook his head. "If a woman killed him, she sure knew how to do it."

"Like she's done it before," I said.

"That'd be my guess."

I stepped out the door and into the twilight. Swearingen came out behind me and we began back toward the police station. "Where did you find the Ford?" I asked.

"It was parked up the road a couple miles, near where the highway passes over the Truckee River. Let's go to my computer and I'll show you exactly where."

•   •   •

As I drove out of the Fernley PD parking lot, I felt quite pleased with my progress so far. I'd found and inspected the vehicle Manuel Alvarez had supposedly inhabited, and also learned that the driver had been killed. I hadn't expected my foray into the desert would be that productive. I wouldn't have been surprised if the trip had been a total waste of time. So I felt optimistic, despite running into a murder right out of the gate.

I didn't feel the weight of the driver's death at that moment. Whether or not it portended danger or might actually make it easier to find Manuel Alvarez, I had no idea. I was still early in the fact finding stage, and didn't yet have basis for theories.

I clenched my steering wheel with sore knuckles and accelerated out of town. The cooperation I'd received from both the Fallon captain and, even more so, from Lonnie Swearingen at Fernley PD, was not something I took for granted. As often as not, the police treated me as if I suffered from a disease that rendered me incapable of either ethical or intelligent behavior. But while it's true that law enforcement professionals commonly view private detectives as greedy, manipulative, law-skirting degenerates who don't have what it takes to be real policemen, cops occasionally see me as a benign ally, someone who can be helpful in solving a case.

It was almost full dark when I turned off the highway onto a frontage road. It ran alongside the highway for a mile, then became a dirt road leading beneath an overpass built over the Truckee River. The road ended in a circular turnabout just beyond the overpass, where the steep, rocky banks of the river were still covered with snow.

I stopped and got out of my truck. There were no buildings visible from this spot, and the angle didn't allow a view up to the passing cars on the highway. If there was any traffic, I wouldn't have been able to hear it above the roar of the river, which was rushing with early snowmelt.

This dirt roundabout marked the terminus of the journey for the Ford minibus. It was probably the place where the driver was stabbed to death. I squinted out at the vast plains surrounding me. The sky was purple and the moon was glowing over the flatlands. I tried to imagine the Ford stopping here, perhaps around three in the afternoon a week ago. Were there four people aboard at that time, including Manuel Alvarez? Did they meet someone else here, in this secluded spot in the high desert outside of Reno? Was the driver killed because of a dispute among the passengers, or were others involved?

And what happened to the occupants after the stabbing? Did they simply gather up their belongings and hitchhike down the road? It seemed unlikely. Maybe they walked the couple of miles back to Fernley and caught a bus to Reno, or some other destination. Or maybe the event was pre-planned, and they were picked up by someone at this location.

I got back in my pickup and fishtailed around the turnabout, spraying gravel until I straightened down the dirt road. Once I reached the pavement, I called the number on the business card Lonnie Swearingen had provided.

"Sheriff Swearingen."

"It's Dan Reno, sheriff. I've got another question or two, if you don't mind."

"I figured I'd hear from you again."

"Do you have any thoughts on what happened to the Ford's occupants after they abandoned the vehicle?"

"Well, first of all, I didn't naturally assume there were any occupants. Suppose the driver was alone. He could have pulled over to nap, and someone could have robbed and killed him."

"I guess that's possible."

"But I did check with Uber and our local taxi company. Neither picked up anybody suspicious last Wednesday."

"How about buses?"

"We checked with three different bus lines that run through Fernley. Problem is, none track customers by name. You pay a fare and get on. And being that we have no idea who we're looking for, it's pretty hard to get any meaningful response."

"Huh," I muttered.

"You have any ideas?" he asked.

"Not at the moment. But I'll keep you posted."

We hung up, and I swung onto USA Parkway 439, which cut south through twenty-five miles of deserted terrain to Highway 50. Once I passed the Tesla battery factory, I entered a black sea of desert scrub. I hit my high beams and drove with a heavy foot while I thought about Lonnie Swearingen. He seemed without a professional or political agenda, which made him different from most cops I dealt with. He also seemed like a good guy to have a beer with, maybe a few beers. I decided I liked him, and more importantly, could trust him. And if there's one thing I've learned, having a trustworthy cop on your side is a valuable commodity in my business.

·   ·   ·

When I got home, it was later than our usual dinner time, but Candi had waited for me. She was on the couch, her legs tucked beneath her, when I walked in. Smokey, his fur billowing in great puffs, lay with his paws resting on Candi's thigh.

"Sorry I'm late," I said, hanging my coat. "My new case."

"I made dinner," Candi said. "Let's eat, I'm starving." When she stood, I could see the three-month swell in her belly. Her face had a happy glow, and her eyes looked radiant. I followed her into the kitchen and stood behind her, cupping her breasts. Then I stepped back. "Sorry," I said.

"For what?" She lifted a skillet from the stove and set it on the counter.

"I need to control myself better."

"We can have sex until month eight. I already told you that, dumdum."

"I know, but..."

"Can you put this on the table?" Candi pointed to the counter, then walked around and spanked my rear.

"Okay, babe," I said.

.   .   .

After we finished dinner we went to our bedroom and undressed. Then Candi pushed me down onto the bed and sat astride me, her face flushed, her dark hair falling around her cheeks. Her breasts and pink nipples looked larger than usual, and her hips were a bit fuller. I found myself more aroused than I expected, as if I was experiencing an altered, erotic version of my fiancée. Candi gyrated and moaned and then fell forward, her belly touching mine, her breasts bumping my face. When we climaxed we were both breathing hard and I realized I was clutching her ass so tightly I could feel the bruised knuckles on my right hand.

We lay in bed for a while, her head on my chest. The drapes were partially open and I could see stars around a sliver of moon in the black sky.

"Tell me about your case," she murmured.

"A missing person. I wouldn't have taken it, but the guy paid me a cash retainer."

"Why wouldn't you have taken it?" When I didn't respond right away, she said, "I mean, it's been a month or two since your last case."

"I've had a few small jobs in between."

I felt her teeth on my skin. "Do you want a bite?"

"I ran a people search on the guy and nothing came up."

"On the guy who hired you?"

"Yeah."

She raised on her elbow and looked down at me. "What does that mean?"

"He gave me a phony name. I don't know why."

She sighed and lay her head back on my chest. "I wouldn't worry about it," I said.

"I'm not. Are you?"

"Not in the slightest, doll."

· · ·

The next morning I made breakfast for Candi and carried her bags out to her car. It was a little past eight when she left for the campus. I stood in our front yard watching her car disappear around the corner. It was not quite freezing but the morning felt very cold and puffs of vapor poured from my mouth when I exhaled.

I went back inside and refilled my coffee mug and began typing my case notes. The only reason I had to doubt what Luis Alvarez told me was because I doubted that was his real name. I tapped my fingers on my desk. People using assumed names almost always have something to hide. And they are almost always criminals.

I found the picture I'd taken of the rental car he'd driven, and called their main number. It took a few minutes, but eventually I was connected to a man who introduced himself as a local manager.

"I'm Nick Galanis at Douglas County PD," I said. "We pulled over a man in one of your cars, and his license doesn't check out. Can you tell me who rented it?" I recited the license plate number.

"Yes sir," he said, and I smirked while listening to the click of his keyboard. Nick Galanis was a corrupt, narcissistic Nevada detective who died the previous winter. I'd watched his estranged son stab him to death.

"Claudia Merchan. Florida driver license."

"Can you provide her address, please?"

"1740 Northwest North River Drive, number 419, Miami."

"Date of birth?"

"October 2, 1982."

"Great, thanks."

"Is the car okay?"

"Yeah, no worries. Thanks again."

I finished jotting down the info, then entered the address into Google maps. In a moment I was looking at a picture of a six-story apartment building called Serenity by the River. It was just west of the Miami International Airport, and was overlooking the Miami River, which ran southeast through downtown Miami before flowing into Biscayne Bay.

I spent a few minutes studying the map. Serenity by the River was in a neighborhood called Allapattah. Less than a mile northeast was Little Haiti, and immediately south was Little Havana. I pulled up pictures of the neighborhoods, more out of curiosity than anything else. I'd never been to Miami. The closest I'd been was New Orleans, where I was thrown in jail after getting blotto drunk in the French Quarter, back before my first marriage.

Serenity by the River appeared to cater to middle-class renters; it was neither luxurious nor a slum. A Google search for Allapattah revealed that the word originated from a Seminole Indian language, and meant alligator. The area called Allapattah was also sometimes referred to as Little Santo Domingo for its high Dominican-American population.

Next I logged into a people search site and entered Claudia Merchan. There were only three individuals listed, and one was for a woman in Miami. I downloaded her file, which included a photo, and residence, employment, and arrest history.

I recognized her immediately. The face in the picture was recent, and looked like it may have been a mugshot. She wore heavy makeup around her small eyes, and her lips were painted and appeared more full and sensual than I recalled from our meeting. She stared straight forward, neither smiling nor frowning. I printed the photo, then clicked on the tab for her background.

Claudia Merchan had a spotty employment record, consisting of waitressing and retail jobs. Evidently she had alternative income sources, for her sheet was scattered with prostitution arrests, a bust for credit card fraud, and most recently, a charge of identity theft related to an IRS tax refund scam. She'd been convicted twice for prostitution, but the fraud charges were still pending.

I paged down to a section listing related people. There was no record of her being married, and no mention of anyone named Luis Alvarez.

I printed the entire report and dropped it into a hanging file folder in my old metal file cabinet. Returning to my computer, I stared blankly before I opened my safe and looked at the stack of hundred dollar bills given to me the day before. After a minute I muttered, "Cash is cash." Then I closed the safe and considered my next move.

3

By 11 A.M. I was back in Fernley. I'd believed Lonnie Swearingen when he said he or someone in his department had spoken to Uber and taxi drivers, and also to some people working for the bus lines that regularly passed through Fernley. But that didn't mean they had expended maximum effort on the task. How motivated and committed might the Fernley PD be to resolve the murder of an unidentified man from out of town, especially a non-white male? Fernley, like many small towns in the northwestern U.S., was predominantly white, and no doubt harbored some degree of racist inclination. If this sounds like a casual and irresponsible assumption, go spend some time hanging out in bars in places like Winnemucca, Nevada or Twin Falls, Idaho. Listen to local business owners talk after a few drinks have loosened their tongues. You might think you've been transported back to Mississippi circa 1960.

I started at the only bus station in town. The address was at the end of a strip mall, and inside the glass doors it was large enough for perhaps four people to stand. A middle-aged woman with bloated arms sat behind a counter reading a gossip magazine.

"Yes?" she said.

"I'm looking for a missing person." I put the picture of Manuel Alvarez on the counter. "He may have caught a bus here eight days ago."

She looked down at the sheet of paper for a moment. "I don't remember the face, but I can hardly remember yesterday." She picked at a red spot on her arm with a broken fingernail.

"Think about it. He doesn't look like he's from around here, does he?"

She stared back me through spectacles smudged with fingerprints and white flakes, but she said nothing.

"Thanks anyway," I said.

I left the cramped space and spent the next three hours talking to taxi drivers, Uber drivers, and then I waited at a bus stop and quizzed a bus driver. I got absolutely nowhere; not a single person recognized Manuel Alvarez. At two P.M. I stood at an intersection off Main Street, fighting my impatience and trying to figure the next logical course of action. I prided myself on my willingness to undertake the drudgery of investigative work and knew that seemingly futile efforts were often necessary before clues presented themselves. But I was running out of options in this small town, and for a long moment I considered if I was wasting my time here.

I was hungry and decided to give it a rest for a while. I was thinking of fast food, but instead I spotted a sign on a peeling gray building advertising cocktails, slot machines, and bar food. I crossed the street and walked into the joint. The interior was all wood planks, and the room was half full with customers, mostly middle-aged or older, and all white. The brume of cigarette smoke that hung over the cocktail tables was so dense that I stood for a moment holding the door open, hoping I might introduce some fresh air.

A wizened woman with stringy hair and missing teeth looked up at me from her perch at a slot machine. "Either come on in or don't, but close the damn door," she said. I waded in and took a seat at the end of the bar.

Fernley is not a city that attracts much in the way of tourists, and I saw no sign that any of the patrons were out-of-towners. This was purely a local's joint, and as if to reinforce the point, the bartender ignored me for a couple of minutes until he finished his conversation with an elderly man in a cowboy hat.

"You got non-alcoholic beer?" I asked when the barkeep finally came my way. He was the youngest person in the place, still in his twenties, but his bushy mustache looked like it belonged to an older man. He was also the biggest dude in the room; I would have bet he played on the line of his high school football team. He raised an eyebrow at me.

"Nope. No demand for it."

"How about a Coke, then. You got a menu?"

"The cook went home already. Sorry about that."

He placed my soda on the bar and I gave him a five, along with my business card. "I'm looking into the murder of a man here a week ago."

He looked at my card, then back at me. "I heard about that," he said.

"Have you ever seen this guy?" I laid a copy of Manuel Alvarez's photo on the bar. He lowered his head, then picked up the sheet of paper.

"Looks like the guy my brother gave a ride to."

"Really?"

"Yeah. Guy came in here, says he's looking for work, says he works on boats. He wanted to know where the nearest lake is. He wasn't from around here."

"The nearest lake?"

"Yeah. He paid my brother a hundred bucks to drive him to Tahoe."

"No shit? Is your brother around?"

The bartender smiled. "He's the cook, but he split about half an hour ago."

"Well, hell. Can I call him?"

He shrugged. "I guess so."

A minute later I was sitting at a table in the corner behind the pool table, talking to the barkeep's brother. The man seemed like a dullard. His responses to my questions were brief and without opinion or context. He had given a ride to a stranger for a hundred dollar fee. There was no one with the stranger, it was solely him. Their conversation during the hour and forty minute-drive was minimal, and he couldn't recall anything specific his passenger said. He had dropped him off at the casinos in Stateline, a short walk to the southern shores of Lake Tahoe.

Before I took off, I tipped the bartender ten bucks.

"Hey, thanks," he said. "Sorry the kitchen's closed, but to be honest, my bro is a lousy cook anyway."

I waved at him, then hit the road, skipping lunch and fleeing west across the desert and back toward South Lake Tahoe, where the boat rental or tour companies on the alpine lake could likely offer employment to an individual who knew how to repair and maintain boats, or drive them.

. . .

It was 4:30 when I pulled into my driveway, and I went straight to my computer and did a Google search for Lake Tahoe boating. Eleven companies came up in South Lake, and at least that many along the north shore of Tahoe. I printed a page with the addresses and jumped back in my truck, heading toward the lake. It was getting late and the businesses might soon be closing, but I felt the winds of momentum at my back and wanted to press forward. If I found Manuel Alvarez tonight, maybe I could wrap this thing up and be done with it.

4

Two months before he ever set foot in Nevada, Manuel Alvarez was locked up in one of the worst jails in the Dominican Republic. The cell that he'd inhabited for thirty days was dank and musty, the humidity so thick he could almost see it. He sat on a thin mattress that was damp and never dried. The mattress was stained dark in the center from sweat, urine, and semen. The moisture had caused the green paint on the walls to peel, and strips hung limply, as if pleading for removal, but no one ever bothered.

Manuel sat shirtless, scratching at the newest bites on his arms. He had lost weight during his incarceration and had not fully recovered from a bout of dysentery that assailed his bowels shortly after he began eating the meals served at the Higüey Jail.

The three men sharing Manuel's cell had been arrested for drug offenses, but they spoke of having connections and seemed confident the necessary bribes would be paid soon and they'd be released. They'd arrived at Higüey around the same time as Manuel. Without money to buy special privileges, they became weaker with each passing day from the poor food and living conditions. But one still had the strength to beat one of the cellmates bloody the previous night, the result of a pointless argument. The injured man lay curled on his mattress, trying to breathe through his broken nose, blood caked around his mouth.

The rules Manuel had learned since his arrest now defined his life. He had been arrested for stealing a melon from a street vendor. He was innocent of the crime; he had paid for the melon, but that didn't matter. He had been processed quickly through the system, moved from the *Palacio de La Policia* to the jail at Higüey within 48 hours. Without money or connections, he was at the mercy of a process that could sentence him to years in prison for the slightest infraction. Since he couldn't afford a defense attorney, whether he was innocent or not made no difference. A judge could decide his fate based on issues having nothing to do with the alleged crime. For instance, if the judge was annoyed at being denied a bribe in his previous case, he could simply punish the next suspect who stood before him.

Still waiting for his day in court, Manuel tried hard to maintain his physical strength. But equally important was preserving his sanity. Contemplating what his future might hold in store would not serve this purpose, for he now knew that a sentence of more than a few years would likely be a death sentence.

If Manuel had known someone with influence, a prominent businessman, a politician, or anyone in the justice system, or even someone who knew one of these people, he might have been released with a small fine. But Manuel had always been dirt poor. Born into poverty in Pedernales, a coastal town on the Haitian border, Manuel was raised in squalid conditions by a woman who claimed not to be his mother. He never knew who his true father or mother were, or if they were still alive. Manuel was ten years old when the woman caring for him died. He found her body, still and cold, upon awaking one morning.

Afterward, Manuel was taken in by a local family that lived in a shanty and survived by raising chickens and goats and growing banana and mango. When Manuel was thirteen, he lost his virginity. This occurred when the family's fifteen-year-old daughter straddled him one night in a room separated only by a hanging tarp from her parent's bedroom. While she squirmed and thrusted her hips, she held her hand over his mouth. When Manuel came, he wondered if this is what it felt like to fall in love. But when he woke the next morning and looked for her, he was met with the father's angry glare. By the end of the day Manuel knew it was time to leave.

Penniless and relying on his wits to survive, Manuel found employment fishing, working for an older man whose sons had moved away. For three years Manuel lived on the beach, often sleeping in a hammock strung in a grove of broadleaf trees. He spent his days on the ocean in a small craft and became proficient in line and spear fishing. He learned to rig sails and repair small marine motors and found extra work painting boats.

Shortly after turning sixteen, the man Manuel worked for collapsed while they were sanding the hull of an old skiff. When Manuel went to him, the man exhaled his final breath with a labored hiss, jerked once, and then stared with unblinking eyes into the clouds. Manuel stayed by him until it turned dark. The man had never spoken an unkind word, and had taught Manuel many things, including the basics of the English language.

Before dawn the next day, Manuel set sail, heading for Santo Domingo, the largest city in the Dominican Republic. Hugging the coast, he sailed the calm, warm waters, drifting around the southern tip of the Jaragua National Park. Then he tacked north, up the coast to Barahona, and then east across the bay to where the tropical forest met the shoreline. He stopped and tied the boat at a jetty in the tiny city of Palmar De Ocoa and spent the night sleeping on the sand. The next morning he was sailing east again, and by noon, from five miles out on the Caribbean Sea, he could see the skyline of Santo Domingo on the horizon.

With only the barest of possessions and never having been in a building of over two stories, Manuel stared at the tall structures set back from the beach. He wondered about the lives of those who lived or worked on the upper floors. Lacking formal education, Manuel was mostly self-taught, and he imagined that the glimmering steel and glass skyscrapers were the domain of rich men in business suits who understood things about money Manuel couldn't even imagine.

When he reached the beaches of Santo Domingo, Manuel tied off his boat and wandered about, never leaving the sand. There was much activity and many businesses on the shoreline. His goal was simple; find a job fishing or working on boats and make enough to survive. He had no aspirations beyond that, for he had learned that the bare necessities of food and shelter were challenge enough.

On his second day in Santo Domingo, Manuel spoke to a man running a water taxi company. The man's name was Hugo Trinidad. He was a native, his skin dark, his face pocked with craters, his eyes cold and scrutinizing, as if he viewed life through a lens of suspicion. He asked about Manuel's skills, and when Manuel said he could speak some English, Hugo Trinidad paused, his eyes turning contemplative.

"That may be helpful," he said.

.   .   .

For the next five years, Manuel worked for the water taxi company. He was provided a bed in a small room in the back of the tin and plywood building that served as the company's store front. In the mornings, customers would walk to where the sand turned to dirt and step up to a counter shaded by a tin awning. Here they would make arrangements with Hugo Trinidad to charter trips to different cities along the Dominican coast. Manuel maintained the three company boats, and within a year he proved himself capable of piloting each craft. From that point he spent much of his time on the sea, often shuttling tourists and businessmen to the turquoise waters and pristine beaches of *Isla Catalina,* and further south to *Isla Sauna.*

His seafaring skills improving, Manuel began venturing to the far eastern tip of Hispaniola, to Punta Cana, the primary Dominican resort destination. When an older pilot left the company, Manuel took his routes and began traveling on the open sea, to both Puerto Rico and Jamaica. He braved difficult seas on occasion, especially in the early fall, when hurricanes ravaged the Caribbean. He nearly lost his life to Hurricane Maria, returning to Santo Domingo alone on a 25-foot catamaran in forty knot winds, the swells nearly swamping the boat.

To aid in communication with non-Spanish speaking clients, Hugo Trinidad told Manuel to improve his English, and gave him books and tapes.

Manuel thought that mastering English could lead to greater things, as few Dominicans spoke anything but their native Spanish. He devoted himself to learning this second language, and became proficient at not only speaking, but also reading English.

As Manuel grew older and became more confident in his value to Hugo Trinidad, he began paying more attention to certain things occurring in the building where Trinidad spent much of his time. A pair of men, Spanish speaking but of fair complexion, began visiting regularly. They would meet with Trinidad in his office, and occasionally voices were raised and Manuel could overhear snippets of conversation. Over time, Manuel began to suspect that Hugo Trinidad was involved in a secondary business, one that might be far more lucrative than the water taxi company.

But Manuel was not interested in learning what his boss was involved in. For Manuel, his life was as good as he thought it could ever be. He loved being on the sea, and lived comfortably, not wanting for food or shelter. He'd even begun dating a plump *señorita,* a waitress at a seaside restaurant. After his boss went home in the evening, Manuel would invite her to his room, and they'd make love with the passionate but clumsy exuberance of teenagers.

While he was with this girl, Manuel sometimes felt strangely detached. He thought she had strong feelings for him, but it was not reciprocal. He enjoyed her company, and she even made him laugh, but there seemed to be a hole in his heart. He would never hurt her, but also could never feel much toward her. In a rare introspective moment, as he lay beside her one night, he wondered if the absence of his parents had left him incapable of loving another human being.

It was around this time that Hugo Trinidad taught Manuel how to drive. There were numerous errands that required trips into the city, and Trinidad assigned Manuel to the task. When Manuel was not on the sea, he would drive Trinidad's work truck into the interior of Santo Domingo to pick up various supplies, and sometimes sealed cardboard boxes from men who appeared in dark doorways and did not speak.

As he turned twenty-one years old, Manuel began to think of his future. On his own, he'd become a savvy seaman, learned to read and write in a second language, mastered rudimentary math, and could navigate a rickety truck safely around the chaotic streets of Santo Domingo. His confidence blossoming, Manuel no longer considered himself a poor, helpless peasant. He had survived a parentless upbringing in one of the poorest towns in the Dominican and had come to the big city to forge his way. He had proved himself capable of learning many things. He felt the time was coming where he would move on from Hugo Trinidad, and perhaps one day open his own company. Of course, this would require money.

Although he had a roof over his head and never wanted for food, Manuel was paid very little. When he needed new clothes or shoes, he was provided some extra pesos, but this was only on an as-needed basis. Manuel had no money saved and knew he was being underpaid. The unfairness of this situation began to dominate his thoughts.

It was on a typically warm mid-February morning that Manuel finally decided he would address the compensation issues with his boss. He fully expected Trinidad to reject his request for more money and was ready to leave the water taxi company. But his boss's response came as a surprise.

"I've been thinking the same thing," Trinidad said, standing at the counter. He turned from his computer screen and looked directly at Manuel. "You've done good and you deserve more. Here's a list of things I need. Take the truck and drive into the city, and when you return, I'll have a new wage for you. I think you'll like it."

Manuel put his hand to his chin and watched Trinidad's cold eyes shift away as if he'd lost interest in the subject. Manuel's boss had never lied to him and had truly provided for him. So why was it that Manuel didn't trust him?

It was later that morning that Manuel was arrested.

·   ·   ·

The inmate hierarchy at the Higüey Jail was based almost entirely on wealth. Money was necessary for survival and comfort at Higüey. With enough money, an inmate could live quite well. The richest inmates bought *goletas,* private luxury cells with fans, televisions, fancy furniture, and king-sized beds. Wives, girlfriends, or prostitutes could visit *goletas* for an extra fee to the warden. The most palatial *goletas,* some as large as two-bedroom apartment units, were commonly owned by wealthy white-collar criminals or drug kingpins who were serving long sentences that would be reversed after an obligatory year or two. Less expensive *goletas* were available to inmates with more modest means.

For those who couldn't afford *goletas* but still had some degree of familial support, the most critical need was food. Only the destitute ate the food at Higüey, which consisted mainly of rice mixed with *alumbre,* a fattening starch designed to keep poor convicts from starving. Meat or other protein sources were almost nonexistent. If not supplemented by outside food, the jail fare didn't contain enough nutrients to maintain an individual's health. To add insult to injury, inmate cooks frequently spit in the clumpy rice dishes or the morning *cocoa* drinks.

Clothing also needed to be brought in by outside sources, as the jail provided no clothing whatsoever; there were no standard-issue inmate outfits. If you had nothing but the clothes on your back when you arrived, that's all you would have unless you had the means to acquire additional garments.

For prisoners without money, commonly called *ranas,* or frogs, the situation was truly dire. The lucky had filthy, rancid mattresses, and the less fortunate slept on floors. Rats and cockroaches were abundant. While those in *goletas* had private bathrooms, the *ranas* used open trenches and emptied their bowels in public. Shower water was rationed and fought over.

After thirty days, Manuel knew that it was only a matter of months before illness overtook him. Without money, medical care was unavailable. Those who became sick were not treated; they would either recover without medication or die. If an infectious disease took hold among the *ranas,* the jail authorities would not intervene. They considered inmate death a means to manage the ceaseless overcrowding.

With increasing frequency, Manuel found himself in a trancelike state, lost in daydreams. These visions would always start the same way: his boat gently rolling in the swells, his body caressed by the salty air that rose from the tranquil sea. He would feel the tropical sun on his skin, and the only sound was the splash of water against the hull and the occasional call of a seabird. He would catch his dinner and reel it in from the ocean, then cook it on a gas burner set on the deck. The taste of the fresh fish was like a godsend.

Manuel sat on his bed, staring at the layered filth on his pants. There was nothing to do but sit and stare and wait for his inevitable demise. He had called Hugo Trinidad daily with his allotted phone call and left messages. He had never heard back from his boss. After five years of loyal service at low wages, apparently Trinidad had no interest in helping his employee. He recalled that Trinidad had once told him that life is unfair, as if that simple comment could explain any misfortune. Manuel now appreciated the wisdom of the remark. No longer wallowing in confusion or disappointment, he simply accepted his situation. All he could do is live one day at a time and hope that someone or something would rescue him from his undeserved fate. He knew it would require a miracle.

A shadow fell over Manuel, and he looked up. Outside the cell stood a guard and two inmates. The guard opened the cell door and walked away.

One of the inmates was so massive he barely looked human. Fat spilled over his sides and his chest was so thick he appeared to have no neck. Tufts of black hair escaped from his collar, and the hair on his back looked like matted fur through his clinging sweat-stained shirt. His forearms were nearly the size of Manuel's thighs, his hands as big as hams. He smiled, his shaved head gleaming, and stepped into the cell, followed by a slender man about six feet tall. This man had a disfigured face that caused his expression to be set in a hideous sneer. Manuel immediately recognized it as a case of *acido del diablo,* a corrosive chemical readily available at Higüey and commonly used in attacks among inmates.

"Do you like my face?" the man said. Manuel pushed himself back against the wall. His three cellmates, who liked to talk like hardened criminals, seemed to shrink into a corner.

"This is Gomez," the man continued, jerking his thumb at the massive man. "His job is to pick out a *puta* for Señor Guzman. He's very good at identifying who will look pretty in makeup. He'll also insist on a test run first, of course."

The fat man looked around the room slowly, and his eyes settled on Manuel. "You," he said. "Don't fight it, I need you in good, clean shape. Don't worry, we'll give you a shower and a shave and new clothes too. They will be women's clothes, but they'll be fresh and clean and smell nice. Señor Gomez likes *maricones* who smell nice."

In a moment that occurred with a flash of clarity, a moment he would long remember, Manuel thought, *so this is how it ends.* He would fight to the death before he'd let himself be assaulted. He had a sharpened piece of metal hidden in a hole in his mattress, and he lunged for it. But the disfigured man was surprisingly quick, and he grabbed Manuel's arm, and then the fat man lifted Manuel, pinning him against his sweaty mass. The blade was pried from Manuel's fingers, and he was carried out of the cell, squirming and struggling vainly for a way to inflict pain on an adversary more than twice his weight.

As they proceeded down the walkway, the prisoners in the cells to either side began jeering and whistling, grabbing their genitals and pressing their bare buttocks against the bars. His mind raging, Manuel kicked and flailed madly, and felt his heel make solid contact with the fat man's shin. But the man only tightened his grip to the point that Manuel had to fight to breathe.

They turned down a dark hallway away from the cells and Manuel let his body go limp, hoping to convince his abductor that he would no longer resist. When the moment came, Manuel intended to ram his heel into the man's testicles. After that he would run and hide, and if necessary he would run for the fences. If he was shot by the guards, then that was meant to be.

"Don't try anything stupid," the disfigured man said. "Gomez can crush you if he wishes. But you might have an option. We're taking you to the warden."

"The warden?" Manuel sputtered. "Why?"

They turned another corner, and a guard opened an iron door. "Shut up and you'll find out."

A minute later Manuel was seated in a wood-paneled room. The warden sat behind an expansive desk and told Manuel's abductors to leave. His head was too large for his thin body, and his thick jowls made Manuel think of animals that tore flesh from their prey. He wore an olive suit coat with a red emblem on the chest and puffed on a cigar. The smoke billowed in the light pouring in from a large window.

Standing at the corner of the desk was Hugo Trinidad.

"As you can see, your boss is here," the warden said. "Maybe he can save you from the *goleta* of Señor Guzman. But that is up to you."

Manuel looked at Trinidad, who was freshly shaved and dressed in white, his pants and shirt pressed and spotless. When he returned Manuel's stare, his eyes showed little sign of recognition.

"What do you want from me?" Manuel said

The warden leaned back and crossed his legs. "Señor Trinidad has a mission for you. If you do exactly as you're told, it won't be necessary for you to return here. However, if you disobey or fail, we will have you back, and this time there will be no hope. Señor Gomez, who you met, will be very disappointed that I would not allow him to make you a punk. You know what? I don't think you would last too long as a punk. Maybe a week or two. Then your insides would be all tore up and you might bleed to death." The warden smiled. "That would be a very painful way to die."

Trinidad took a step forward and sat one of his haunches on the corner of the big desk. When he spoke his voice was quiet and intense. "I need you to pilot a boat to Miami. And after that, there will be another journey. We will know where you are, we'll be watching. We have ways to watch you that you know nothing about. If you do exactly as you're told and all goes well, you'll be a free man. But make a mistake and you'll be back here getting ass-fucked to death. We will see to that."

Manuel stared round-eyed at the two men. He felt weak with relief. In the back of his mind he wondered what brought Trinidad here this day, but at the moment he didn't care. Whatever they proposed, he would do. He'd gladly accept whatever danger or challenge that awaited him. For he knew the alternative was so grim and excruciating that he may well take his own life.

5

Sometimes, good, old-fashioned detective work pays off. I hit pay dirt at the third boat rental company I visited, in the Tahoe Keys. I didn't even have to show a picture or ask a question. I simply spotted Manuel Alvarez walking toward me from a wooden pier stretching a hundred feet out on the lake. He carried two small buoys attached to a rope looped over one shoulder, and on the other shoulder he balanced a pair of oars.

He looked up and our eyes met. I looked away and retreated to the doorway of the boat rental outfit. Luis Alvarez had specified that I not alert Manuel to my reason for being there. I tried the door, but it was locked. I considered turning away and returning to the parking lot, but I needed to confirm that Manuel was in fact employed at this company. So I waited for him.

He came within ten feet of where I stood, then before he could turn down a path that led to the side of the building, I said, "Excuse me, I'm looking to rent a boat."

He stopped and looked me up and down. I smiled and shrugged, hoping to put him at ease, but I saw a hint of alarm in his eyes. I didn't know if this was due to what I said or how I said it, or how I looked, or any aspect of my demeanor. But the fear on his face was unmistakable.

"What kind of boat?" he asked.

"Oh, a power boat," I replied, cursing myself for the hesitation.

"Come back tomorrow. We open at nine o'clock."

"Okay, thanks," I said. I waved and headed toward my truck. As soon as I climbed behind the wheel, I called Luis Alvarez.

"I found your nephew," I said.

"Where?"

"Action Boat Rentals, in the Tahoe Keys. He works there."

"He's there now?" His tone was curt and demanding.

"Yes, but I believe he'll be leaving soon. They're closed for the day."

"Did you talk to him?"

"I just said I wanted to rent a boat. He said come back at nine tomorrow."

"That's all you said, right?"

I was looking out my windshield, and at that moment I saw Manuel at the corner of the building, half his body hidden, watching me.

"That's right. I found your nephew, Mr. Alvarez, as you hired me to do. I consider this case closed."

"I'll contact you if necessary," he said, and hung up.

I tossed my phone on the passenger seat and turned out of the parking lot. Whatever Luis Alvarez's motivations were, whatever his relationship truly was with Manuel, that wasn't my concern. Likewise, if any police agency in Nevada was seeking Manuel Alvarez as a witness to or suspect in the death of the man in the minibus, that also wasn't my problem. I'd performed as I was hired to, within the law. My obligations ended there.

As I drove home, I told myself to ignore the unanswered questions in my head, and to instead focus on the positives in my life. I had used my determination and skill to complete a job in a minimum of time, and I'd been well-compensated for it. Within a few minutes I'd be returning to the house I shared with the woman I loved, a woman who was pregnant with our child. We'd have dinner together, then I'd mix a drink, and we'd watch the sun set over the meadow behind our home. We might put on our coats and spend a few minutes on the deck, basking in the scent of spring wildflowers and pine as the sun dropped behind the distant ridges. If I could ask for more, I couldn't fathom what it would be.

By the time I pulled in my driveway, I'd concluded my psychic inventory taking, and found everything in stock and accounted for. I then went inside and spent a quiet evening with Candi and did not think again about Luis or Manuel Alvarez.

· · ·

At ten the next morning, my cell rang. I looked at the 305 area code and my brow constricted.

"Dan Reno."

"I went to Action Boat Rentals this morning," the voice said without introduction or preamble. "Manuel did not show up for work."

I sighed and walked out to my deck. "Who did you talk to, Mr. Alvarez?" I asked.

"The man working there. He said Manuel didn't call in."

I watched my neighbor back out of his driveway. "I see," I said.

"Do you?" he replied.

"What is it you want from me, sir?"

"I hired you to find Manuel. I paid you in advance, in cash."

"That's right. And I found him at his place of employment."

"But it seems he no longer works there. I'm wondering what you said to him."

"Like I told you last night," I said, staring at a trail of sap dripping down the bark of the tree in my front yard, "I just asked about renting a boat."

"And now he's not there."

"Is it a meeting you want me to arrange? Is that it?" I walked to the tree and kicked at a chunk of bark hanging off the trunk. It tore free and went flying across the lawn.

"I want you to find him and hold him until I can get there," he said, his words tight, as if he was fighting to keep his voice from rising.

"Hold him?" I replied. "That constitutes kidnapping. That's not part of the package."

The phone went silent, then he said, "Find out where he's staying. I hope that's not too much to ask for the two grand I paid you."

"All right," I said. "I'll let you know when your retainer is exhausted."

"You do that," he said.

I stuffed my phone in my back pocket, crossed my arms, and began pacing the perimeter of my yard. I crunched through some snow along the fence line and opened the rear gate to the meadow. The thick field grass was dense with moisture from the snowmelt and I could hear the rush of water from the stream a hundred feet out. I picked up a softball sized stone, flung it toward the stream, and listened as it crashed through a mass of deadfall. Then I walked out until I stood looking at where the rushing green torrent was rapidly eating away at the ice along the banks.

After ten minutes passed, I returned to my house, went straight to my truck, and drove out to Action Boat Rentals. The morning chill was waning as the sun rose above a haze of low clouds. The lake was a deep blue beyond the rows of docks in the Keys.

The boat rental company lobby had plastic racks along the walls stuffed with activity brochures for tourists. The lobby was empty except for a man behind the counter. He had a suntanned face and sunglasses resting on his forehead.

"Good morning," I said.

"How can I help you?"

"Detective Dan Reno, South Lake Tahoe," I said, pushing aside my coat to show the shiny gold badge on my belt. "I understand Manuel Alvarez works here."

"He did until he went AWOL today. He never showed up this morning."

"Can you provide his home address, please?"

"Is he in some sort of trouble?"

"Might be."

"Hold on, it's on his application. He only worked here for five or six days." He went to a file cabinet in the corner and returned with a single page employment application. The handwritten letters were chicken scratch, as if the author had lifted the pen each time a change of direction was required. But the words and numbers were legible enough. I took a picture of the document.

"Thanks," I said.

"Why are you looking for him? Anything I should know?"

"I want to help him," I said, handing him my card. "Have him call me if you see him, please."

"You're the second guy looking for him today."

"I know."

Just as I opened the door to leave, the man said, "Hey, I thought you were a cop." I turned, and he waved my business card at me.

"I wouldn't worry about it," I said.

· · ·

The home address on the application was for the Royal Flush Inn. I was sorely tempted to call Luis Alvarez, give him the address, and tell him we were done. Instead I drove the six miles to the hotel. It was tucked away on a side street near the state line, between two other low cost lodges.

The Royal Flush looked more like a pair of deuces, and that was being generous. The wooden sign out front was faded and peeling, and the green room doors on the first floor looked warped and bowed, perhaps by the weight of the second floor's sagging balcony. I parked in the nearly empty lot and walked by an overflowing garbage bin on the way to the office. This was the kind of place where the walls were paper thin, the towels threadbare, the hot water a roll of the dice.

The attendant at the counter was a teenager with black eyebrows and a shock of platinum dyed hair. He wore a nose ring and half-inch gauges in his ears. I pulled my coat aside as I approached, showing my badge.

"Is this guy checked in?" I said, laying a picture of Manuel Alvarez on the counter.

"Yeah, I think so," the kid said.

"What room, please?"

He looked at a computer screen, and said, "108. But I saw him hiking away, lugging his bag earlier today. He's paid up through last night."

"Did he pay with a credit card?"

"No, cash."

"He didn't happen to say where he was headed, did he?"

The attendant raised his eyebrows and shrugged. "Why would he?"

I walked back to my truck, leaned against the fender, and called Luis Alvarez.

"He spent last night at the Royal Flush Inn in South Lake Tahoe, room 108," I said.

"You're sure?"

"I just confirmed it."

"I'm on my way. He better be there."

I straightened and took a step away from my truck. "Or what?"

"Or we're not done."

"No, sir, you're wrong. You hired me to locate your nephew, without alerting him. I've now done it twice. But he doesn't seem inclined to stay anywhere for long. There's nothing I can do about that."

"I'll let you know," he said, and the line went dead.

. . .

As soon as I got home, I prepared my final bill for Luis Alvarez. I'd only used $1400 of the cash retainer, so I owed him $600, which I intended to return to him without delay. I printed the statement and stuck it in an envelope along with six of the hundred-dollar bills he'd given me.

I sealed the envelope and sat weighing it in my hand, then I put it in my desk drawer. I took no satisfaction in ending an investigation and leaving a client without resolution. It made me feel like I'd left a job undone, or worse, like I was less than committed. But I'd begun drawing conclusions about this case, none of which suggested it was in my best interest to stay engaged.

The man who hired me was likely using a phony name, and in conjunction with the death of the minibus driver, it spelled bad news. I was not willing to be drawn into a situation with serious criminal implications, including murder, unless I knew exactly what I was getting into. And the man who went by Luis Alvarez was no doubt being less than forthright.

But it was the expression on Manuel Alvarez's face that made up my mind. I'd been trying to discount it, but he looked genuinely frightened when he saw me. I wondered what about me elicited that response. At six-foot-two and 210 pounds, I'm not overtly physically imposing. I don't think I look like a mean son of a bitch, or a cop. Candi thinks I'm handsome and says I have an easy smile. But I know I don't have a great poker face, and something about my presence alarmed Manuel. Which meant he had something to be afraid of. And I was willing to bet that the man who hired me was the source.

I walked out to my deck, thinking about having lunch at the picnic table in the sun, but it was still too cold. Instead I went back inside and called Candi, who was on her lunch hour at the college. But my thoughts were distracted, and she eventually asked why I was calling.

"Just to say hi, babe."

"Well, hi to you."

After we hung up, I called the number I had for Luis Alvarez. He didn't answer.

•　　•　　•

By the time Candi got home late in the afternoon, I was no longer thinking about the case. I'd spent a couple hours pulling weeds and reseeding the lawn, then I sanded and painted a section of wood siding damaged by sun and snowmelt. And then I vacuumed the rug in our family room where Smokey rolled and left wisps of gray fur.

We enjoyed a tranquil evening, full of familiar banter and touching that was intimate but not sexual. We sat on the couch after dinner, and I rested my hand on her belly, wondering if it was too early to feel any movement. The television was on but I couldn't say what we were watching. Instead my head was consumed with a profound sense that I was entering a new phase in my life, one that would involve parenthood and a level of responsibility that would define me moving forward. Given the transgressions of my past, which included borderline alcoholism, a ruined marriage, and violence that many considered unnecessary, I felt oddly serene with the prospect. It felt like a normal transition, one that I'd been working toward and was ready for. And I had no doubt that Candi was the right woman to spend the rest of my life with, for she understood and accepted me, and brightened my life with each moment we were together.

It wasn't until eleven P.M., while I lay reading in bed with Candi asleep next to me, that Luis Alvarez called.

6

I muted the ringer so Candi wouldn't wake, threw the blankets aside, and took the call in my office.

"Reno."

"Manuel is not at the Royal Flush Inn as you claimed. I've been waiting here for hours."

"Sorry to hear that."

"I'm now staying here in town. I want you to find Manuel and keep him under surveillance until I arrive. Please start first thing tomorrow morning."

"Thanks, but I'll pass. I've got your invoice plus six hundred bucks coming back to you. Let me know which hotel you're at and I'll bring it by tomorrow."

"You're quitting me?"

"With the invoice is a report detailing my activities and what I've learned about Manuel and his potential whereabouts."

"You found him once, you can find him again."

"You don't seem to be hearing me. I won't be continuing this investigation."

"And why not?"

"Because I don't think you are who you say you are, and I don't like working for clients who hide their identities. And second, I don't think Manuel wants to be found."

The phone went silent for a moment. "Why wouldn't he?"

"That's a question I'm sure you can answer better than me."

I heard a female voice in the background, and a brief, muted discussion. Then the man said, "You've done nothing but waste my time and money."

"And you've misrepresented your motives."

"How so?"

"I don't think you're related to Manuel Alvarez, if that's really his name. That means you're looking for him for reasons different than you described. And I think Manuel knows he's at risk."

"What did you say to him?"

"Like I said before, I just asked about renting a boat. But I think he was suspicious of me."

"I thought I'd hired a pro."

"Is there anything else?"

"Yes. You are still under contract to me. I want you to find Manuel tomorrow and keep him in sight until I get there. Despite your issues, you seem capable of that."

"This conversation is over."

"Yes, it is. I'll be waiting for your call tomorrow," he said.

"Or what?" I said. When he didn't reply I looked at my screen and saw the call was still connected. I heard him take a couple breaths before the line went dead.

.　　.　　.

The next morning I received a call from a man who was certain his younger wife was having an affair. He was a wealthy restaurateur and wanted pictures in anticipation of divorce proceedings.

I met him at a popular restaurant with a great bar up off Kingsbury Grade. We discussed the case in his back office.

"I mean naked pictures, the dirtier the better," he said. He handed me a photo of his wife.

"How old is she?" I asked.

"Twenty-four." I raised my eyebrows. In the right lighting, he might have passed for sixty.

A few minutes later I drove down the grade, pleased with the prospect of a new case, sordid as it may be. I rarely had jobs back to back and often spent weeks inactive between cases. I wondered if the spring might bring a flood of work, allowing me to put aside at least a few thousand for new expenses I'm sure would come with the baby.

I reached the intersection at Highway 50 and turned right. The restaurateur's home was in an exclusive neighborhood in a gated community in Zephyr Cove, five miles into Nevada. I picked up a sandwich at the grocery store in Round Hill, then continued north until I turned onto the road leading to the man's house. I gave his name to the woman at a security booth, and the gate swung open. I drove around a few sharp bends, climbing upward.

The house was a multilevel wood and stone structure obviously worth millions. I stopped at the curb and looked the place over, then turned to take in the splendid view of the forested hillside and the lake. The home was representative of Lake Tahoe's affluent residents, who typically made their fortunes elsewhere and decided to relocate here.

The house appeared empty, but the restauranteur had assured me his wife was there, as she never left before noon. I followed the road up above the house, looking futilely for a dirt shoulder, then I was forced to retreat when I hit a dead end. I finally found a place to park below the house, on a turnout that gave way to a dirt trail.

I grabbed my pack and started hiking up the trail. It took twenty minutes to climb roughly a thousand feet to a boulder outcropping. I tightened the straps on my pack and wedged myself up a crack, skinning my palms on the granite. Then I found a good handhold and pulled myself to a flat perch on top of a rock ledge. From there I was roughly level with the house, and only a couple hundred feet away. I removed my pack and trained my binoculars through the trees, looking at the three garage doors, then at the large windows facing out from the structure.

An hour passed, and at noon I sat where the sun warmed the rock and ate my sandwich. Then I shimmied back down the crack and leapt the final six feet to the forest floor. I had not glimpsed anyone during my surveillance, but I hadn't expected to. My efforts to reach a suitable vantage point might seem pointless, but I always want to study the angles of whatever location I'm working. It's a habit.

For the next three hours I sat in my truck. I had backed in until my tailgate touched the trunk of a pine at the foot of the trail. If a car was to come down the road, it would be easy for me to follow it. During that time, only two cars passed by, neither of which was the black BMW SUV the man told me his young wife drove.

It wasn't until four P.M. that the BMW glided around the sweeping corner. I started my pickup and followed it at a distance, knowing it would need to stop before turning onto the highway.

Fifteen minutes later, I followed her into a neighborhood less than a mile from where I lived. She turned onto a street where I had rented a house for a few months before I bought my home. I pulled over when she parked in front of a house with a blue Dodge pickup in the driveway. The Dodge had oversized tires and rust on the quarter panels.

The wife climbed from her SUV. She had long blonde hair and her tight clothes showed off a body that would make any man look twice. I rolled my eyes. Her husband, nearly three times her age, married a trophy wife and then wondered how she could cheat on him. I guess he thought his money could buy her loyalty.

When the front door opened, it was obvious the husband's suspicions were correct. The man in the doorway was about her age, my height and probably twenty pounds lighter. He had dark hair and was handsome and his teeth were white when he smiled. The blonde took a quick glance behind her, then disappeared into the house.

I left my truck and walked toward the house, then cut across a grass field between two homes. From there I was able to get to the back fence of the house. Like my place, it had a gate which opened to a stretch of meadow. The fence was chain-link, and the gate was unlocked. I went through it and darted to the back wall, where there were windows to either side of me.

I peeked into the nearest window and saw the couple standing in the kitchen. He held a bong and offered it to her. She put her mouth to it, and when he lit the bowl, I could see smoke billowing through the clear plastic. She held the hit for a long moment, then exhaled a white plume. I snapped a picture with my cell. Then he took her by the hand and led her out of my sight.

I moved to the window to my right, hoping it was a bedroom with open drapes. It was, but it was vacant. So I crept around to the side of the house, to another bedroom window.

The curtains were partially open, and they were standing and undressing each other. Once the man removed her jeans, she lay on the bed, and he knelt before her spread legs and buried his face between her thighs.

From my position I was able to hold my cell to the window and snap photos, and I almost considered switching to video mode. But then they changed positions, and I ducked down. When I peeked back in, she was on her knees pleasuring him. A minute later they were having intercourse. Then my phone blared at full volume. I'd forgotten to turn the ringer off.

The loud ring made the woman's closed eyes jump open, and she spotted me.

"Ah, shit," I said.

.   .   .

I hightailed back to my truck, chiding myself for my slipshod preparation. Lack of attention to detail during a surveillance is the mark of an amateur, and surely I knew better. I stopped a few blocks away and looked at my phone, angry and fighting the urge to blame whoever had called.

It was the 305 area code number belonging to Luis Alvarez. I stared at the screen for a long moment before I muttered, "Go fuck yourself." Then I drove out of the neighborhood and to Whiskey Dick's.

When I walked into the bar, the murky lighting and familiar odors made me feel like I was wading into my past, into a welcoming world where guilt and regret could be washed away for the price of a drink or two. Or many more, if I was inclined. For years that had been my gig. A couple of drinks to take the edge off, to blur my ire and replace it with a happy numbness. And then late into the night, until I was drunk to the point that I could barely remember who I was.

I sat at the end of the bar and motioned to Pam, a woman in her forties who'd been tending bar there for as long as I could remember. She came to me and filled a glass with ice.

"Double?" Her face was narrow and wrinkled beyond her years, but her blue eyes were hard and knowing.

"Yeah."

"How's Candi?"

"Just fine."

A flicker of doubt creased her face before she left me with a whiskey-seven. I drained it in two swallows, then stood and walked past the pool table to the jukebox. I rolled my neck and looked blankly at the song selections. And then, almost like a recording preset in my brain, I heard the voice of my best friend, Cody Gibbons.

"Use it like medicine, drink it slow," he said.

"That, from you?"

"I know you better than you think."

I straightened and returned to the bar, but this time I told Pam to make it a single. Then I got my notebook computer from my truck and took a table near the front window, where a pool of light provided a respite from the fuzzy darkness that shrouded the handful of locals at the bar.

I downloaded the pictures I'd taken onto my hard drive and began typing a case report for the restauranteur. I deployed the standard legal language in my description of the sex acts I'd witnessed, and provided explicit detail, as it's often valuable in court cases. I did so without hesitation, detailing the estimated length of each individual act: oral sex–male to female, oral sex–female to male, sexual intercourse–missionary position, etc. It took an hour to complete the report, and I made damn sure to include every detail I could recall. I still felt like an ass for not muting my phone, and I wanted to atone for it by making my report as thorough as possible.

When I was done, I drove down the street to a business that offered printing services, then I headed back to the restaurant off Kingsbury Grade. I walked into the restaurant with the report, but was told that the man who hired me had already left. When I called him he asked that I meet him at another restaurant he owned, this one all the way around on the west side of the lake, near Camp Richardson.

It took almost half an hour to get there. "What did you get?" the man asked from behind his desk. Errant gray hairs above his ears stuck out from his skull as if electrified.

"Everything," I said, and placed a manila envelope in front of him. He opened it and his face fell when he saw the pictures.

"You're surprised?" I asked.

"No," he said, his eyes like large droplets of rain. "I just hoped I was wrong."

"Sorry to bring bad news," I said.

"I guess that's what I hired you to do," he said, and the age spots on his bald head seemed to darken. Then he paid me in cash, and I left him to deal with his grief, be it self-inflicted or otherwise.

It was getting dark when I pulled out of the parking lot, but a band of fluorescent blue still glowed above the ridgelines. I turned from 89 onto Lake Tahoe Boulevard and was stopped at a light when Candi called.

"Hey, sorry I didn't call earlier. I got a new case and—"

"Dan, some guy was just here," she said. Her voice was brittle.

"What guy?"

"He pounded on the door and wanted to know where you were."

"When?"

"He just left. He said you better call him."

"What else did he say?"

"He scared me, Dan. He had that look, like he was mad and might hurt me."

I paused. "Did he leave his name?"

"No. He said you'd know who he is. Then he said, '*for the safety of your family,*' you better call him."

I felt the cords in my forearms tighten, and I accelerated with a jerk when the light turned green. When I spoke, I tried to keep my tone relaxed. "It's nothing to worry about, babe. Just lock the house. I'll be there in ten minutes."

I blew through a yellow light, and when I hit the next red, I turned into a residential neighborhood and rolled through stop signs for another two miles. The twilight was in full bloom, the clouds backlit with orange and pink hues, when I finally turned onto my street. I opened my eyes wide as I pulled into my driveway, then rubbed my forehead, hoping to stem a growing tightness.

Candi was sitting on the couch when I came into the family room. She stood abruptly when she heard me.

"Take it easy, there," I said. I walked to her and put my arm around her, and we sat together. She leaned her body into mine and grasped my hand. "I'm glad you're here," she said. "Would you like dinner?"

"This guy, what did he look like?"

"Pudgy face, curly dark hair, with a scar between his eyes."

"And he threatened you?"

"No, not exactly. Although that was definitely what he meant. I mean, he said, 'for the safety of your family.' Sounded threatening to me."

When I didn't respond, she said, "What are you going to do?"

"I'll go have a talk with him. It's just a little misunderstanding. How about if I bring dinner home?"

"Pizza?"

"Sure."

I went to my office and grabbed the Alvarez case report and the six hundred dollars I intended to return to him. Then I walked into the garage, opened the locked tool box welded to the bed of my pickup, found the lead sap I call 'Good Night, Irene', and fit it into the chest pocket of my black work coat. After that I started my truck and called Luis Alvarez.

"Yes?" he said after a single ring.

"I think we should have a meeting," I said.

"I'm staying at the Hotel Becket. Not far from your house." He enunciated the last sentence with emphasis, as if to make sure his meaning was not misunderstood.

"What room?"

"120."

"I'll be there in five minutes."

The Hotel Becket was right at the state line, on the California side. The building was newly built, part of the renovation of the prime real estate near the casinos. It was a two-story hotel boasting an upscale bar and restaurant. The exterior was done in mountain-chic stone and timber. It was not the most expensive hotel in South Lake Tahoe, but it was probably in the top twenty percent.

I drove around the block, circling the hotel and searching for a parking space. On my second lap, I found a spot on a dark street bordering a closed ski rental business behind the hotel. I wedged Alvarez's $600 into my pants pocket, but left the case report on my passenger seat. There was a rear hotel guest door close to where I'd parked, but it was locked, so I had to walk out to the main drag before I found the front entrance, which led through the lobby and into a large courtyard.

Room 120 was in the center of a row on the right side of the courtyard. I stared at it for a moment, then walked across a section of brick inlays and rapped on the door. The woman named Claudia Merchan appeared in the doorway, and behind her I saw Luis Alvarez sitting at a small table. The room was dimly lit by a single lamp behind him.

Claudia stood to the side so I could enter. I walked to where Luis sat and dropped the folded bills on the table.

"Here's the portion of your retainer I didn't use," I said. "If you want, I can give you a verbal account of what I learned during my search for Manuel."

"You owe me that."

I sat across from him and stared at his face. He looked impassive, or maybe a bit smug. I didn't know if that was because he knew he'd motivated me to respond quickly. But at that moment I didn't really care.

"I learned that Manuel paid someone to drive him from Fernley, Nevada, to South Lake Tahoe," I said. "You told me he knows boats, so I visited boat businesses until I found him."

"What was he doing in this place, Fernley?"

"It's where he chose to not continue in the minibus."

Luis's brow pinched, creasing the C-shaped scar between his eyes. To my right, Claudia was sitting on the edge of the bed watching us. "Why would he not continue in the minibus?" Luis asked.

"Because someone stabbed the driver to death."

Luis blinked, then he glared at me, his eyes glowing with suspicion. I glanced at Claudia, who was round-eyed and frozen.

"How do you know this?" he asked, his lips raised, an eye tooth glistening.

"I asked the right people the right questions."

Luis clicked his nails on the table in a rapid cadence. "Then tell me, where is the minibus?"

"Yes," Claudia said. She was now leaning forward, her elbows on her knees, her phony breasts pushed outward between her thin arms. She looked at me eagerly.

"Take your eyes off her and answer my question," Luis said.

"You didn't hire me to find the minibus. And I'm not in the mood to be charitable."

"And why is that, *señor?*" His Spanish accent was now more pronounced, as if something about my response prompted his return to his native language.

"You visited my house and scared my fiancée. I don't take it lightly. So, our relationship ends here and now."

"Here," Luis grunted, shoving the six hundred dollars at me. "Where is the minibus?"

"To the best of my knowledge, it's still in Nevada somewhere," I said, shoving the bills in my coat pocket. "Contact the police if you want."

I pushed my chair back to leave, but Luis was already on his feet. For a moment I thought he might lash out at me, and my hand was moving to my sap. But apparently he thought better of it.

"*Adios,*" he said.

I left the room and walked out the front entrance of the hotel, then turned down the side street that led to the rear of the building. I fully intended to call Lonnie Swearingen the next morning and tell him to expect a call or a visit from Luis Alvarez. I'd advise the sheriff that Alvarez was likely using an assumed name and should be considered a person of interest in the murder of the minibus driver. I would also tell Swearingen that Alvarez would probably be uncooperative and should be held and interrogated. I'd make the call first thing in the morning.

I paced through the cold darkness and turned down the street behind the hotel. Just as I got to my truck I was startled by a voice.

"Hey, there," Claudia Merchan said, emerging from the shadows at the front of my truck. She wasn't wearing a coat, and her shirt was low cut and showed ample cleavage, her nipples extended in the cold and pushing against the cloth. "You shouldn't worry about Luis, he's like that sometimes. Would you like to have a drink with me?"

I shook my head. "No, thanks," I said, keys in hand. I began inserting the key in the door lock, then heard a sound and sensed motion behind me. I turned just as Luis Alvarez rose from behind my bumper and leapt at me. In his right hand I saw the silver flash of a blade.

I reacted instinctively, jumping back and facing him. He jabbed with his right, trying to stab me in the gut, the tip of the blade just nicking my coat. When he retracted his arm, I feinted a left hook, and he slashed with the knife, hoping to slice my forearm. But I pulled back the punch, then threw a right cross, my fist arcing in a blur. My knuckles slammed into the side of his face, and his features contorted as his head spun nearly 180 degrees. Then his body followed, and he twisted in the air and landed face down on the pavement.

"What the..." I breathed, stunned, my heart racing. I looked to where Claudia had been standing, but she was gone. Then I saw her run past me, her foot nearly hitting Luis's head. She sprinted off into the moonless night.

My eyes fell back to Luis. I tapped his shin with my boot, and he didn't move. He was out cold.

"Attempted murder," I said out loud. Then I called 911.

.　　.　　.

A South Lake Tahoe PD squad car arrived within two minutes, followed by an ambulance. Luis Alvarez was still unconscious. I stood talking to two uniformed cops, both of whom I'd met before, but neither whose name I could remember.

"He was a client of mine," I said, standing in the bright glare of the patrol car's spot lamp. "We had a meeting in his hotel room, then I left out the front entrance. He must have come out the back door there and hid behind my pickup, waiting for me. He came at me with a knife, tried to stab me in the gut."

Two paramedics knelt beside Luis Alvarez. "A woman he claimed to be his wife also was here. She tried to distract me."

"Where is she?" one of the cops asked.

"After I knocked him out, she sprinted away."

"From her husband?"

"He tried to kill me, for Christ's sake. She's an accomplice."

One of the paramedics ran back to the ambulance.

"You said he tried to stab you?" the second cop said.

"That's right."

"Where's the knife?"

"Probably lying around here somewhere," I said, but the area was flooded with light, and I didn't see it. The cops and I stood looking around.

"I'm sure it flew from his hand. Maybe under a parked car. Or maybe underneath him."

The paramedic returned to Alvarez with an oxygen mask attached by tube to a steel canister. A minute later the other paramedic looked up at us. "He's not breathing. We need to get him to trauma."

The paramedic who'd been holding the mask to Alvarez's face began pushing rhythmically on his chest, just as two more patrol cars arrived. Then they placed Alvarez on a gurney and fed him into the back of the ambulance.

. . .

I rode to the police station in the back of a patrol car and was placed in an interview room with an on-duty detective named Bolo Jones. He was a tall, square-headed man with bristly hair that looked dyed, and he had a protruding mole on his chin that must have made shaving difficult. When he spoke, only one side of his mouth moved, as if the other side of his face was paralyzed.

I sat across from him and answered his questions, speaking into a digital recording unit on the table. When Jones was finished with the interview, he switched the device off.

"You intend to press charges?" he asked.

"What do you think? He tried to kill me."

"I'll let the D.A. know."

"Tim Cook?"

"Cook? No, he moved away a couple months back. The new district attorney is Magnus Swett."

"Where's he from?"

Jones shrugged, then looked at me with a curious gleam in his eyes. "You've never heard of him?"

"Nope. Why?"

"I overheard him talking about you the other day."

I stared back at Jones. His forehead was grainy, his eyes almost color- less. "Can't imagine why," I said after a moment.

"Really?" Jones replied, a crooked smile beginning on his mug.

At that moment the door opened, and one of the patrolmen I'd rode with entered the room.

"It's bad news, Reno."

"What?"

"The man you punched didn't make it."

I blinked. "Didn't make it where?" I asked, feeling like my intelligence was draining out of my ears.

The patrolman raised his eyebrows, probably wondering if my com- ment was a lame attempt at humor. Then he replied, "The doctor said cause of death was traumatic brain injury. You must have really clocked him."

I studied the tabletop. "That's unfortunate," I said. "You mind giving me a lift back to my truck?"

"Not tonight. Sorry, but you're under arrest."

"What the hell for?"

"Voluntary manslaughter."

"It's a bullshit charge. Self-defense is not manslaughter."

"You're gonna have to work that out with our new prosecutor."

"Magnus Swett?"

"That's right. He'll be here tomorrow morning, nine A.M."

"I want to talk to him now."

"Not gonna happen."

I stared down at my clenched fists and blew out my breath. "I need to make a few phone calls."

"That'll have to wait," he said, then he read me my rights.

.   .   .

It's a funny thing, being arrested. From the moment you are held prisoner your social status changes, as if all an individual has achieved in his life, every virtuous act, every shred of earned respect, has been wiped off the board. A new set of labels are now assigned to you: liar, loser, greedy, stupid, deplorable—the list goes on and on. And those are the polite terms. For those less charitable, including most in the law enforcement trade, the language of the day is much more colorful.

As I went through the booking process, I saw a number of people I knew, mostly uniformed cops and plainclothesmen. Some I'd worked with on past cases, with positive outcomes. But regardless of our history, all either averted their gaze or stared at me blankly, as if I was a subspecies unworthy of recognition. The sole exception was a detective I'd butted heads with some months ago. When our eyes met, he smiled broadly, grabbed his crotch, and shook his genitals at me.

In the four years I'd lived here, I'd spent plenty of time in the building off Al Tahoe Boulevard that served as South Lake Tahoe police headquarters. But I'd never had the pleasure of residing in their jail. It wasn't until ninety minutes after my arrest that I was led, thankfully without handcuffs, through a steel door and into a hallway where three payphones were mounted on the wall. From around the corner I heard a hubbub of male voices, and then I was assaulted by the wafting odor of unwashed clothes, urine, and vomit.

A middle-aged uniformed officer with a beer gut, bad breath, close-set eyes and a toilet brush mustache stood close enough to listen as I made my calls. The first was to my fiancée.

"The arrest is bogus, Candi. There's a new D.A. I never met. For some reason he wants to take me over the hurdles."

"Why would he?"

"My guess is one of the cops here had nothing better to do and brought up my name in a bad way."

"What kind of dipshit cop would do that?"

"I think you just answered your own question. Listen, I expect to be out of here by ten A.M. tomorrow. You don't need to worry about anything."

"Should I call anyone?"

I glanced at the mustachioed uniform, who was picking his nose. I didn't know how many calls he'd allow me.

"Yeah, call Sam Ruby, my lawyer. Then call Marcus Grier. Their numbers are in the black book on my desk."

"I'll tell Marcus to get over there and have you released."

"Okay," I said, knowing that wouldn't happen. I looked again at the cop. "Candi?"

"Yes?"

"I'm not sure how many calls they'll let me make. So please call Cody Gibbons too, let him know."

When we hung up, I smiled, despite the situation. In times of crisis, Candi never overreacted, never burdened me with panic or unanswerable questions. She simply focused on what she could do to help. I suspected she acquired this trait from her mother, who'd been married to a Houston sheriff for thirty years.

Before my next call I glanced at the list of 24-hour bail bondsmen affixed to the wall. I knew most of them. They were a heartless and cynical breed whose sole purpose was to extract money from those unfortunate enough to be arrested. Their success was based on the ability to both assess flight risk, and when required, to hunt down fleeing bail skips. I once worked as a skip tracer for a bondsman in San Jose. It's a no-bullshit, hardcore business, and not one given to flexibility or charity. Unless I was owed a big time favor, which I wasn't, I'd be paying a full rate of ten percent. I knew the typical bail for voluntary manslaughter was a hundred grand. That meant it would cost me ten grand to avoid a night in jail.

Next I called my attorney's cell. Sam Ruby split his time between San Jose and Sacramento, and could be here in a few hours if necessary. But his voice mail recording said he was out of the country on vacation, and wouldn't return calls until the following week.

I muttered a curse and called Sheriff Marcus Grier's mobile number. If anyone in town could discourage an overzealous district attorney, it was Grier. He was the highest ranked cop in the local force, and in effect served as the police chief for South Lake Tahoe. Our history went back almost five years, to when I helped him get rehired after he was fired by a corrupt county sheriff. Since then we'd crossed paths frequently on local cases, and although he wasn't always thrilled with my methods, he definitely viewed me as one of the good guys. I'd even met his wife and two daughters, and Candi and I had been to their house for summer BBQs a few times. I considered him a friend and ally.

But I also realized there was only so far that Grier would bend over backwards to aid me. This was due both to Grier's career priorities (above all, he valued keeping his job and providing for his family), and to the political reality that Grier was required to serve the district attorney's prosecutorial agendas.

When my call went to voice mail, I began what I intended to be a concise message, but my words meandered and seemed inadequate to describe the situation. I finally said, "Look, Marcus, your D.A. wants to screw me and I need your help. Can you call this guy, Magnus Swett?"

"That's it," the cop said when I hung up. "It's time to meet your bunkies."

He followed me around the corner to the holding tank. This is where new arrivals spend a short amount of time before moving to the next phase of their detention, which offers all sorts of pleasantries, including a full cavity search, a lice bath, and the issuance of jailhouse clothing. Soon afterward, the prisoner will be made available to detectives who will try to extract a confession. Concurrently, a court date will be set.

The holding tank was a windowless room about twenty by thirty feet. Benches lined the walls, where six men were spread out. Two lay curled beneath the benches, one snoring loudly. The other had his hands over his ears. Across the room, another pair were in their twenties and dressed fashionably casual. Their hair was neatly styled, and I assumed they were tourists busted for scoring coke or some other minor infraction. In the near corner, a man in a suit and tie sat silently, holding his head in his hands.

It was the sixth man who took it upon himself to define the evening. He was built like a haystack, at least three hundred pounds of pale flab. He wore a black T-shirt beneath gray bib overalls secured by chrome buckles. His forearms were scrolled with tattoos, including a lovely bit of artwork displaying a swastika above a tombstone.

"What you in for, white brother?" he said, as I sat on a section of bench near the iron bars that separated us from the hallway. When I didn't respond, he took a step in my direction. "Not that I really give a shit."

"You wouldn't believe me if I told you."

"Try me."

"I threw a beer can in a ditch."

His lips pursed and his beady eyes grew even smaller in his round head. "That some kind of joke?"

I leaned against the wall and looked up at him. "Do I look like I'm in the mood for joking?"

I kept my eyes on his while he took a few more steps forward. He stopped about ten feet short of where I sat. "You got a smart mouth, pal," he said.

I dropped my gaze to his lower body. If he came forward in a rush, I'd drop to the floor and slam my heel into his knee. If he was lucky, he might avoid surgery. Depends how hard I kicked him.

"You smart, you'll keep it shut," he said, but he was standing in the middle of the room, and if he had an inclination to test me, he had clearly reconsidered.

"Nothing would please me more than to end this conversation," I said.

He scowled, his lips puckered like an asshole. "I sure hope we meet down the road, motherfucker. Maybe we're headed to the same joint, where my people are waiting. Then we'll all get on the same page, hear me?"

I resisted a response and just nodded in agreement, hoping he'd view it as a conciliatory gesture and one that allowed him to save face. Apparently it served that purpose, for he grunted and returned to the opposite side of the cell. And I was glad for that, for I didn't need to make my situation worse than it already was.

I lay on the bench, stared at the water-stained ceiling, and tried to think positively. But after a few minutes it seemed like nothing more than a delusional exercise, and so I just let my mind wander where it may.

All my life I'd enjoyed hand-to-hand combat. The earliest fight I remember occurred on my first day in high school, when I was thirteen years old. An older kid decided to victimize a friend of mine. Back then, the ritual was to grab a younger student and stick him head first into a garbage can. Then two students would hold him by the legs, pushing him down and spinning to ensure maximum coverage. This would usually happen at the tail end of lunch hour, when the cans were full of discarded cafeteria food. When the victim was allowed free, his clothes and hair would be smeared and matted with custard, ketchup, peanut butter, melted ice cream, soda pop, lettuce, and the entree of the day, which could range from spaghetti in tomato sauce to BBQ beef sandwiches.

Some defenseless students viewed this as little more than a friendly public hazing. I didn't buy into that, so when my friend was chosen for the ordeal, I stepped up to defend him. The ringleader was a tall, gangly teenager, older and bigger than me. But his advantages proved inadequate, for I was still reeling from my father's murder and full of unrelieved rage. Plus, despite having no formal training, the athletics of fighting seemed natural to me.

By the end of the day, the teenager was in the hospital recovering from a concussion and his family was threatening my mother with a lawsuit.

The school counselor thought football would be "therapeutic," so I joined the team and played middle linebacker. I enjoyed the experience, but was ambivalent about the overbearing coaches and what I felt was artificial comradery. So I switched to wrestling.

If it was therapy I needed, wrestling provided it, for it allowed me to exercise my demons to the point of exhaustion. Few sports are as demanding, both physically and mentally. But what really inspired me was the challenge of the simplest form of combat: one-on-one, man against man, may the strongest, most skilled, and most determined win. No reliance on teammates; every man wins or loses on his own merits. And no excuses for losing, for there is nowhere to hide in the ring.

I lost a single match while in high school, to a Brazilian kid who told me afterward that he was a brown belt in jiu-jitsu. Within a week I enrolled at a martial arts school. The jiu-jitsu skills I learned were critical to my winning a spot on the university wrestling team, where I participated in tournaments for four straight years.

I heard a noise from outside the cell, then two guards arrived with folding cots. They entered the cell while a third guard stood watch outside the bars. Once the cots were unfolded and situated about the room, the guards left and the lights were dimmed. Within a minute, my cellmates moved to the cots, their shadowy figures reluctant but resigned. I was the last to take a cot, and I knew I wouldn't sleep for hours. But I lay down anyway, for I was in jail and had nothing else to do.

When I finally grew drowsy, I was replaying the fight in my mind. There was no doubt that Luis Alvarez's intention was to kill me. To set me up, he'd sent Claudia Merchan outside as a distraction. She'd come out into fifty degree weather in a low cut top, hoping to captivate me with her cleavage. But the diversion had failed, and Alvarez didn't realize it until it was too late. He also probably didn't know I was trained in self-defense and not an easy mark. It all added up to a series of fatal mistakes on his part.

But I certainly hadn't tried to kill Alvarez. I threw an appropriate punch, a disabling punch. I meant to knock him down, not kill him. I'd hit plenty of men that hard, and none had died. Just my luck, he had a glass jaw.

I rolled over and tried to get comfortable on the lumpy mattress. The only witness to the fight was Claudia Merchan, who'd run away after I struck Alvarez. Why had she run? Was she scared I would attack her? Or hold her for the police? Or had she just panicked?

Magnus Swett would definitely seek Claudia as a witness. But so would my attorney, once I told him what really happened. If Claudia was brought to stand, would she perjure herself? That would depend on the true nature of her relationship with Luis Alvarez. But whatever her inclination, Sam Ruby would be ready. He was one of the best defense lawyers in California. He'd take the dirt I'd found on Claudia and dig deeper. By the time Ruby was done with her, no jury would give her much credence.

This will all blow over tomorrow, I told myself. No need to kill my brain cells with worry. After all, I was innocent, and I needed to be home with Candi, for she was pregnant and my absence was unacceptable. Our life together would soon include marriage and parenthood, and I wouldn't let anything stand in the way of that. The bearers of justice and righteousness would surely rise in our corner. I repeated this refrain every time doubt and worry clouded my thoughts.

I wish I could say I slept well.

7

The lights came on at seven A.M., followed by trays of cold breakfast and weak coffee. Over the next ninety minutes, a jailer released all six of the men sharing the cell with me. Whether they were released on their own recognizance, or to meet with bondsmen, or to be interviewed by detectives, I didn't know or care. I just wanted out as soon as possible, and I was already annoyed that I was the last one there. I reminded myself that impatience doesn't work in jail, but as a licensed private investigator and bounty hunter, I considered myself part of the local justice system, and that should have afforded me preferential treatment.

As the minutes ticked by, I wondered where the hell Marcus Grier was. Unless he was dealing with a major emergency, he should have shown up by nine A.M. No matter what the situation, I couldn't imagine him abandoning me.

It was 10:30 when the jailer finally came for me. He pointed me down the hallway to the same room where I'd been interviewed the night before. When I went through the door, I stood facing three men, one whom I didn't recognize. He was sitting at the table and wearing a black pin-striped business suit. Standing behind him were Marcus Grier and Detective Bolo Jones.

"Well, good morning, Marcus," I said, trying unsuccessfully to keep the frustration out of my voice. Grier frowned and put his hand on his gun belt near where his .38 rested in its holster. He had recently regained the thirty pounds he'd lost in last year's diet and looked like an overfilled inner-tube, his jowls round, his arms massive, his midsection tight against his shirt. Grier had grown up in the Deep South and battled an addiction to fried food.

"Dan, this is D.A. Magnus Swett," Grier said, his eyes bulging from the walnut shine of his face. "Take a seat, please."

I sat across from the prosecutor. His head was round and hairless and sectioned with scars and ridges that made it resemble a soccer ball. His blue eyes were small and deep-set above a bulbous nose. When he looked at me, his colorless lips tightened, as if he was sucking on something sour. His necktie was red and his suit looked like something an undertaker might wear.

"Pleased to meet you," I said. "You're new in town?"

He kept his still eyes on mine. "I read the statement you provided Detective Jones."

"Yes?"

"There was no knife found at the scene. Can you explain that?"

I felt my skin tighten. "I can only assume Claudia Merchan grabbed it before she ran off."

"Without the knife, I can't substantiate your claim of self-defense."

"Have you found Claudia Merchan?" I asked.

"We're looking for her."

The room fell silent except for the sound of my feet scuffling on the floor. "My P.I. and fugitive recovery agent licenses are up to date. I gave a full statement voluntarily, without an attorney present. I have a clean record. I'm perplexed at why I was arrested."

Swett's eyes rolled. "Your clean record includes involvement in no fewer than fourteen deaths in the Tahoe-Reno area. You seem to take your licenses very liberally."

74

"That's not true," I said. "Some of those deaths were not by my hand. The others were either self-defense or involved other mitigating circumstances."

"Yes, I've read your file carefully. And that includes the carnage that occurred in San Jose and Utah last year."

"Mr. Swett, I've never been charged with any crime in those cases. I operate within the law and within the codes and guidelines of my profession."

"I hope you'll forgive me, but that line sounds practiced."

"Besides, I suspect the man who tried to stab me is using an alias and is a criminal."

"So you feel justified in killing someone if you suspect they're a criminal?"

"Only if they're trying to kill me."

"We have no evidence that was the case, Mr. Reno. All we have is a dead body with your name on it."

"Have you identified him yet?"

"No. He wasn't carrying ID. Our detectives searched his room and came up empty."

"I suspect he has a history of violence. I doubt this was the first time he tried to kill someone."

"Your suppositions as to your victim's character and background suggest you were predisposed to do him harm."

I took a deep breath and looked up at Marcus Grier, who met my stare with a furtive glance. Then I shifted my eyes to Bolo Jones. He formed an O with his mouth, his eyebrows raised, then he winked and smiled.

Magnus Swett leaned forward on his elbows, his hairless pate knotted with furrows. "You have one chance to plead out, Mr. Reno. Voluntary manslaughter carries an eleven-year sentence in state prison. I'm prepared to offer you six years."

"You're serious?"

75

"Yes, and you better be, too. The manslaughter charge can be replaced by a murder charge, depending on what Claudia Merchan has to say once we find her. That's twenty-five to life."

"I'm not pleading to a goddamned thing."

"That's a decision you'll likely regret. Do you have an attorney yet?"

"Mine's on vacation."

"How unfortunate. You better find an alternate. Either that or we'll assign you a public defender."

"I'll take him back to the tank," Grier said.

.   .   .

We stopped in the hallway near the payphones. My mouth was dry, and I felt a hollow lump in my stomach. "Marcus, what's the deal with Swett? Why's he busting my balls?"

Grier rubbed at his lips. "I don't know much about him. He's only been here a couple months."

"Look, you know me. I did nothing wrong. Can't you go talk to him?"

When Grier looked at me, his expression seemed disjointed, as if he was caught in an anomalous storm and was trying to navigate his way to shelter. "I'll try," he said. "But you need to be ready to post bail. You'll appear before the judge at two."

"I can't believe this."

"Go this way. Candi is waiting for you in the visitor's room."

"She is? How long has she been there?"

"Since 8:30."

.   .   .

When I saw Candi sitting in the room where prisoners were allowed visitors, I was struck with a wave of shame and regret so powerful that my knees nearly buckled. She was dressed in jeans and a white blouse, her hand resting on the swell of her belly, and an almost magical light seemed to radiate from her body. It was as if the angelic glow of her pregnancy had risen to a new level, and the fact that I was witnessing this moment in this room left me feeling as if I'd been hit in the gut by a wrecking ball.

I glanced at the other two occupied tables in the room. At one sat a skinny white punk covered in tattoos, talking with a man who could have been his brother. At the other table a stout Mexican man was conversing with two *cholos* in oversize clothes, bandanas tied on their heads, and gang tats on their fingers. They all looked like typical, run-of-the-mill criminals, exactly the kind of repeat offenders you'd expect to see in jail. Their eyes shined with undisguised jailhouse rut when they looked at Candi.

I sat across from her at the round white table and put my hand on hers. "You've been here all morning?"

"Yes. What's going on?"

"I'm scheduled for arraignment at two. That's when I can post bail."

"They won't let you free on your own recognizance? After all you've done for Marcus? After all you've done to serve law and order in this city?"

"The new D.A. doesn't see things that way. And I don't think there's much Marcus can do about it."

"I'd like to have a word with this D.A."

"I know, babe," I said, trying not to think about what I'd like to do to Magnus Swett. "Once Sam Ruby gets back in town, he'll take care of this mess in a hurry. But for now, the best thing is to not worry and just take it easy."

"Does the D.A. really think he can convict you?"

"I don't know. But I'm innocent."

"You'll need to prove that."

"Yeah," I conceded, and her face was flush, her eyes both vulnerable and angry. "Look, this is just an occupational hazard. I've been accused of crimes before. I'm not worried about it."

"Dan, how can you say that? Don't treat me like I'm stupid."

"Listen," I said, clasping her hands and leaning close to her. I dropped my voice to a whisper. "I am not going down for this. My attorney is the best in the business. I'll be home this afternoon, and everything will be fine. You have to believe that."

"But…" she said, then her eyes welled with tears. I wrapped my arms around her and held her head to my chest. "Don't get wrapped up in the what-ifs, Candi. You can't think that way. It will drive you crazy."

She held me tightly, and we sat that way for a long time.

.   .   .

At two P.M. I was led to the adjoining courthouse building, where I was introduced to the public defender. She was a slight woman with black hair in a bun and eyes like slits. I estimated her age as twenty-six.

We went to a small room across the hall from the courtroom and sat at a table.

"Just passed the bar?" I asked.

"Four years ago," she replied.

"Oh. You look younger."

"We only have a few minutes. This court appearance will serve as your arraignment. The judge will also rule on whether the probable cause is sufficient to warrant the charges. If the judge rules that probable cause is sufficient, then bail will be set. In that case, I need to convince the judge you're not a flight risk."

"I've lived here for four years and own my home. I live there with my fiancée, who's pregnant. I'm not going anywhere."

She looked up with a cocked eyebrow. "That's what they all say, right?" I said.

"More or less."

"Besides, the deceased came at me with a knife. I punched him in self-defense. It was a fluke that he died."

"If the D.A. believed that, you wouldn't have been arrested."

"To be honest, I don't know what his problem is."

"My understanding is there was no knife found at the scene."

"That's because the woman at the scene probably grabbed it before she ran off."

She held her eyes on mine. "At this hearing, the D.A. will present the details of the complaint to the judge. We don't get to argue at this stage, although I may be allowed to comment. If the judge agrees to press charges, I'll request R.O.R., no bail."

"Who's the judge?"

"Phil McIlroy."

"Never met him," I said.

We walked into the courtroom, and I sat in the row reserved for the accused. For the next ninety minutes, I watched while a dozen defendants were brought before the judge, a man about sixty with a full head of silver hair and a country club tan. For the most part, he looked bored to death. I would have bet that he spent his off hours on a tennis court and sipping cocktails with South Lake Tahoe's upper crust.

The defendants were accused of a variety of common crimes, covering a wide range of what police generally refer to as "lesser dirt-bag offenses." That included shoplifting, drunk driving, drug possession, passing bad checks, vandalism, disturbing the peace, failure to pay child support, and so on. The junior D.A. handled these cases, and it wasn't until a few minutes before my name was called that Magnus Swett entered the courtroom.

I stood while the judge's assistant read the charges. Across the aisle Magnus Swett waited in his black suit, studying a sheet of paper in his hand.

"Mr. Swett?" the judge said.

"Yes, your honor. On April 14 at approximately 8:15 P.M., Dan Reno was involved in a physical altercation with a man, presently unidentified, at Cedar Avenue approximately one hundred feet southwest of Park Avenue. When paramedics arrived, they found the man unresponsive and rushed him to the hospital, where he was declared dead due to massive head trauma. The state contends the defendant killed the man with a punch to the head."

"Do you have anything to add, Miss Li?"

"Mr. Reno was purely defending himself against a knife attack, and he called 911 himself."

"There was no knife found at the scene," Magnus Swett retorted.

"Duly noted. The defendant is bound over to the district court for trial. How do you plead, Mr. Reno?"

I stared at the judge for a moment. "Not guilty, your honor."

"Are you prepared to post bail?"

"Your honor," my assigned counsel replied, "We request Mr. Reno be released on his own recognizance. He is a licensed private investigator and fugitive recovery agent. He owns a home here and lives with his fiancée, who is expecting a child. Plus, he deals with criminals on a regular basis, and was only defending himself when the unfortunate event occurred. He is not a flight risk."

Magnus Swett leaned forward, his knuckles on the table. "Dan Reno, your honor, is a man who leaves dead bodies in his wake wherever he goes. He's been involved in fourteen deaths in the greater Tahoe region in the last four years, plus at least that many in the Bay Area, Nevada, and Utah. There is no doubt he has excessively violent tendencies, and he needs to be held accountable. The state requests remand."

The judge rapped his gavel on his desktop. "Bail set at two hundred thousand, cash or bond." He stood abruptly and exited through a door behind his bench, clearly in a hurry to declare his work day finished.

Stunned, I looked down at the public defender. "A hundred thousand is standard bail for voluntary manslaughter," I said. Before she could reply, Magnus Swett walked past us. "See you in court, Reno," he said.

·   ·   ·

I spent the next two hours arranging my bond. It involved sending Candi to the bank to pull twenty grand cash from my safe deposit box. It was money I had put away for the future. It was money I was saving to help us raise our child. It was money I had literally risked my life for.

And now, by grace of his title, Magnus Swett, a man I'd never met and had no history with, had taken that money from me. The fact that he'd done so legally made it no less grievous. In fact, I considered it a criminal act. Swett didn't have to arrest me; he could have instead waited for an investigation to be completed before determining if any charges were warranted. Then, to add insult to injury, Swett requested remand, meaning incarceration until trial. It was as if he had a personal vendetta.

When I finally was released and made it back to my truck, I felt like a barbwire tourniquet was wrapped around my skull. I had moved to Lake Tahoe to escape the San Jose rat race, where I made barely enough to rent an apartment. I had escaped the congestion and overpriced real estate to live in a valley where a picturesque alpine lake was surrounded by the towering splendor of the Sierra. I had mined a niche in investigative work, taking cases that sometimes involved direct conflict with violent criminals. I had made a living, bought a home, found a woman to marry, and was ready to start a family. And Swett wanted to take it all from me.

No, I thought, staring through my dirty windshield. Swett's act was worse than criminal; it was an act of war. At that moment, if I could have plotted a surefire way to get away with it, I would have driven straight to wherever he lived and killed him.

8

Better late than never, I brought a pizza home for our dinner that evening, and Candi and I spent a quiet night together. I reassured her and acted as normally as possible, for I was concerned that stress could impact her pregnancy. But I repeatedly found myself staring off, immersed in my own thoughts and not hearing her comments. After the sun set and the windows turned dark, I sat next to her on the couch, our bodies pressed together. We watched television until she went to bed around eleven P.M. Then I poured three fingers of Canadian Club, put on my coat, and went out to the deck.

The sky was cloudless and dark, the air cold on my face. I took a long swallow and felt the whiskey burn my throat. I stared out past my back fence and heard a series of staccato yips from a family of coyotes that roamed the meadow. Other than that, the night was silent.

My cell rang, its electronic tone shattering the calm. My eyes clicked when I saw it was my vacationing attorney returning my call.

"Thanks for calling, Sam. Where are you?"

"Florence, Italy. Just finished breakfast and listened to your voice mail while trying to enjoy a cappuccino. What have you got yourself into?"

I recited the events leading up to my altercation with the man who went by Luis Alvarez and then told him about Magnus Swett and his intentions.

Then I added, "I ran a people search on Luis Alvarez, couldn't find a match. I think it's an alias."

"He wasn't carrying ID?"

"No, and the police couldn't find anything in his room, either."

"How about the woman, Claudia?"

"They said they were looking for her."

"And you think she picked up the knife before she ran off."

"Yeah. Only other possibility is one of the cops or paramedics took it, but I don't know why they would."

"Hmm. Is it possible a security camera might have recorded it?"

"I doubt it, but I'll check."

"Have they set a trial date yet?" he asked.

"Yeah, in two weeks." When he didn't reply, I said, "What do you think my chances are?"

"Assuming the woman testifies, do you think she would tell the truth?"

"I doubt it. She has a criminal background—prostitution, credit card fraud. Plus, if she tells the truth, it could implicate her in attempted murder."

I heard Sam Ruby sip from his cappuccino. I imagined he was sitting on a quaint stone terrace, or perhaps a balcony, looking out over a tranquil, picturesque Italian landscape. But when he spoke his voice was hard and focused.

"I can rip her to pieces on cross, but I'll need as much dirt as you can dig up on her. But more important is Luis Alvarez. You're pretty sure he's a criminal?"

"He came at me with a knife. Set it up nice, but I was too quick for him. But it's not the first time for him."

"Then you need to find out who he is, and document everything. If we can show him as a man with a violent history, your claim of self-defense stands up a lot better."

"That's your strategy, then? Smear the victim?"

"In a case like this, it's crucial. Plus, it's all we got. Simply your word against Claudia's. But it sounds like your D.A. doesn't like you. He'll try to use your background against you."

"Fuck him."

"The best way to do that is show the jury that you're a saint compared to the deceased."

"What if I can't find out who he is? What if he remains a John Doe?"

The line went silent for a moment, then my attorney said, "Not good for you."

.   .   .

The next morning I awoke before Candi and left the house immediately, not even bothering to comb my hair. I drove straight to the scene of the altercation. The sun had just risen, and the cars parked behind the hotel were coated in dew. I stood at exactly the spot where the fight had occurred. The nearest building, thirty feet from where I stood, housed three businesses along the street. One was a ski rental shop with a neon sign in the window advertising *Rossignol.* To its left was a sandwich shop, and to the right a tattoo parlor. I walked over and carefully checked each business for security cameras facing the street. Finding nothing, I crossed the street to the back wall of the Hotel Becket and walked its length, searching for cameras installed beneath the gutter. Although it had been very dark when the fight happened, I knew that some modern surveillance cameras could capture images in near total darkness. But it was a moot point, since I didn't find a single camera.

I went back to my truck, which I'd parked in the same spot as when I was here last. I got down on my belly and looked under the nearby cars for the shiny blade of a knife, although I knew it was likely a futile effort. Then I peered up and down the street. Seeing nothing, I turned in a slow 360, and then once more, like a bewildered tourist. What I was searching for, I didn't know. Maybe a cosmic clue beaming in from the stars beyond the morning sky, to show me the path to innocence and freedom. Or maybe I was just hoping that immersing myself in the scene of the crime might spur a thought that I wouldn't otherwise have.

What I got instead was a phone call. I looked at my ringing cell and saw it was Cody Gibbons.

"Cody," I said.

"That must mean you're out of the gray-bar hotel," he replied.

"Got out yesterday around five. My bail was two hundred grand."

"What? What kind of rat fuck is that?"

"A twenty grand kind, at ten percent bond rate."

"Fuckin' A, Dan."

"There's a new D.A. in South Lake Tahoe. Seems he's read up on me and decided to punt a railroad tie up my ass."

"Who is this jackass?"

"Magnus Swett. Ever hear of him?"

"No. Should I have?" Cody asked.

"I don't know, but he wants to put me away."

"That ain't gonna happen. Look, Dirt, I'll be there in about two hours."

"You're on the road?"

"Just passing through Sacramento."

"I can take care of it, Cody."

"No worries, I need to blow Dodge anyway. I had a little misunderstanding with the Lopez brothers."

"You mean Fatty and Skinny?"

"Right. It seems Skinny got tired of rejection and never getting laid, so he raped a housewife in Atherton. But the house has security cameras all over the place, and the whole thing got recorded. So Skinny calls me from lockup and says the housewife wanted it and it was consensual and he wants me to make sure she understands the charges need to be dropped. And I told him, 'Listen, you rat-faced pervert, I think you've been sniffing the glue bag too long, because you smacked her around and it's on tape, and you're nuts if you think I'd go to bat for a scumbag rapist.'"

"What do you owe him?"

"Nothing. I mean, him and his brother, those genetic misfortunes, have been feeding me street G2 for a long time. And I admit it's been helpful on occasion. But I've paid them for it, and besides, I feel I need to wear a body condom every time I deal with them. Anyway, Fatty calls me, and he's losing it, because, you know these two are twins, right?"

"Twins? They don't look like it," I said, leaning against my truck bed.

"Yeah, it's strange, since Skinny is a hundred-forty pounds dripping wet, and Fatty, the bag of whale shit, weighs four hundred. But they're exactly the same height, and if they weighed the same, they'd probably look real similar. So they got this twins thing, right, like when one is fucked the other feels his pain. So Fatty is getting a little irrational."

"He really expected you to coerce the woman his brother raped?"

"Yeah, until I set him straight. And then he basically lost it, said all sorts of crazy shit, and I would have busted him up, but I don't need the headache, you know?"

"Best to let them cool down for a while, huh?"

"Yeah, Fatty's in meltdown mode, and I could use a change of scenery anyway. So how do you beat this thing?"

"The man I punched is a John Doe, probably from Miami. I need to find out who he is, and hopefully he's got a sheet full of felonies."

"Sounds pretty straight forward. Did you tell Grier to send his fingerprints to Miami PD to look for a match?"

I rubbed at my temple. "No, I need to call him," I said.

"Get on it, buddy. Don't let him forget he owes you."

We hung up, and I called Grier's cell. When he didn't answer, I left him a message asking that he contact Miami PD and send them Luis Alvarez's fingerprints. Whether or not he would prioritize it, I couldn't say. Every time I asked Grier for support, he weighed the potential consequence carefully. If Grier felt contacting Miami PD could cause him problems with Magnus Swett, he might default to letting me solve my problems on my own.

•   •   •

When I got back home, Candi was sitting at the kitchen table in her bathrobe. I had hoped to make coffee while she was still in bed, but she'd beat me to it.

"Where were you?" she asked, sipping from her cup.

"At the Hotel Becket, scouting around." I poured myself a cup and sat across from her. "Cody called while I was there."

Her eyes widened. "Can he do anything to help you?"

"He's on his way here."

"Why?" she asked.

I looked back at her silently.

"I mean, what's your plan?"

"Sam Ruby called late last night. I need to find out who the deceased is, dig up the dirt on him. If he's bad news like I suspect, no jury will convict me."

"That's what Sam said?"

"More or less."

"Do you need Cody's help?" she asked, doubt edging her voice.

I exhaled and looked at the steam rising from my cup. "I don't know yet."

Candi crossed her arms. "It's just that, his methods are a little extreme. I mean, you don't need any more trouble."

I reached across the table and grasped her hand. "Cody is my best friend," I said. "And he always has my back. He's also the most effective investigator I've ever met."

"I know," she said, smiling weakly, "but you understand my concern?"

"Yes. But I'll be far better off with Cody by my side. He's very resourceful."

"Okay, my guy."

"You have nothing to worry about, I promise." I came around and encircled her with my arms. She leaned her head into my face and we stayed in that position for a long moment. I was used to Candi questioning my relationship with Cody, and I always forgave her, for it was only natural. Actually, it would have felt strange if she didn't have reservations about my best buddy.

Cody's investigative technique often seemed like a wrecking ball flying free of the chain. But while it would be easy to view his actions as impetuous and impulsive, I'd learned that he was always thinking a step ahead. The problem was, that next step usually involved violent confrontation. This was Cody's method of operation; rattle your opponent's cage, piss in their punch bowl, stick a finger in their eye, and wait for their response. While this type of corner cutting presented certain risks, it usually brought investigations to a close quickly. Cody made this work well business-wise, as he often charged clients not by the hour, but based on expedient resolutions.

On occasion though, the mayhem resulting from his provocations made the network news stations. The most recent example was when two carloads of gangbangers from Compton riddled Cody's San Jose home with machine gun fire. I was there at the time and emerged uninjured, while Cody was wounded in the thigh. He was back in action within 48 hours, albeit with a slight limp. The injury didn't stop him from shooting dead a perp who was an instant from pulling the trigger and putting a bullet in my chest.

If it was solely Cody's professional conduct that concerned Candi, that would have been enough. But Candi was also familiar with Cody's personal life, which had derailed after his divorce and was akin to a runaway train trenching a path of destruction through bars and picking up loose women at every stop. I suspected that in his dark, hungover hours alone, he might wish for a more stable existence, but if so, his attempts at this were always halfhearted and temporary.

Whatever Cody's professional or personal ethics, I'd long accepted him for who he was, and I loved him like a brother. When I told Candi that I'd be better off with Cody by my side, I considered it an understatement.

·   ·   ·

It was 10:30 when I heard the diesel rattle of Cody's fire engine-red Dodge truck. I walked out my front door as he was parking on the street. When he climbed out of the cab, I did a double-take. He had shaved his beard. The last time I'd seen him beardless was in high school.

"New look?" I asked, rubbing my jaw. I stepped off my deck and met him in the driveway.

"Yeah. I was on a date the other night, and this woman convinced me to shave it."

"Let me guess, that's what it took to get laid."

Cody smiled, his big jaw shiny in the sunlight. "Now, Dirt, you always default to that kind of thinking. Did it ever occur to you I might have other motivations in life?"

"Sure, like finding the next bar."

"Well," he said, clasping my shoulder with his huge paw, "I'll have you know I'm on a personal quest for life, liberty, and the pursuit of happiness. Those are my unalienable rights."

"Where did you hear that one?"

"It's in the Declaration of Independence. I thought you went to college."

"I must have slept through that class."

"Is Candi home?" he asked, eyeing the front door.

"No, she's working."

"Still teaching art at the college?"

"Yeah. She said she intends to until she goes into labor."

"Tough broad," he said.

"Looks like you lost some bulk."

"I'm down to two-eighty. It's my fighting weight. Let's sit here," he said, stretching his six-foot-five frame. "It's nice out."

We sat at the redwood picnic table on my deck. Cody stared out past my back fence at where the cloudless blue sky met the western flank of the ridgeline. I sat next to him, resting my arms where the sun warmed the rough wood.

"Start at the beginning," Cody said.

"It all starts with Manuel Alvarez, if that's really his name. He was supposedly driving from Miami to Reno with another man and two women in a Ford minibus."

"Why?"

"According to Luis Alvarez, Manuel wanted to come out west to try his luck."

"That's it? What about the other people in the bus?"

"I don't know. Luis Alvarez said they were Manuel's friends."

"No names or descriptions?"

"Nope."

"You said you found Manuel, right?"

"Yeah. Luis told me he was a boat guy, and I spotted him working at a boat rental company over in the Keys."

"You talk to him?"

"No. I think he made me, and I wouldn't be surprised if he left town."

"You think he's running from something?"

"I think he didn't want to be found by Luis."

"Tell me again about the minibus and the dead driver."

"He was found in the vehicle, parked at a turnout near an overpass in Fernley. It's about eighty miles northeast of here, out in the desert. Stabbed in the neck from behind, it looked like."

"Any ID of the body?"

"The Fernley sheriff said he was a John Doe when we talked a couple days ago."

"Christ, you got all these people, all unidentified?"

"The only verified name I got so far is the woman, Claudia Merchan."

"That's a starting point. Let's track her down. You think she's still in town?"

I ran my fingers over a weathered patch on the tabletop and pried free a splinter. "I suspect she's bailed. She was posing as Luis's wife. I think that's the reason she was here. To pose as his wife."

"Maybe she was his girlfriend."

"Yeah, maybe. My guess is she took the first flight she could get back to Miami."

"Let's find out, then."

"You got anybody works at an airline that owes you a favor?"

"It wouldn't matter if I did. There's only one way to get an airport to share passenger information. The request has to come from a verified law enforcement official."

"No way to fake it?"

"Nope. The airlines are paranoid about security, for obvious reasons. But lucky for you, I've got an ace in the hole."

"Your girlfriend at Vegas PD?"

"Huh? I don't think so. I haven't spoken to her in a while."

"Who then?"

"Abbey."

"Your daughter?"

"Yeah, didn't I tell you? She just got formally hired as a uniform at Vegas Metro. Give her a few years, she'll be running the department."

"Wow. I suppose congrats are in order."

"Damn right, Dirt. And for reasons beyond me, she thinks you're hot stuff, so I'm sure she'll be willing to stick her neck out."

I looked at Cody's big mug, his green eyes lighted with humor and self-assuredness, his lips pressed together in a cocksure smile, and I thought back to the case we had worked in Vegas a few months back. Cody had just met his daughter for the first time. She had been the result of a teenage fling, and Cody didn't know of her existence until after she graduated from high school. When he met her, she was twenty-one years old, attending UNLV and doing an internship with Las Vegas PD. She had inserted herself in the case Cody and I were working and was kidnapped by Russian mobsters and nearly killed. While it was true she owed Cody and me her life, I never considered it a debt I would call on. She was simply my friend's daughter.

"Don't get her in trouble," I said.

"You worry too much," Cody replied, jabbing at his cell phone. He stood and walked to my back fence. I watched him kick and stomp a series of gopher mounds near the fence as he paced. After a minute he lowered the phone from his ear and returned to the table.

"It's done. Abbey will see if there's any record of Claudia Merchan flying in the last couple of days. She says hello and asked how you're doing."

"What did you tell her?"

"I said you're just peachy, except for some problems with the local D.A."

"I guess that sums it up."

"Abbey said she'd call back in the afternoon. What do you want to do until then?"

I stood and hiked my boot up on the bench. "I want to see if I can find Manuel. I'd like to sit him down for a nice, long chat."

"I thought you said he probably left town."

"Maybe, maybe not. Let's go."

We climbed into Cody's oversized pickup and drove out to Highway 50. It was a fine spring day, the air crisp and tinged with the scent of pine. We turned left and drove away from the state line. To our right Lake Tahoe was a stunning blue, as if the color rose from the depths of the cold water. We passed the gym where I worked out, the grocery store where Candi and I bought food, and then we came to Zeke's Pit, where I still occasionally tended bar and kept an eye on my minority investment. It was here where my problems with Luis Alvarez began, and for a moment I felt a sorrowful weight in my gut. This was my home, and although I'd dealt with evil intruders before, this time it was different. This time I was engaged to be married, and would soon be a father. And this time, I had a manslaughter charge on my back.

It would have been nice to pull in for an early lunch, maybe have a few beers with Cody. But I had two weeks to uncover information critical to my defense and had no time to relax. Or feel sorry for myself.

Two miles up the road we pulled into the Tahoe Keys, a complex of canals and marinas built to provide boating access to the lake. I directed Cody to Action Boat Rentals, where I had seen Manuel Alvarez.

When we parked and went into the small lobby, I saw the same sun-tanned man who'd told me that Manuel had not shown up for work two days ago. He was speaking with a woman in hot pants and heels, and after a minute it became clear it wasn't a business conversation.

"Excuse me," I said. When he ignored me, I moved next to the woman, so close our elbows nearly touched. "Excuse me," I said again.

"You're the guy with the phony badge, right?"

"Private investigator. Need to ask a couple quick questions."

"I'm in the middle of a conversation, if that's not obvious to you."

"Tell you what, bub," Cody said, "Why don't you ask your lady friend to give us a few minutes? It'll be a wise investment, I promise." Cody winked and stood at the counter on the other side of the woman, sandwiching her between us.

"I'll talk to you later, Jeff," she said, and walked out.

"Sorry, there, Jeff," Cody said. "But I'm sure a smooth operator like you can recover. Should be no problem getting her in the sack, huh?"

The man made a face somewhere between perplexed and angry, but his anger faded as he sized Cody up.

"Have you talked to Manuel since I was here last?' I asked. When he paused, I said, "We don't have time for bullshit, Jeff. That would seriously offend us."

"He stopped by late in the afternoon two days ago to pick up his pay. Said he had family problems and was leaving town."

"He say where to?"

"No, and I didn't ask. I just paid him in cash and he took off."

"Why cash?" Cody asked.

The man frowned and shifted his eyes. "You promise to keep it between us?"

"As long as you're straight up, yeah," I said.

"The guy was an illegal alien. No social security number, no green card, nothing. Worked for minimum wage, cash, under the table. Look, I was doing him a favor."

"Think real hard, Jeff," I said. "Think about everything you know about him. Where do you think he's going?"

The man took a moment, then said, "My only guess would be, somewhere in the Caribbean. He once said it's a lot colder here than there."

. . .

We spent the remainder of the morning talking to the various boating businesses in the Keys. Then we drove around the west side of the lake, stopping at Camp Richardson before climbing the narrow switchbacks above Emerald Bay. Twenty minutes after descending to the rolling straights along the water, we visited the marina in Homewood, got nowhere, and continued north. We made another stop at San Ramon Boat Center, and ten minutes after leaving empty-handed we rolled into Tahoe City.

"Let's see if we can find a small Mexican restaurant with a bar," Cody said. "Like an authentic joint."

"In the mood for a margarita?"

"You said Manuel's native language is probably Spanish. So he might gravitate to somewhere he feels at home."

"He's not Mexican. I think he's from the Dominican Republic."

"They speak Spanish there, right?"

I ran a search on my cell, and we passed the Blue Agave and Hacienda Del Lago before parking at a small standalone building set back in a grove of pines off North Lake Boulevard.

The Habareno Cocina occupied a structure that looked like it had originally been a residential house. Beneath the Spanish tiled roof, the façade was white stucco, and neon signs advertising Mexican beer glowed in the windows to either side of the front entrance.

When we walked in, I spotted an empty six-stool bar in a dark nook apart from the dining room. It was past two P.M. and I would have preferred getting a quick bite, but I followed Cody to the bar without protest. The bartender was a plump fortyish woman with dark hair pulled back close to her head.

"How about two of your house margaritas, *Señora?*" Cody said.

"A couple menus too, please," I added, then I showed her my picture of Manuel. "Does this guy look familiar?" I asked her.

She shook her head. "No, I don't recognize him."

"Thanks, anyway. I turned to Cody, who was staring into the bottles behind the bar.

"When I was with the force," he said, "I was involved in a situation with the San Jose D.A. He asked me to lie on stand." I looked at him curiously. Cody rarely spoke of his time with San Jose PD.

"An ex-con had been stalking this woman, a social worker who spent a lot of time with disabled children. He sent her emails, called her, sent her flowers with bizarre notes, but she could never figure out who he was. His emails were untraceable, the calls made on a drug store cell."

The bartender placed our drinks in front of us. Cody removed the thin black straw and took a long swig. "The ex-con seemed to know everything about her. What food she ate, what cosmetics she used, where she bought clothes. She's starting to freak, right? Then the emails and calls got more threatening. This degenerate started talking about what he was going to do to her. All sorts of sick, perverted shit."

"She called the cops?" I asked.

"Yeah. She had no idea who was stalking her, but within two days I knew it was the ex-con. He was thirty days out of the pen on an identity theft charge. He had hacked her computer, which is how he knew all her buying habits. Plus, he rented an apartment across the street from hers, and had a freaking camera with a zoom lens set up on a tripod to spy on the poor woman."

"So, did you bust him?"

"No, I didn't have enough evidence. And then…"

"What?"

"The woman's calling every day in a panic. She keeps getting the emails, and he says he's gonna kill her. She's begging for police protection. But what can we do? All the evidence we had on the ex-con was circumstantial. Our assistant D.A. wanted this guy back in prison, wanted him bad, but there wasn't enough hard evidence to arrest him."

Cody took another long pull from his glass, the ice cubes rattling. He motioned to the bartender for a refill. Then he looked over at me, his green eyes flat and stoic. "And then she was found dead in her apartment, raped, mutilated, and stabbed."

"I imagine you took it personal."

"You're fucking right I did. And so did our A.D.A. We went after this guy balls to the wall, but he was smart and had covered his tracks meticulously. We were going nuts trying to sort through his digital footprint, we brought in our best forensic computer guy, but we couldn't prove the emails were his. And he didn't leave a shred of DNA at the crime scene. So we had nothing, but we arrested him anyway. We put him in an interrogation room and tried to spook a confession out of him."

"It didn't work, I take it?"

"No, he was hardcore con-wise, and then his lawyer shows up. And then we're really fucked, because this guy is a sharp defense attorney, and he starts tearing us to pieces."

"So he walked?" I asked.

"We had to let him go, but I caught him that night hanging out in a downtown dance club, and I figure he's casing his next victim, trying to decide who turns him on. I grabbed him out in the parking lot, and we spent a few quality hours together back at his apartment. I got a confession out of him, even found the knife he used to kill her. Problem was, none of it was admissible. But I brought it to the D.A. anyway, and you know what he told me? Make up a story that the confession wasn't coerced."

"Would a jury buy it?"

"You better believe it. Because this prick was guilty, and just because the evidence we had was illegally obtained, it was goddamn compelling. So when I said the perp voluntarily confessed, the jury was only too happy to take him off the streets."

"What was the verdict?"

"Twenty-five to life. He's caged at Pelican Bay."

The bartender set steaming plates of enchiladas on the bar. I took a bite and said, "Are you asking me if I think you did the right thing?"

Cody laughed. "That's where you thought I was going with this? Seeking your approval?"

"What then?"

"The perp's name was Malcom Swett."

I put my fork down. "Related to Magnus Swett?"

"How many guys you know with that last name?"

.   .   .

We left after Cody finished his third drink. For some people, three cocktails might render them dysfunctional for the day, or perhaps set them off on a bender. Neither applied to Cody. Over our twenty-year friendship we'd spent plenty of long nights in bars together. I'd seen him swill huge amounts of liquor, but I never remember seeing him drunk. At most, his judgement might become somewhat impaired, usually to the detriment of any miscreants he crossed paths with.

My relationship with alcohol was different. I'd plumbed the depths back when I was new to the trade. I hit my rock bottom after first killing a man, drinking myself out of a job and destroying my first marriage. Cody helped pull me out of the gutter, and I never abused the privilege after that, even rode the wagon for two solid years. When I came back to the booze, I was careful, and learned I could moderate. This was not due to any extraordinary self-control, but simply because my physiology was not prone to addictive abuse. For that I was fortunate.

Talk to a newly recovering alcoholic, and you'll learn that they tend to view the world through the lens of their addiction. They have a hard time understanding that many people can drink and not be addicted. To them, the idea that an individual can enjoy beers and cocktails on a regular basis without sending their life down the toilet is incomprehensible. Such is the mindset of those in the clutches of alcoholism.

"I found out the other day that Brado-boy Turner died," I said as we pulled out of the restaurant parking lot.

"Your old neighbor?"

"Yep."

"He was, what, five or six years younger than you?"

"Seven years, I think. He'd just turned thirty."

"What killed him?"

"Apparently he got blotto drunk and was driving the wrong way on the freeway in San Jose. Hit a semi head on."

"Poor bastard. He had it bad, didn't he?"

"I always felt sorry for his parents. He was adopted."

"What about his sister who jumped your bones?"

"Lusty Lana? She wasn't adopted, but Mrs. Turner couldn't have a second kid for some reason. So they adopted Brad."

"That's too bad. I liked that guy."

"They were just pursuing the American dream. Two kids, a dog, and a house with a white picket fence."

We stopped at a light. "Is that what you're pursuing?" Cody asked, looking at me out of the corner of his eye.

I stared out the windshield at shards of sunlight filtering through the pines. "Right now I'd settle for staying out of jail," I said. "But we're not getting anywhere with Manuel Alvarez. He could be anywhere."

"There's plenty of daylight left. Let's play it by the numbers."

And that's what we did. We hit every boating company between Tahoe City and Kings Beach, and no one we spoke to recognized my picture of Manuel. It was five P.M. when we crossed the state line and entered Nevada at Crystal Bay. We drove by all the old casinos, the Tahoe Biltmore, the Nugget, and the closed Cal Neva, which had been purchased by a Silicon Valley billionaire who hoped to return the casino-hotel to the glory days when Frank Sinatra, Marilyn Monroe, and Joe DiMaggio were among the visitors.

I saw Cody eyeing the casinos wistfully, no doubt imagining the bars inside. Then his cell rang.

"Hey, Abbey," he said. "I'm gonna put you on speaker. Dan's right next to me."

"Dirty Double Crossin' Dan?" she said.

"That's right," I said.

"Do you mind if I call you that, Dan?"

"Your dad made it up, so why not?"

She laughed, and her girlish tone seemed incongruent with her involvement in my case in Vegas and Utah last winter. But, like her father, I sensed she'd already assigned the memory to the past, a cavalier dismissal of the violence and death that had occurred.

"Claudia Merchan flew to Miami last Monday morning. She took the 9:46 flight out of Reno."

"She arrived in Miami late Monday?" I asked.

"At nine P.M."

"Did she fly with anybody?" Cody said.

"Doesn't look like it."

When we didn't respond, she said, "Anything else?"

I tapped my jaw with my knuckle. "Do you have record of what kind of car she owns?"

"I'll have to check the DMV database."

We drove on, hugging the shoreline of Crystal Bay until Abbey said, "2014 Honda Accord. Blue, license plate 276OCZ."

"Thanks, Abbey," I said.

"Good luck, Dirty Double Crossin.'"

Cody disconnected the call, and we continued around the lake, stopping in Incline Village and then heading south along the eastern shoreline. Then the road veered from the lake and into the forest. Shadowed by tall pines, we drove silently as purple streaks appeared in the twilight sky.

"So you think the new South Lake Tahoe District Attorney has a relative in prison for murder?" I said.

"I think it will be easy enough to find out."

"Yeah, but how will that help me?"

"You never know, Dirt. Magnus Swett's got a hard-on for you, right? It'd be nice to make him reconsider his priorities."

I gritted my teeth and stared at Cody's profile. He looked serene and confident. "I'd like to make him regret the day he was born," I said.

Cody smiled. "We'll work on that."

We made one more stop at Zephyr Cove, and saw the large paddle boat called the Tahoe Queen docked at the single jetty. We spoke with the only person we saw, a deckhand, and he didn't recognize my picture of Manuel.

We drove on, and were nearing the border at Stateline when I said, "I need to fly to Miami tomorrow."

"You mean *we*," Cody replied.

9

When we pulled into my driveway, Cody offered to come in and say hello to Candi. I hesitated before replying. "Probably best not to. I'll need to explain to her what's going on."

"I'll get a room at Pistol Pete's. Call me later, let's book our flight."

"Okay, buddy," I said.

I went into my home with a sigh and saw Candi sitting on the couch with Smokey curled on her lap. Her eyes met mine, and I smiled weakly.

"What have you been up to?" she asked.

"Searching for Manuel Alvarez."

"Any luck?"

"Nope." I sat down next to her. "I need to fly to Miami first thing tomorrow."

If she was surprised or dismayed she didn't show it. Instead, she grabbed my arm and said, "You don't worry about me. I'll be fine. You do what you need to do."

"I know, it's just that…"

"Dan, you can't let me be a distraction. I'm only three months pregnant. It's not like I'll be going into labor while you're gone."

I rested my hand on her belly. "I wish I didn't have to go. I keep thinking, how could I have avoided this trouble?"

"Just focus on what you need to do to get out of it." The words bounced off my face like conflicting stabs of encouragement and recrimination. "You know what?" she added, "You did nothing wrong. But you need to put your blinders on and defend yourself." She lay her hand over mine. "For us."

"For us," I repeated, as if in a daze.

.   .   .

By ten o'clock the next morning, I was sitting on an American Airlines flight, climbing out of Reno. Cody sat on the aisle, and fortunately no one was crammed in the middle seat between us. I gazed down at the barren high desert mountains as the plane made a sweeping turn and headed south toward Phoenix, where we'd lay over for two hours. Our scheduled arrival in Miami was nine P.M. We were on the same daily flight that Claudia Merchan took three days ago.

I'd stayed up late the previous night after packing my bag, reading up on Miami. I'd never been there, never set foot in the state of Florida. I studied maps of the greater Miami area, noting the proximity of the airport to the many sections of the city, including downtown, Little Havana, Little Haiti, Allapattah, and the tourist-party destination of South Beach. I always invest myself in understanding as much as I can about a new town before arriving for a job.

I skimmed the history of South Florida, beginning in the 1500s when the native Seminole tribe were the sole residents. Things began to change for the natives when Spanish explorers arrived in the 1600s, followed by the British in the 1700s. Once Florida was acquired by the U.S. in 1820, the Seminoles, despite fighting valiantly, suffered the same fate as all Native American tribes; they were defeated and forced to resettle, in this case to Oklahoma.

Miami was formally founded by a local businesswoman in 1896. The barrier islands of Miami Beach, one of the United States' most popular tourist destinations, was created in the early 1900s by an agriculturalist named Collins. With aspirations beyond farming, he and his family replaced his coastal avocado farms with resort hotels, and the area evolved into a rich commercial and cultural hub. Chartered in 1915, its man-made beaches frequently have to be replenished with new sand, an investment the city has always maintained. A tourism-spurred real estate boom collapsed after a hurricane in 1926, but despite the economic challenges, the Art Deco district was established during the peak of the Great Depression in 1935. Post-WWII, Miami's growth was heavily weighted by an influx of Latin American immigrants, particularly from the Caribbean islands.

Of more interest to me was the modern history, especially the events of the late seventies and the 1980s. The Mariel boatlift, which occurred in 1980, was a mass emigration of Cubans to the United States from the Cuban port of Mariel. Set free from communist Cuba by dictator Fidel Castro, 125,000 Cubans poured into South Florida, making the ninety-mile journey to Key West on often dangerously overcrowded boats. The number that were released from prison or mental health asylums has never been exactly determined, but some estimates run as high as 20,000. No one debates that Castro took advantage of the United States' liberal immigration policies to rid his nation of those he deemed undesirable.

It was bad timing for Miami. The arrival of thousands of immigrants with dubious backgrounds coincided with the beginning of Miami's explosive drug trade. The genesis of this business was in Colombia, where in 1975 Pablo Escobar began building a cocaine operation that would later become the Medellín Cartel. Once Escobar realized the massive opportunity awaiting in the U.S. market, he established a smuggling network, controlling the cocaine transportation from his processing plants in the Colombian jungle and onto planes and boats heading to South Florida.

By the time American law enforcement officials conceded that Miami was flooded with cocaine, violence on the streets had already broken out. Cuban gangs, along with enterprising local criminals, were fighting for turf. A bloody broad daylight shootout at Miami's Dadeland Mall prompted a policeman to refer to the shooters as 'Cocaine Cowboys.' This marked the beginning of a wave of blood-spattered killings. The bodies were typically left on Miami's streets as a warning to rival gangs.

Despite increased efforts by local police agencies, the relentless flood of cocaine into Miami made countless Miami hoodlums into multi-millionaires. It would take an entire decade for the cocaine business to be brought under control, and this only occurred after President Ronald Reagan created the South Florida Drug Task Force and assigned George Bush to lead a coordinated federal offensive.

By most accounts, the Feds won the war against cocaine smuggling by the early nineties. Either that or the smugglers scaled down their operations, got smarter, found ways to minimize or hide the violence. Because it was the violence, the gruesome spectacle of dead bodies on the street, that truly killed off the original cocaine cowboys. It had reached a scale that was intolerable to U.S. authorities. Pablo Escobar and the Medellín Cartel may have used their massive financial power to nearly destroy Colombia, but the United States was a different story.

After we touched down in Phoenix, Cody and I made our way to a noisy airport restaurant serving southwestern cuisine. We took two open seats at the end of the bar.

"Remember when you were a little kid," I said, "Nancy Reagan's 'Just Say No' campaign?"

"Part of the War on Drugs," Cody said, motioning at the bartender. "Big waste of energy."

"You think? Do people still use hard drugs like they used to?"

"Two Coronas," Cody said to the barkeep, pointing at the taps.

"I don't want a beer."

"They're for me. Have a glass of milk if you want."

"You see much blow on the street in San Jose?"

"Yeah, but more meth. And prescription drugs, lots of Oxycodone. Pot's everywhere too, but hell, now it's legal."

"When I think criminals in Miami, I think cocaine," I said.

"I think you've watched too many reruns of Miami Vice."

"All right, wise ass. Then where does the coke come from?"

"Mexico," Cody said. "Colombia may still produce the most cocaine, and Afghanistan the most heroin. But most of it flows through Mexico."

"Why?"

"Because that's where the most powerful cartels are. Los Zetas, the Sinaloa Cartel, and the Jalisco New Gens are the big players. When the Colombian cartels got smacked down, the Mexicans filled the void."

I turned from Cody and my eyes settled on the amber glow of a whiskey bottle that the bartender had just poured from. I could have reached out and grabbed it.

"You think Luis Alvarez was in the coke biz?" Cody asked.

"I don't even know for sure that he's from Miami," I said. "All I know is Claudia Merchan lives there."

"Maybe Luis was from Mexico. Maybe Juarez."

"The murder capital of the world?"

"It's a short flight from here. Right across the border from El Paso."

"You suggesting we cancel Miami?"

Cody held up his beer mug and drained it in a single pull. "What do I know? It's your party."

•　　•　　•

We hit turbulence as we descended into Miami, and it got worse as we punched through the clouds. The plane bucked and shuddered, and when we finally landed with a jolt, I looked out my window and saw rain hammering down on the runway.

"We must have come through a thunderstorm," I said.

"Whatever. Get me off this death trap."

Once we deplaned, Cody made a beeline for the first bar we saw. "Just a quick one, for my nerves," he said. I waited while he gulped a double shot of whiskey, which cost $18 and was about the same size as a single at Whiskey Dick's. Then we made our way to the baggage claim area to pick up the large bag I'd checked through. I lugged the suitcase off the carousel. It was heavy with firearms, ammunition, our bullet-proof vests, and a variety of gear we commonly used while working. It weighed 75 pounds, and I'd had to pay an extra fee to get it on the plane.

We walked for about half a mile before reaching the airport's rail system, which took us to the rental car center. Fifteen minutes later we drove out of the garage complex in a gray Toyota SUV. It was almost ten P.M. and it was raining so hard I couldn't see the road signs or the lines on the pavement.

"This is nuts," I said.

"You ever see rain like this in California?"

"Once or twice. And I've lived there my whole life."

Somehow we made it through the blinding deluge, running lights, missing turns, swearing and arguing, until we finally found our hotel. As soon as we parked, the rain abruptly stopped.

We stepped into the balmy night in front of the Holiday Inn, a mile northwest of the airport. "Why did you pick this joint?" Cody asked.

"Cheap and conveniently located."

"How so?"

I pulled the big suitcase from the back of the SUV and set it between two puddles. "We're only about a mile from the address I have for Claudia Merchan."

We waited behind a couple speaking Spanish at the reservation counter. Behind us was a dining area and a bar.

"How's your *Espanol?*" Cody muttered.

"Passable."

I'd reserved adjoining rooms, for I knew from experience that I could not sleep through Cody's chainsaw snoring. We took the elevator to the fourth floor.

"Meet me in the bar in fifteen?" he asked.

"Get a coffee. I want to work tonight."

"Okay, *señor.*

· · ·

The skies were heavy with rolls of white clouds when we left the hotel. It was eleven P.M., and the air was pleasantly warm. I tossed my coat and a small backpack into the back seat, and we headed west on Hialeah Drive, then turned right on NW 27th. The houses we passed were all small and single-story. Their stucco walls were painted blue, pink, and yellow, but the gay colors clashed with the security bars mounted to the window frames and piles of rubbish in some of the yards.

The streets were quiet, only a few cars out, and it took no more than five minutes to reach North River Drive. I drove along a white concrete wall with teal trim, then pulled into a narrow entrance that led to a blue awning over glass doors. On the awning, white lettering spelled *Serenity by the River*. We parked in a visitors spot to the side. Nearby was a gated driveway that likely led to a basement parking garage.

"You got her unit number?" Cody asked.

"Yeah."

"How do you want to play it? Go knock on her door?"

"I'd like to bug her place."

"What if she's home?"

I stared out the windshield at a growth of large frond plants at the base of the six-story structure. Above us, rows of balconies with scrolled white iron bars stretched up the face of the building.

"If she's home, we'll chat with her. If not, let's plant bugs."

Cody shrugged. "Fifty-fifty. Either way works."

I grabbed my backpack from the rear seat, slung it over my shoulder, and we walked to the glass door of the apartment lobby. It was locked. A card entry unit was mounted on the wall. I rattled the door and peered inside. The floors and walls were covered in glossy tan tiles. I looked around for security cameras, my eyes roaming past an open stairwell, a bank of mail boxes, and a metal elevator door.

"No cameras," I said, "but I can't beat this lock."

"What's plan B?"

"We'll have to wait for someone to open the garage."

We walked around to the garage gate and I futilely tried a locked steel door. Then we found a convenient hedge to crouch behind. Neither of us spoke. We had no way of knowing how long we might wait for a pair of headlights to appear, either entering or exiting the garage.

As luck would have it our patience was barely tested, for within five minutes the gate opened to allow a car to leave the structure. As soon as the gate began to close, Cody and I darted behind it. I looked to the right and quickly spotted the stairwell next to an elevator.

We hiked to the fourth floor and entered the deserted hallway. It was quiet; no sounds came from behind the walls of the apartments. We paced silently to unit number 410. I rapped on the door, just loud enough. We stood waiting.

"Maybe she's asleep," I said.

"You told me she's a hooker," Cody said. "They usually keep late hours."

"You'd know," I said, and knocked again.

"Maybe she's got a john in there."

"Her prostitution busts were a few years ago. I don't know if she's still selling herself."

"Old habits die hard," Cody said.

"Tell me about it." I knocked one more time, wishing there was a door-bell. When no one answered after a minute, I removed my backpack and selected a zippered nylon pouch from the outside pocket.

"If anyone comes out, tell them you lost your key and I'm a locksmith," I said.

"Okay, kemosabe."

I knelt and began working on Claudia Merchan's door lock. Picking locks is an imperfect science; some common residential locks can be opened in less than thirty seconds, while similar locks may take five minutes or more. Whatever the case, the process takes patience and concentration. If I try to hurry, it never pays off.

I worked the small tools methodically, ignoring the concern that a tenant could step into the hallway at any moment.

It seemed like longer, but it only took two minutes for the tumblers to fall. We quickly stepped into the dark unit. I held a flashlight in my left hand, and a stun gun in my right. I moved to the single bedroom and found it unoccupied. The apartment was empty.

"You plant the bugs," I said, handing Cody my backpack. "I want to see what I can find."

Cody grunted and knelt at the coffee table in the sitting room. There was a depression in the seat of the green couch, and the arm looked dirty and worn. I saw Cody's eyes take it in, then I walked down the short hall to the bedroom. I hit the light switch and wasn't surprised to see a twin bed, which was too narrow to comfortably accommodate two adults. The bedspread had a frilly fringe, as did the pillows. I opened the closet door and saw it was packed with a shoe rack and garments on hangers. The shoes were all womens', as were the clothes.

The dresser was under the single curtained window in the room. I went through the drawers and found nothing but underwear, stockings, blouses, bathing suits, and jeans. In the final drawer there was a jewelry box overflowing with bracelets, rings, and necklaces. It all looked like costume jewelry, nothing expensive.

The only other piece of furniture was a nightstand. If I was lucky, I might find an address book, or maybe a handwritten letter. I would have been pleased with any paper document that might point me in a direction. But there was nothing except a vibrator, a small bag of marijuana and a glass pipe, a few loose condoms, and two books of matches. I took pictures of their covers and went back out to the main room.

"You want one in the bedroom?" Cody asked, holding one of my dime-sized bugs.

"Yeah, try behind the nightstand," I said, walking to where a printer rested on a wood grain cabinet along the wall. If there was a place here where Claudia Merchan kept paperwork, this would be it.

The cabinet's top drawers were indeed stuffed with papers, but they were mostly old receipts and bills that she may or may not have paid. I sifted through the papers, searching for something that might provide a clue to the nature of her relationship with the man who claimed his name was Luis Alvarez. The only thing I found that made me pause was a letter spelling out the details of her parole. The letter was almost four years old.

"I stuck the receiver under the couch," Cody said, coming up behind me.

"All right. Let's roll."

"Find anything interesting?"

"Nope.

"She was here earlier today," Cody said.

"How do you know?"

"Grocery bag on the counter, with a receipt. Today's date, transaction at two P.M."

We left the unit and headed to the stairs. As we descended, I said, "Let's go out through the parking garage."

"What for?"

"I want to see if her car's here."

"She's not here, why would her car be?"

"Who knows? Maybe someone picked her up, or she took a cab somewhere."

We went down past the lobby and exited the stairwell into the garage. It was dimly lit, the air warm and musty. Cars were crammed into slots barely large enough to allow entry. We walked the rows, looking for Claudia Merchan's blue Honda Accord. After ten minutes of futile searching, we walked up the on-ramp and out the door beside the gate. Before letting it close, I jammed a folded card over the latch mechanism to prevent it from catching.

We stood and looked past a row of palm trees to the deserted street. "What now, you want to wait until she returns?" Cody said.

"You hungry?" I asked.

Cody looked at his watch. "It's 8:30 California time. Let's find some chow."

"All right. Then I want to come back and look for her car again."

As we walked to our rental car, Cody pointed down a passage way between the apartment complex and another building, and said, "There's a boat slip over there."

"It's the Miami River."

"Let's take a quick look." We walked between the buildings until we reached a pier where about a dozen boats were moored. The vessels were all roughly the same length, about thirty feet, and were a mix of cabin cruisers, speedboats, and fishing craft. We continued down the length of the pier until we reached the river. From there, we could see more docks stemming from the waterway. The black water was quiet, its surface rippled with silver glints. The river cut a dark swath through a sea of muted lights on either side.

"It leads out past downtown Miami to Biscayne Bay," I said, looking at the river's eastward path.

"How do you know?"

"Because I studied the damn map."

"Very proud of you," Cody said. "I'd like to see what this looks like in daylight."

"Let's go find a restaurant," I replied.

We drove away from the Serenity by the River apartments, and after cruising the darkened streets for a couple minutes, we concluded that even the fast-food restaurants were closed. Cody worked his phone and said, "I found a place a mile away that stays open until three A.M. Honduran food."

"Is it any good?"

"We'll find out. Take a right at the light."

We drove to the northeast corner of Allapattah and parked at a single story, rust-colored stucco building. There were satellite dishes on the roof and white-painted security gates installed at the doorways. A sagging vinyl banner advertising $4 lunch specials hung just below the flat roof. Next to the building, used cars were for sale in a lot secured by a chain-link fence topped by barbed wire.

The parking lot for the *Rincon Progreseno Restaurante* was half full. "Makes me a little homesick for East San Jose," Cody said as we walked toward the entrance. I could hear music from inside.

When we went through the door, we entered a rectangular room painted red. Phony brickwork lined the walls, oscillating fans were mounted on support pillars, and Roman tiles that looked plastic were installed above a small bar. A trio of men in white Panama shirts were on a stage in the corner, singing to guitars and playing percussion instruments. A half-dozen folks danced in front of the stage, their movements graceful and exuberant. Hung on the wall next to the bar were pictures of menu items with accompanying prices. The descriptions were in Spanish.

We grabbed menus and sat at a table, our chairs scraping against the tile floor. After a minute it became apparent that there was no wait staff on duty, so we went to the bar and ordered plates of *carne asada,* rice, red beans, and at my insistence, *tajadas de platano.*

"What's the big deal with fried bananas?" Cody asked.

"They're plantains, not bananas. They're part of the banana family, but more like potatoes. You can't eat them raw."

"Gee, you're certainly a fountain of information."

"It's your lucky day."

We got a couple of Heinekens from the bartender and headed back to our table. From the middle of the floor, I scanned the patrons. I concluded we were the only out-of-towners in the place, but no one gave us a moment's glance. I sat silently with my beer in my hand, listening to snippets of Spanish and wondering if someone in this joint might recognize my picture of Luis Alvarez. I knew the chances of that were nil, and that Miami had a huge population of Latin American residents, but I was tempted to pull the picture from my pocket and start canvasing the place.

Without thinking further, I unfolded the picture on the table.

"What's up?" Cody asked, guzzling from his bottle.

"I need to find out who he is," I said, rapping my knuckle on the page.

"No shit, Sherlock."

"Couldn't hurt asking around here."

Cody raised his eyebrows, then he laughed and shook his head. "Dirt, listen, it makes no sense to start asking random people. I know you're under the gun, but keep in mind, we're waiting with a purpose. After we chill out here for a while, we'll go back to the apartment, and we'll wait all night for Claudia if we have to. Then you can put a tracker on her car, or hell, let's just go have an intimate conversation with her."

"We confront her, there's no guarantee we'll get anywhere. And then she'll know she's being watched."

"True," Cody said. "But she won't know her apartment's bugged."

I sighed, sipped off my beer, and tried to rub away the tension that had been building behind my eyes.

"I got advice for you," Cody said. "Chug your beer and go get us two more."

"We're not gonna confront Claudia, understand?" I said. "We stay in the shadows and let her lead us to the next step. If we spook her, there's no telling what she might do. Maybe leave town, take a vacation. Then it's my ass."

"No problem, it's all copacetic, *amigo*. I'll be right back," he said, and ambled off to the bar.

I took a long swig from my beer, sat with my eyes closed, and tried to ignore the worry that had propelled itself to center stage in my head. I wanted to push my thoughts aside and make my mind still, but I knew the effort would be futile. But I also knew I'd drive myself crazy if I let myself surrender to the pressure. And just as important, I couldn't afford to be distracted, couldn't afford to think illogically and make mistakes.

Hoping to find at least a temporary respite, I kept my eyes shut and concentrated on the music, which had an upbeat tempo and sounded like a celebration of sorts. The Spanish lyrics were about a woman who left a rich *bandito* for a poor man and was happy to trade her material possessions for true love.

Immersed in the tune, I rested my chin on my chest and tapped my foot to the beat. When the song ended, I looked up and noticed two curvaceous women had entered the restaurant. They were in marked contrast to the rest of the patrons, who were a scattered mix of blue-collar laborers, their wives, and a few nondescript single men occupying tables along the walls. The ladies, both provocatively dressed, moved to the bar where Cody held two bottles in his hand. In a moment one of them was engaged in conversation with him. A short white dress clung to her ample curves, and she had a head of lustrous black hair, the curls framing her face and falling over her bare shoulders. The whiteness of her dress was startling against her deep bronze skin. She wore a silver necklace, and a large pink stone rested above her cleavage. Her heels were at least four inches, but she was still a foot shorter than Cody.

The second woman was slender and taller. Her hair was short and blonde and looked dyed. She wore jeans and a tube top made of a sheer material that highlighted the shape of her small breasts.

I finished my beer and waited for Cody, who was smiling and talking. Then a man from the kitchen put two plates on the bar, and Cody brought the food to our table.

"I'm starting to like this place," Cody said. "Friendly people."

"Hookers?"

"Possibly. Either that or that hot *señorita* just found me irresistible. She asked if I was in the mood to party."

"That's a dangerous question."

"You'll be happy to know I told her I have other obligations tonight. I also asked her if she knows Claudia Merchan."

I took a bite of sizzling red meat. "Any luck?"

"No," Cody said. "But she was a little hard to understand. She has this crazy accent, all rolls of the Rs. Very sexy."

We concentrated on our food, and I noticed the slender woman eyeing me, probably sizing me up as a potential customer. I did nothing to encourage her, but a few minutes later, once our plates were taken away, the pair approached us.

"Can we join you?" the one in the white dress said.

"We were just leaving," I said.

"But we still have to finish our beers," Cody said, pulling out a chair. The ladies sat, and the slender one said, "Where are you handsome men from?"

"All the way from sunny California," Cody replied.

"Business or pleasure?"

"A working trip," I said.

The slender woman leaned her shoulder against mine, and then her hand was on my thigh. "You look like you need to relax," she said.

I took a deep breath. The hooker in the white dress was saying something to Cody, and they were smiling as if sharing some profound joke. She was nearly beautiful, and for a moment I felt sorry for her. She reminded me of many attractive prostitutes I'd met in the course of my work. I imagined her career choice was the result of an unfortunate upbringing and maybe dire financial circumstances. Possibly she was molested as a child and taught that the only thing she had of value to offer this world was sex. Then again, maybe she didn't see herself as a victim at all. Maybe she had other options, but rejected the notion of a regular job, and chose instead to sell her body. Whatever the case, I was struck with an unexpected twinge of sadness.

I stood and went to the bar to pay the bill. When I returned, Cody was holding a card with a handwritten phone number.

"I have a picture I'd like you to look at," I said, addressing both women. I unfolded the sheet of paper in my hand. "Do you know this man?"

The women looked at Luis Alvarez and both said no, they'd never seen him.

"Thanks, anyway," I said. "We have to go now."

"Next time," Cody said, winking.

We walked out into the early morning. It was past one A.M. and the weather hadn't changed. It was still mid-seventies and balmy.

"The nights always get cold in Cal," Cody said.

"Especially in the mountains."

"I like it here. No need for a coat."

"Let's go back and check the garage for Claudia's Honda."

We made the short drive without hitting a traffic light and parked on the street. I slung my backpack over my shoulder and we walked down the ramp into the garage. After ten minutes of futile searching, we returned to our rental car.

"Looks like she keeps late hours," I said.

"She went grocery shopping earlier today," Cody said. "She's definitely in town."

"Park across the street and let's wait her out," I said.

· · ·

At 3:30 A.M., Cody said, "We could go get some shut eye, come back around nine in the morning."

"I'd rather put the tracker on her car while no one's around. Let's give her another hour."

"I'm gonna have a smoke," Cody said, and opened his door.

"I'll join you," I said.

I usually only smoke when I'm drinking to get drunk, but I bummed a cigarette from Cody out of sheer boredom. We stood on the sidewalk, blowing streams of smoke into the still, heavy night.

"I might have to give Aisha a call tomorrow night," Cody said.

"Who?"

"The bombshell in the white dress."

"Why don't you call her friend too, go for a ménage à trois?"

"Sounds expensive."

At that moment a pair of headlights turned down the street. I ducked low behind our rig, and Cody knelt beside me. We watched the car move toward us and slow at the garage entrance.

"It's her," I said.

We stood once the car disappeared into the garage, and I checked my watch. We waited ten minutes, then I said, "Be right back."

I entered the garage through the door I'd rigged to stay open. It took two minutes to spot her car, jammed into a spot far from the stairwell. Holding a penlight in my teeth, I lowered myself beside the car and felt around for a suitable nook in the chassis. Then I took a rag presoaked with degreaser and wiped the spot as clean as I could. Once I determined the spot was as free of grime as I could make it, I stuck a magnetized tracking unit onto the steel frame. I pushed on it with my fingers, testing its hold.

Satisfied, I rose to my feet and left the garage. The tracker would alert my cellphone with GPS data whenever the car moved. Its battery would last for 72 hours.

"Let's go get some sleep," I said to Cody. He nodded, and we drove back to our hotel.

10

It was eight A.M. when sunlight invading from around the curtains woke me. I'd slept less than four hours, but I knew I'd be unable to fall back asleep. I sat on the edge of the bed for a minute, then I brewed the single cup of coffee the hotel provided to guests. If that wasn't enough to get me going, I'd have to go downstairs and find another source of caffeine.

I listened to the gurgle of the small percolator, then did a hundred pushups, huffing and puffing and clearing the cobwebs from my head. I took the Styrofoam cup into the shower and drank it down as I stood beneath the water. Ten minutes later I was dressed and had opened the curtains wide to let the Florida sun pour into the room. It was so bright I was tempted to put on my sunglasses. Instead, I pulled the drapes closed so I could see my computer screen without glare.

I pulled up the Miami-Dade police website and found their headquarters was about ten miles away on 25th Street, which looked to be a main thoroughfare in Doral, a city just west of Miami. I clicked around the site, hoping to find the name of a detective in drug enforcement. Given Miami's history as a smuggler's gateway, I was hopeful that they might have a task-force committed to narcotics, but the only thing I could find was a tab for D.A.R.E., a national program for drug education that most large cities offer. At the bottom of the section was an email address and phone number for the lieutenant in charge. Although this person would likely not be responsible for investigating crimes, I entered the name in my computer's contact folder. I spent another fifteen minutes clicking around, but was unable to find another name.

I left the hotel a few minutes before nine, driving west. I navigated around the airport, battling morning traffic, until half an hour later I found 25th Street and saw the sprawling police HQ building. I turned into the parking lot, peered at the different buildings along a circular road, then parked and hiked back to the building nearest the boulevard. Black letters next to the entry defined it as the Midwest District Station.

A middle-aged couple sat silently on a bench along with a young man who may have been their son. Their faces looked grimly stoic. They were the only people in the lobby. I approached the counter and behind a glass partition an older uniformed cop was typing on a computer, apparently in deep concentration.

I picked up the phone on the wall and pressed zero. The officer looked up, his eyes flickering with impatience above his spectacles while he waited for me to state my purpose.

"I'd like to talk to a drug enforcement or homicide detective," I said.

"You'll need to ask at the building next door," he replied, pointing to my left.

I left the lobby and strode across a broad brick walkway to the Miami-Dade Police Headquarters Building. Clusters of lush palm trees rose against three stories of mirrored glass. I went inside and saw the lobby was configured identically to the building I'd just left. But this lobby was far more crowded, and I was forced to wait ten minutes before I could get to the phone and speak with the desk sergeant.

"I'd like to talk to a detective about the death of a Miami resident in California," I said.

The cop looked at me with a quizzical expression, his salt and pepper mustache twitching.

"A homicide?" he asked.

"No. He was killed in self-defense. He's a John Doe."

"But you know he's from Miami?"

"Yes, sir."

"I'll have to take your name and number and ask a detective to get back to you."

"All right. It might be best if I talked with a drug enforcement detective."

"Drug enforcement doesn't operate out of this building."

"Really?" I asked. "Where, then?"

"We don't make that information available for security reasons."

"I see," I said. "Can I leave you a picture of the deceased?"

"No, you'll need to wait for a call from one of our investigators."

·　　·　　·

I walked back to my car, hands thrust in my pockets. If I could meet with a detective, I might convince him to run the photo of Luis Alvarez through a facial recognition system. All it would take is one hit, and he could be identified. Then I could have Marcus Grier request his record, which hopefully would show a long history of criminal acts.

I reached my car and stood staring at the line of stopped traffic on 25th Street. What were the chances a detective would call me back? How high on their priority schedule would they rate a John Doe death in California?

At that moment my phone rang, and for an instant I felt a surge of hope. But then I saw it was Candi calling. I stared at the call screen, thinking she must have just woken, and might still be in bed.

"Hey, Candi."

"Hi. Good morning," she said, but it sounded more like a question.

"Good morning."

"How's it going?"

"Making progress," I said, making my voice upbeat. "Everything fine at home?"

"Sure. Do you think…?" Her voice tailed off.

"Think what?"

"I'm sorry, I shouldn't have called. I know you're busy. I'm just worried."

"Don't be, Candi. I'm making good progress, and I haven't even been here twenty-four hours."

"I know you'll get done what you need to."

"Damn right, babe," I said, hoping my artificial cheer wasn't obvious.

"Dan? Just promise to keep me updated, okay?"

"Of course. As soon as I have something definite."

"I love you."

"Love you, too. Talk to you soon."

I tossed my cell on my passenger seat and drove out into the traffic. But I was unsure where I was headed and took the first right I came to, onto 92nd Avenue. It ran along the right side of the police complex. Despite the heavy congestion on 25th, there wasn't a car on the road, as if it led nowhere. To my left, a herd of cattle grazed on a large plot of grassland. I drove slowly, then pulled over onto the grassy shoulder. I got out and stared at the black cows. The field was about half-a-mile square, and how it ended up next to police headquarters in Doral, I couldn't fathom. The city catered primarily to import-export businesses, and every street I'd driven by was lined with office buildings.

"Weird," I muttered. I crossed my arms and gazed out at the field, perhaps waiting for my mind to hit upon an idea or revelation, anything to provide direction on what to do with my time this morning. Because for now I was only waiting, either for an unlikely call from a Dade County detective, or for an alert that Claudia Merchan was driving her car.

I leaned against my car, and when no epiphany occurred, I was resigned to drive back to the hotel. But before I could get in the vehicle, I saw a squad car pull out from the parking lot and turn in my direction. The car rolled onto the shoulder behind me and two patrolmen got out.

"Everything okay here?" one asked.

"Yeah," I said. "Just looking at the cows."

"There's no parking here."

"Sorry, I didn't see a sign. I was just leaving."

They nodded and turned back to their cruiser. "Hey, officers," I said.

"Yes?"

"I'm a private investigator from California. I'm waiting for a call from one of your detectives. I'm trying to identify a Miami John Doe who died in California last week." I held out a picture of Luis Alvarez.

They looked at the sheet of paper and then at me with blank expressions. "I suspect he's a violent criminal," I said. "Possibly a drug dealer."

One of the patrolmen, a tall, clean-shaven white man, shook his head, returned to the cruiser, and began talking on his radio. The other, a stocky Latino, took the page from me and said, "You got his prints?"

"No, but I should be able to get them."

"When you do," he said, handing me a card, "call me at this number."

"Thanks, I'll do that." We shook hands, and he turned to leave, but stopped when I said, "I know of Miami's history in the cocaine trade. Is drug dealing much of an issue here anymore?"

He looked down and seemed to weigh his reply. "Yes, it is," he said after a moment.

"Anyone you can recommend I can talk to who might help me find out who this guy is?"

He paused, then said, "I don't know if this will help you. There's a reporter at the Miami Herald who focuses on the narco business. Goes by Vasquez. If he thinks there's a story in it, you never know."

"Thanks for the tip, officer. I'll let you know when I have the fingerprints."

"Be safe," he said.

•   •   •

It was eleven A.M. when I arrived back at the Holiday Inn. I called Cody from the parking lot and he said he'd be in the lobby in ten minutes. I went inside, took a seat on a couch opposite the reservation counter, and called

Marcus Grier. When he answered the background noise made it difficult to hear his voice.

"I'm trying to shave," he said.

"Sorry," I said glancing at my watch. "I'm in Florida, it's three hours later here."

The background noise ceased. "I hope you have permission to be out of state," he said.

"I was never told not to leave town, Marcus."

"What are you doing there?"

"Gathering information to aid in my defense. Did you contact Miami PD and send them the deceased's fingerprints yet?"

"Yes, I did. They couldn't find a match."

"Are you sure?" I sputtered.

"I'm sure that's what they told me. I spoke with a clerk at Miami-Dade PD who took it to a detective yesterday. They just called me this morning. No hits."

I didn't say anything, until he said, "Are you still there?"

"Can you send me the prints?"

"Really?"

"I'll be talking with a Miami detective sometime today. I want to ask him in person to run the prints. I need to make sure."

"Christ," he said, under his breath.

"As a defendant, I have a right to all evidence. Right?"

"I don't know," he said. "But I'll email it to you."

"Thanks. Talk to you later."

At that moment Cody walked into the lobby. He was wearing tan slacks, running shoes, and a blue flower print shirt.

"Sleep well?" I asked.

"I always do," he replied. When he reached up to scratch his ear, his huge bicep looked ready to tear through the sleeve. "Any pings on the tracker?"

"Nope. Claudia's probably still in bed."

"What have you been doing?"

"I went to Miami PD, left my number for a detective."

Cody sat in the chair next to me. "I also called Grier," I said. "He said he sent the prints to Miami PD, and they found no match in their database. I told Grier to send me the prints. He said he would."

"Any alerts on the bugs we placed?"

"Not yet. It usually takes 24 hours to update."

Cody stood and stared out the front doors. "Let's get out of here," he said.

"Give me a minute," I said, working my smartphone. Then I said, "All right, let's go."

"Where to?"

"The Miami Herald. It's about five miles away, a straight shot down 36th Street."

"A newspaper?"

"That's right. I want to see if we can talk to their crime reporter."

Cody shrugged. "Killing time, but what else we got to do?"

We drove off, hitting the lights on 36th along the airport, until I turned left on 87th and found the Miami Herald headquarters, a long, two-story building with an American flag flying high outside the main entrance. I parked, and we went through the front doors. The receptionist was a pretty woman with dark hair and red lipstick.

"Hello, miss," Cody said. "We were hoping to speak with one of your journalists."

"Mr. Vasquez," I said.

"We don't have a Mr. Vasquez."

"No? I thought he was a crime reporter here."

"We have a *Señora* Vasquez," she said. "And you are?"

"Dan Reno, investigations." I handed her my card.

"*Un momento.*" She spoke on her phone for a minute, then said, "She is not available now, but promised to call you."

"*Gracias, señorita,*" Cody said, and she gave him a look somewhere between confused and skeptical.

"You need to work on your accent," I said as we left the building.

"Why bother?"

"Good point."

I turned onto 36th and began heading back toward our hotel. We were stopped at a light when Cody's cell rang.

"Shit," he said. "It's Fatty Lopez." Cody stared at his phone, his face pinched. "I'll let the douchebag leave me a message."

"He's still freaked about his rapist brother?"

"I'm sure he is."

"Maybe he should join him in prison. That would cure his separation anxiety."

Cody cut his eyes at me, then the crease above his brow receded. "Hmm," he said. He rolled down the window and lit a cigarette. "What's in a Cuban sandwich?" he asked.

"It's basically a ham and cheese with pickles."

"Let's go get one. I only had coffee for breakfast."

"All right."

A minute later I turned into a newer strip mall and parked outside the El Tropico Cafeteria. Inside, the décor was modern, ferns hanging from above, flat screen televisions mounted on the wall, and a sliding door refrigerator full of soft drinks and bottles of Dos Equis.

We sat at the counter and ordered from the menu. I checked my phone to make sure I hadn't missed any calls, while Cody listened to his voice mail from Fatty Lopez. After he set his phone down, his scowl slowly turned to a grin. "Yeah, I'll have to have a heart-to-heart with that young man."

"He's really losing it, huh?"

"He never really had it. That's the problem."

"What's the remedy?"

Cody laughed and patted me hard on the back. "I don't know, Dirt. You think of something, let me know."

"I'll tell you what I'm thinking. I'd like to see if we can dig up some dirt on Magnus Swett."

"It's in the works."

"How so?"

"You remember I told you about Malcom Swett, the rapist and murderer I put away? I made a few calls, and it seems Magnus and him are indeed related. Possibly cousins, or maybe even brothers. I'll nail it down soon enough."

The waitress put plates in front of us. Cody took a huge bite from his Cuban sandwich, then washed it down with a long guzzle from a bottle of Dos Equis. I sat staring at him, my food untouched.

"What else have you found out?" I asked.

"The Swetts are from Denver. Guess who else is from there?"

"No idea."

"Russ Landers."

I felt my jaw drop. "Is there a connection?"

"Landers was a detective in Denver when Magnus Swett was an assistant DA there."

I pushed my plate away, leaned forward on my elbows, and rubbed my forehead with my fingertips. "You don't think Swett would come after me because of my history with Landers?"

"Anything's possible. What do you think?"

I brought my fists up to my mouth. Russ Landers was Cody's boss at San Jose PD and had railroaded Cody out of a job when Cody refused to take dirty money. Eventually Cody testified against a number of corrupt San Jose cops in a major police scandal, but Landers somehow avoided the fallout and kept his job. During the course of events, Cody slept with Landers's wife, who despised her husband and wanted to screw him over any way she could. To this end, she asked that Cody film their illicit couplings and distribute CDs to everyone at SJPD. Cody claimed that the idea of humiliating Landers turned her into a raving nymphomaniac.

The events surrounding Cody's exit from SJPD surely would have justified a lifelong grudge by Landers, but that wasn't the end of the story. Less than two years ago I had my own trouble with the corrupt San Jose precinct captain. In the midst of a case involving a heroin-dealing army deserter and an attempted terrorist bombing in San Jose, Landers had me arrested for killing six gangbangers. All six were participants in the drive-by shooting at Cody's house. After spraying his home with machine gun rounds, they left their cars in an attempt to finish us off. It was a critical mistake on their part. If they had simply driven away, I never would have had the chance to return fire.

Landers thought he could put me away for murder, but when I told him I'd videoed him getting it on with the heroin dealer's sister, the charges were dropped. But we had a pointed conversation first, and he advised me to never cross his path again. I responded by providing full disclosure to FBI and CIA agents, along with the San Jose District Attorney. Landers was terminated from the force shortly afterward.

. . .

When Cody and I left the diner, he was talking about the food, but I couldn't process his words. I felt discombobulated, my thoughts jumbled and scattered, and even my physical sense seemed unbalanced. I stopped at our rental car and thought, *you need to get it together, get focused.*

"That sandwich wasn't half bad," Cody said. "I wouldn't mind getting another one to go."

"Let's go back to the hotel. I need to figure some stuff out."

"You want to draw a diagram on a big sheet? That's what you usually do, right?"

"Sometimes," I said. "Let's stop at a store and buy some paper."

"Okay, partner."

We found a drug store a block away, and I picked up a large pad of drawing paper and a pack of colored felt pens. Within a few minutes we were back at the Holiday Inn, the pad lying on my bed as I hovered over it.

In the center of the white sheet I wrote two names: *Manuel Alvarez* and *Luis Alvarez.*

"Pseudonyms?" Cody asked.

"I ran searches in people finder databases and couldn't find matches."

"So you assume they're both criminals using aliases?"

"I didn't necessarily assume that about Manuel."

"But you do for Luis."

"Yeah. But I couldn't find either of them in the search engines."

I began writing on the sheet, but Cody said, "Hold up for a second. Did you use an international people finder?"

I straightened. "No," I said. I shook my head. "I've never used one for international. Have you?"

"Once, yeah. A tech company hired me to track an executive who fled to China or Taiwan after he was indicted for stealing trade secrets. This was over a year ago. I used a bunch of different sites."

"Did it work?"

"Yes and no. The guy's name was Chen, which is one of the most common Chinese names. So when I searched I came up with literally thousands of hits."

"There can't be that many Alvarezes worldwide," I said.

"Especially if you limit the countries. Didn't you say something about the Dominican?"

"Liz overheard them mention the Dominican Republic."

"Who?"

"Liz, the bartender at Zekes. That's where I first met Luis and Claudia."

"No shit, huh?"

"Yeah. And Claudia's apartment is in Allapattah. It's also called little Santo Domingo. That's the big city in the Dominican."

I bent to the pad, wrote *D.R.,* and drew lines connecting to Luis and Manuel.

"I'll grab my notebook," Cody said.

. . .

Thirty minutes later Cody was muttering curses at the desk in my room, while I continued to fill the sheet of paper with words, most of which ended in a question mark: *Drive minibus from Miami to Reno. Why? Who was in bus besides Manuel? Who was killed in bus and why? Death by knife wound – Luis experienced with knife? Why Luis looking for Manuel? What crime connected? What is Claudia's involvement? Really married to Luis? Are Luis's fingerprints really not in the federal database?*

"I think I got something," Cody said.

I went to the desk where Cody was typing. "Look," he said. "It was in Spanish, but I used the English translator."

On his screen was a website for a Santo Domingo company called Trinidad Transport. It offered sea taxi services up and down the coast of the Dominican, as well as to nearby islands, including Puerto Rico, Cuba, and Jamaica. Cody scrolled down and put the pointer on two names: Hugo Trinidad, President, and Manuel Alvarez, pilot.

"This is the only Manuel Alvarez I could find in the D.R.," Cody said.

"Can you find a picture of him? Or anything else, like age?"

"I'll keep looking."

I turned back to my sheet, which was now filled with ideas and open-ended questions. It was my habit to create diagrams during the direction-seeking phase of an investigation. It helped calm my mind and organize my thoughts. As I stared at my jottings, it occurred to me that my personal stake in the investigation was preventing me from applying my full skills and focus to the task at hand. It was a distraction I couldn't afford.

I squeezed my eyes shut, relaxed my facial muscles, and blew out a deep breath. "How about a Dominican driver license for Manuel? Or any high school attendance records?"

"I'm digging," Cody replied. "But the access to public records is sketchy. It ain't exactly the USA."

I checked my phone to make sure I hadn't missed a call or an alert from Claudia's car. It was two P.M. I opened my notebook, thinking I'd try my hand at finding a clear indicator that Manuel Alvarez lived or worked in the Dominican, when my cell rang. It was a Miami area code number.

"Dan Reno, investigations," I said.

"Nate Esparza from the Miami Herald. You were here earlier asking for Mrs. Vasquez?"

"That's right."

"For what purpose?"

"I'm a private investigator from California. A man from Miami, or possibly a Caribbean Island, died last week in California. He's a John Doe, and I need to learn his identity. I suspect he's a violent criminal, possibly involved in the drug business."

"Have you alerted Miami PD?"

"Yeah, but that hasn't got me anywhere."

"What else can you tell me?"

"The deceased hired me to find a man he claimed was his nephew. That man had driven from Miami to Nevada in a minibus with some other folks. The minibus was found abandoned, with a man dead in the driver's seat. He's also a John Doe."

The line was silent for a moment. "Give me a few minutes. If *Señora* Vasquez is interested, I'll let you know."

I shrugged. "All right."

"The newspaper?" Cody asked.

"Yeah. It was some guy, not the lady."

"Whatever," Cody said. His eyes were glued to his screen as he typed. "Come here," he said, and leaned back so I could see. "Looks like your boy."

The image on Cody's computer was that of a blurred driver license. Across the top it read *Republica Dominicana Licencia de Conducia,* and to the left was a photo of Manuel Alvarez. It included an address, his height and weight, and date of birth.

"Nice work," I said. "That's him all right."

"A Dominican citizen."

"That's why I couldn't find any record of him in the U.S."

"Hold on," Cody said, typing, then he looked back at me. "The address on the license is the same as the address for Trinidad Transport."

"He lived where he worked?"

"Either that, or he had some reason not to use his real address."

"Hmm." I straightened and looked at where a spider was spinning a web in the corner of the room. "What about Luis Alvarez?"

"No hits in the Dominican."

"Shit. I'll get on my computer. I want to search every island in the Caribbean."

"That's a lot of countries."

"We might need to try Central and South America too."

"I'll start with Colombia," Cody said.

"Or Mexico."

. . .

I know some old school investigators who still view the Internet as a novelty. One of them was my first boss, a man who taught me many things, including the value of creativity and persistence. I considered him a superb detective, but unfortunately his skills were developed in a bygone era. When trying to navigate the digital world, he admitted it was like learning a new language, and he was sadly incompetent. I spoke with him a few months ago, and he told me that although he wished to continue working, it was time he retired.

Today, it's not uncommon for unwitting crooks to incriminate themselves on social media. While it suggests the peak of stupidity, some lawbreakers find it irresistible to boast on Facebook, Instagram, or Twitter. But even cautious rogues sometimes discount the fact that any social media presence can aid the authorities in bringing them to justice. Hell, I once worked a case where I located a subject purely by his Internet Protocol address.

As for my current investigation, I'd already come up empty when searching for social media links for Manuel and Luis Alvarez. The only digital footprint I'd seen so far was Manuel's place of employment and Dominican driver license, which Cody found. Might that necessitate a trip to the Dominican Republic?

First things first, I told myself. Manuel was not my search target; the man using the name Luis Alvarez was. As I typed on my notebook, I considered that if Luis Alvarez was indeed an assumed name, searching for him online would lead nowhere. But that didn't mean I would treat the task lightly. Lack of attention to due diligence is a trait of weak investigators. So is lack of patience.

For the next two hours, Cody and I worked in tandem on our computers. We found dozens of individuals named Luis Alvarez. Actually, every Latin American country we searched, with the exception of Guyana, Trinidad, and a few other tiny Caribbean islands, had at least one Luis Alvarez listed. Unfortunately, none were a match for the man who tried to stab me in South Lake Tahoe.

Cody shut his notebook and walked over to the window. "Nothing from the tracker on Claudia's car?" he asked.

I stood and joined him in looking out past the roofline at a congested freeway under a pallid sky. "It's 4:30. Who knows if she'll leave today."

"If she doesn't, we may need to pay her a visit."

"What, and force her to talk?"

"Motivate her."

"I'm in enough trouble, Cody," I said, shaking my head.

"We don't need to break any laws, man."

I crossed my arms and felt my resolve weakening. Maybe it was time to shift into a higher gear. But before I could pursue the thought, my cell rang. It was Nate Esparza from the newspaper.

"If you'd like to meet, Mrs. Vasquez and I will be available in South Beach in an hour."

"Where exactly?"

"Go to Mango's on Ocean Drive. I'll find you. What do you look like?"

"I'll be with my partner. He's six-five, reddish blonde hair."

"Okay. See you at 5:30."

11

We drove due east, heading toward where the Atlantic Ocean merges with the Caribbean Sea. The skies were bright and the sun shone down upon a long, horizontal cloud band with a thunderhead rising from its center. We veered south onto 95, and then east again, heading across the causeway over Biscayne Bay. The waters were a sparkling blue, and to our right the downtown Miami skyline looked like spires of turquoise glass. As we neared the island of Miami Beach, I began seeing shorefront homes with private piers.

"Looks like something out of Lifestyles of the Rich and Famous," Cody said.

"Supposedly a lot of it was built with drug money."

"This is a playground for celebrities. I hear the nightclubs in South Beach are something else."

"Where'd you hear that?"

"Just rumors that need validation. How about playing wingman tonight?"

I turned to Cody. He grinned, rolled down his window, and shook a cigarette from his pack. The balmy air rushed into the car.

"Tell you what," I said, "We get to the bottom of Luis Alvarez, we'll go paint the town."

"Deal," Cody said, blowing a stream of smoke into the warm afternoon.

We came off the causeway and crossed Alton Road and drove through a half-dozen lights before taking a left on Ocean Drive. On our left were a row of storefronts, mostly restaurants with sidewalk seating. The buildings were painted in pastel shades, muted yellows, pinks, and blues. To the right was a stretch of parkland and beyond that was the beach. We crept along behind a gold Lamborghini that drove with its winged doors raised, while its occupants, two dark-skinned men in their twenties, took videos with their cellphones and revved the exotic motor. A pair of women strolling the crowded sidewalk in heels and bikinis called out and waved to them.

We passed a neon sign above a sea-colored awning that read, *Mango's Tropical Café*. "Where the hell do we park?" I said. I took my eyes off the road, searching for a sign leading to parking, and had to jam the brakes when the Lamborghini stopped unexpectedly. Two buxom women in sunglasses and tube tops were at the car.

"What the..." I said.

We sat there for a long moment, until it became apparent the driver either didn't understand or didn't care that he was holding up traffic. "I'll go have a word with these dickweeds," Cody said. Before I could respond he opened his door and walked to the passenger side of the sports car. He leaned down under the winged door and I could see him talking. Then he stood and the Lamborghini took off with a jerk. Cody smiled and waved at the two young women, then returned to our car.

"What'd you say?" I asked.

"I told them to move it or I'd lift the car and put it on its side."

I laughed. "Think you could?"

"If I wanted to, sure."

I turned down a side street, found a parking lot, and we began walking back toward Mango's. "What do you expect to get out of this lady?" Cody asked.

"Hell, maybe she'll recognize Luis Alvarez and know his entire life story."

"Sounds like something straight out of *The Art of Thinking Positively*. Didn't you read that book?"

"Not that I remember."

We turned onto Ocean Drive and began navigating through the congestion of tourists on the sidewalk, which was built to accommodate both foot traffic and rows of dining tables. We passed shops selling overpriced clothing, restaurants where waitresses holding menus tried to lure us in, and outdoor bars with DJs and dancing girls and blinking signs advertising 2 for 1 drinks. When we reached Mango's we were greeted by a woman wearing a leopard print leotard that would have been perfectly appropriate in a strip joint. We walked past her into an interior that looked like an orgy in a tropical jungle…on acid.

The walls were florescent green and covered with murals of unworldly foliage and cartoons of naked women. At the end of the U-shaped bar was an oversized section surfaced with glittery tiles. A stairway led to a second floor, where patrons could view the main floor over railings scrolled with vines and flashing lights. I looked upward at rows of skylights sectioned by images of burning clouds. Latin music blared from hidden speakers, the volume just low enough to allow conversation.

We went past a drum set, timbales, congas, and a few amplifiers set up facing tables and chairs with zebra print upholstery, and continued to the far end of the bar. The woman pouring drinks was a brunette with a slight upper body, but her lower body was so disproportionate I couldn't help but stare. Her hips were more than twice the circumference of her tiny waist, and when she turned, her ass was so big and round that her leotard simply disappeared between her cheeks, like a string bikini.

"What a trip," Cody said. I didn't know if he meant the décor, the bartender, or both.

I caught a glimpse of a man looking down at us from the balcony. He promptly came down the stairs and walked to where we waited. He was average height and slender but had wide shoulders and moved athletically. His hair was black against his bronze skin, and he had striking blue eyes. My immediate impression was that he might be a Hollywood actor. But then I saw his right ear. It was a mangled stump of flesh, as if it had been burned away. I looked down, and under his gray windbreaker, I saw the unmistakable bulge of a sidearm on his ribs.

"Dan Reno?" he said.

"Yes. My partner, Cody Gibbons."

"Hello," Cody said.

"Nate Esparza. Let's go upstairs."

We followed him up to a table in the rear corner of the place, where a solitary woman was seated. We were the only ones in the upstairs area.

"Mrs. Vasquez?" I asked.

She nodded. "Your card, please?" She was a large woman, well over two hundred pounds, maybe two-fifty, but she was not obese.

I handed her a business card and Cody and I sat along with Nate Esparza. In our corner, the music was much quieter than downstairs.

"I understand you're from California, trying to identify a man who was killed there." She had a definite Latin accent, but her English was perfect.

"That's right," I said. I laid a picture of Luis Alvarez on the table. "This man died in South Lake Tahoe, California, a few days ago. He was going by the name of Luis Alvarez, and claimed to be a Miami resident. But I can find no record of him."

She leaned forward and studied the picture. "How'd he die?" Esparza asked after a moment, turning the sheet of paper so he could examine it.

"Blow to the head."

"Accidental?"

"The blow was intentional and in self-defense, but I didn't mean to kill him."

"Oh," Mrs. Vasquez said, her eyes widened, but a smile began on her big lips. She had curly brown hair pulled back from her fleshy face.

"He hired me to look for a man he claimed was his nephew. We had a disagreement about the case, and he came at me with a knife."

"Were you arrested?" she asked.

"Yes, and charged with manslaughter."

"I see," she said.

"So that's why I'm here. I'm trying to learn who he was. The way he attacked me, my bet is he has a criminal record."

"Did the police run his fingerprints?"

"Supposedly, and came up with nothing. But I'm not buying it."

"Ah, the plot thickens." She put her beefy forearms on the table and brought her hands together. Then she picked up the photo of Alvarez and looked at it with narrowed eyes.

"Do you recognize him?" Cody asked.

"I need to check something," she said, pulling a black backpack onto the table. She removed a notebook PC and began typing. We sat silently for a couple of minutes, until I said, "What are you looking for?"

"I've been reporting on the drug trade since the late seventies," she said, peering at me over spectacles low on her broad nose. "I'm probably older than you think. In the eighties, before anybody had computers, I kept everything in file cabinets. Pictures, every scrap of information on the cartels, on smugglers, on murders, I kept all of it. A few years ago I had it converted to digital. It's all here, on my hard drive. I have pictures of over a thousand narcotraficante."

"So you might recognize him?" I asked.

"It's the eyes," she said. "Eyes are a funny thing. A man's happy, his eyes look very different than when he's angry. It's almost like a person's voice. Something about your man's eyes looks familiar, I think. But it's very distant in my head, like maybe from twenty years ago."

I sighed and sat up in my chair. "Can you look through your photos and see if anything jogs your memory?"

"Perhaps. But first tell me more about your case. I'm in the reporting business, don't forget."

"Promise to keep my name out of the paper?"

She shrugged. "If you have a story worth reporting, I'll assign you an alias."

"All right," I said. She put a small recording device before me, and I spoke for three or four minutes on my investigation into Manuel Alvarez.

"Good enough?" I asked.

Her features looked impassive, her eyes blunt. "What makes you believe Luis Alvarez is involved in drugs? Is it just that he is a violent man who may be from Miami?"

"Do you find my suspicion irrational?"

"Not necessarily. But you have nothing to support it."

"That's why I've come to you."

She didn't reply, but folded the picture of Luis Alvarez and put it in her computer case.

"Since Manuel's from the Dominican," I said, "I think Luis might be too. Is there much drug trafficking there?"

She looked at me knowingly. "When U.S. drug enforcement cracked down on the original cartels in the nineties, they learned how the cartels were moving cocaine. They uncovered the routes and transport methods, which was key to shutting down the volume from Colombia to Miami. After the Medellín and Cali cartels collapsed, the business became decentralized, with smaller players involved. The islands have become common launch points for inbound shipments, not only to Miami, but up the coast as well. Today the Dominican is a major transshipment point. But so is Haiti, Puerto Rico, and Jamaica."

"But Colombia is still producing as much blow as ever," Cody said, "and most of it is now smuggled into Mexico and then into the U.S."

"I see you're well informed," Vasquez said. "Yes, it's true, Colombian cocaine production has been increasing since 2015, when the government stopped aerial herbicide spraying on the coca fields. But while much of the drugs are now shipped through Mexico, there is still plenty of contraband coming into Miami." She turned her attention back to her computer.

"You look like a lineman for the Dolphins I once knew," Esparza said to Cody. "Ever play ball?"

"I was defensive end for Utah State. Went to work for San Jose PD when I missed the draft. When they shit-canned me, I got my P.I. license."

"No kidding." Esparza smiled. "I worked for Miami PD right out of high school."

At that moment a blast of loud music came from below, the drums pounding away in a clattery Latin rhythm. Esparza rose and motioned for us to follow him.

"Thank you," I yelled at Mrs. Vasquez. She raised her fingers in a wave of dismissal, her eyes locked on her screen.

As we descended the stairs, I saw a man and woman dancing on the tiled section of the bar. The man wore a shirt with purple embroidery opened midway down his chest, flared pants tight at the knees, and pointy shoes. His female counterpart was costumed for festival, her tanned body shimmering in a bikini festooned with sequins, tassels and fringes, and her face was dwarfed by an elaborate headdress topped with peacock feathers.

The bar was growing crowded as we walked out the front entrance. We moved beyond the shade of the awning and stood near the street. "I played baseball when I was a kid," Esparza said, lighting a thin cigarette rolled in brown paper. "At one point I had dreams of going pro."

"I hear you," Cody said. "I thought I'd be drafted, had fantasies of playing for the Raiders. But I had a bad rap for behavioral issues and nobody took me."

"Behavioral issues?"

"I once threw my coach into a trash bin."

Esparza laughed and hit off his cigarette.

"Were you born in the U.S.?" I asked him.

"No, Colombia."

"How about Vasquez?"

"She's Colombian too. She lived there during Pablo Escobar's run of terror."

"She's not a big fan of his, I take it?"

"She watched him nearly tear the country apart. She knew many people who died at his hand, and part of her job as a young reporter was to visit the scenes of his mass murders." Esparza was no longer smiling. "I had some trouble before moving here." He tapped his deformed ear. "I was kidnapped by the *Norte del Valle* Cartel when I was seven years old. My father was in the Colombian government and the cartel wanted his cooperation on certain things. It ended badly."

"Sorry to hear that," I said.

"I don't want to bore you with the obvious, but if you're dealing with drug cartels, you must keep in mind they have no boundaries. *They will do anything* if it serves their needs."

"Looks like you're speaking from direct experience," Cody said.

"Yeah. I've got another plastic surgery coming up next month."

My eyes met Esparza's. "So you and your family left Colombia under duress?"

"We needed to get out."

"I see," I said.

"Are you a reporter or a body guard?" Cody asked.

"A little of both. I help the *señora* with research, interviews, that sort of thing.

"You always pack heat?" Cody patted his ribs.

Esparza tossed his smoke into the gutter. "The drug trade is as violent as it ever was, but the gangs don't feud in public like they used to. There's no bodies left on the streets these days, not in the U.S. But the *sicarios* stay busy, and a few of them are not fond of me. So yeah, I carry twenty-four-seven."

We stood looking out over the traffic on the street. The ocean was no more than a couple hundred feet away. For a moment I considered crossing the street and walking down to where the waves were breaking on the shore. Maybe the natural scenery would provide a brief break from the reality of my situation. If I were here for anything less important than trying to keep my ass out of prison, I definitely would have done so.

I handed Esparza my card and a picture of Luis Alvarez. "I've got to find out who this is," I said. "If you think of anything, will you call me?"

"Sure," he said, but his expression expressed no optimism.

"Hey, you want to get a bite somewhere?" Cody asked him.

"Thanks, but I've got work," Esparza said, pointing with his thumb back toward Mango's.

At that moment my phone buzzed. I yanked it from my pocket and squinted at the screen. "Let's go," I said, beginning down the sidewalk. "Claudia's on the move."

"About time," Cody said.

. . .

By the time we made it back to our rental car and exited the parking structure, Claudia Merchan's Honda sedan was on Interstate 395. She was heading east, toward us. I drove back on the same path we'd taken to Miami Beach. If Claudia did not turn off the Interstate beforehand, we would run into her. But it quickly became apparent that traffic was an issue. While I watched Claudia make steady progress on my tracking application, Cody worked his phone, pulled up driving directions, and said, "It's yellow and red, all the way over the MacArthur Causeway. Rush hour gridlock."

I resisted a curse as we waited in a long line at a stop light. "It doesn't matter," I said. "We'll know where she went, and we'll catch up to her within an hour."

And I was right, but just barely, for we crawled all the way back to the mainland, and it took forty-five minutes before we turned south on Biscayne Boulevard, and another fifteen minutes before we pulled into the parking lot for the Miamarina wharf. It was seven P.M. and the sun was setting behind us as we walked to where Claudia had parked near a locked gate. I rattled the handle and looked up and down a long pier where at least fifty boats were moored. The vessels ranged from thirty-foot cabin cruisers to massive luxury yachts.

"She only parked twenty minutes ago," I said. "She could be on any one of these boats."

"Or she could be at that bar and grill over there," Cody said, pointing to our left.

"Then why did she park way over here?"

Cody and I stood and scanned the boats. A man on a cabin cruiser was arranging fishing poles. On the stern of a forty foot yacht, another man in coveralls wiped his brow, then disappeared below deck. I tried the locked gate handle again and wondered how long it might take to pick it.

"I bet she's turning a trick on one of these yachts," Cody said.

"Let's go park at the end of the lot. I think the view will be better, and I want to use my binoculars."

"All right," Cody said, staring in the opposite direction. We got in our rental car and drove about a hundred yards to a chain-link fence. I parked facing the water and got my binoculars from my gear bag. From the slightly elevated vantage point, I could see up and down the wharf. I methodically viewed each vessel in the marina, but only saw a few people.

After a couple of silent minutes, Cody poked at his phone and said, "I want to see if I can get a decent connection in the restaurant over there."

"Bring me back something to eat, would you?"

Cody nodded, grabbed his backpack, and climbed out of the car. "And be ready to go if I call," I said. He waved and paced briskly toward the bar and grill.

I put the lenses back to my eyes and continued scanning the boats. The sun was hot on my neck. The minutes ticked by and I began to wonder if Claudia might be planning to spend the night aboard one of the yachts. Of course, it was also possible she met someone in the parking lot and drove off in another car. Either way, I'd probably be sitting here for hours.

I'd never met a detective, private or otherwise, who enjoyed the drudgery of surveillance. The task can test the patience of the most seasoned investigator. But over the years I'd learned to apply a specific mindset to the chore. I don't allow creeping doubts to enter my head. I keep my thoughts in a narrow band focused on the sole purpose of my activity. If the surveillance wasn't worth the time, I wouldn't do it. So the fact that I was doing it justified the hours of inactivity and boredom.

This was doubly true in my case, for I was beginning to think that Claudia might be the only viable pathway to discovering the identity of the man I'd killed. So far, everything else I'd tried had produced nothing. If clues didn't pan out soon, I might be faced with the prospect of forcing Claudia to talk. That could necessitate a wide variety of crimes, including kidnapping and assault and battery. If I decided to confront Claudia, I needed to make damn sure she'd talk. That would require planning.

I don't routinely commit crimes during my investigations. Doing so would be stupid. But sometimes hard choices must be made. The key for me is always a careful calculation of risk and reward. If risk must be taken, it needs to be minimized. That means no witnesses. Of course, if I got Claudia alone and subjected her to physical duress, she would perhaps be a very willing witness. So I'd need to give her good reason to not report our interaction to the police.

I felt a knot begin in my gut as I contemplated what would happen if I interrogated Claudia Merchan. If she was a man, I could simply crank her arm behind her back and threaten to ruin her shoulder. It's not creative, but plenty effective. But this is not something I'd ever done to a woman.

I grimaced, lowered the binoculars, and rubbed my eyes. Behind me, the sun was an orange ball and had burned through a hazy line of clouds above the western horizon. It was still bright enough to cast a blinding explosion of light over the water. I tried to keep watching, but it was like sandpaper on my pupils. The best I could do was focus away from the glare, on the farthest end of the marina, where there were mostly smaller craft.

As I stared mutely at the boats, the events of Luis Alvarez's death began replaying in my head. Like many fights, this one had unfolded quickly, leaving no time for strategy or tactical considerations. Alvarez had clearly meant to catch me unaware and stab me to death. I assumed he'd instructed Claudia to distract me. I also assumed Claudia had picked up the knife as she'd ran off. Not only was Claudia complicit in attempted murder, she'd also absconded with the key piece of physical evidence. If she hadn't taken the knife, maybe I'd never have been charged.

I got out of the car and set my arms on the roof. My very life was now in jeopardy due to the actions of this woman. I flexed my shoulders and felt my face twist into a scowl. If and when the time came, I'd not give her a pass. Hopefully she would cooperate before it got too bad.

I thought fleetingly about what I might do to Luis Alvarez if it was him I'd be interrogating. He'd thrown all in when he visited my home and scared Candi. I recalled an event last year when I caught two men who'd entered my home, unaware I was waiting for them. Their intentions were of a nature I don't wish to revisit. Suffice to say that they forfeited any right to mercy. When I was done with them, I was certain I'd extracted all they knew on the case I was working.

All things considered, Luis Alvarez was probably lucky he died without prolonged pain. If he'd lived and continued to push me, things might have gotten very ugly for him.

But why had Alvarez tried to kill me? The thought had been lurking in the back of my mind ever since our altercation. I could think of only two motivations: Either I'd offended him so grievously he felt compelled to murder, or he determined I knew things that put him in jeopardy.

I couldn't imagine what I'd learned about Manuel Alvarez that would give Luis Alvarez reason to permanently silence me. That left me to consider that my unwillingness to cater to Alvarez, my insubordination and lack of respect, were things he considered intolerable.

I shook my head. What kind of person tries to kill someone over a disagreement? Someone in the throes of a psychological meltdown, maybe. Or maybe someone who felt he commanded respect, and would kill without hesitation if he was disrespected. The profile fits those in criminal gangs, where status is earned and maintained via a harsh code of honor and obedience. Is that where Luis Alvarez was coming from? Was he bound by a machismo so extreme that contempt was punishable by death? If so, could that help me learn who he was?

I stared at a row of mastheads etched against the twilight sky. My circuitous ruminations were getting me nowhere. I needed real clues leading to hard information. So far I'd uncovered nothing of the sort.

For a moment I felt a swoon of sorrow, for I imagined Candi at home by herself, her hand resting on her pregnant belly. I imagined her contemplating the possibility of raising our child with a father in prison.

"No," I said out loud. Then I saw a pair of cars pull into the parking lot and park next to Claudia's blue Honda. A black Maserati sedan stopped first, followed by a white Alpha Romeo coupe. I climbed back into my car and trained the binoculars on the two cars.

The driver of the Maserati stepped out. He was a tall Caucasian with a wispy build. My immediate impression was that he might be gay. The man that emerged from the passenger side was of a different ilk. He was medium height and powerfully built, and he moved with a tense purposefulness, as if on full alert. His face was ridged and angular, his facial bones exaggerated and pushing against the skin. His Adam's apple was a large knot in his throat and his lips were thick and jutted outward. Above his pocked cheeks his eye sockets were cavernous. When he turned I saw his black eyes, glistening with an angry intensity, roving up and down the pier.

"Someone's having a bad day," I muttered.

The driver of the Alpha Romeo was a Latino nearly my size. He had a closely trimmed beard and wore a black leather jacket even though it was at least 75 degrees outside. But I paid more attention to his passenger, a man about fifty in white slacks, tasseled loafers, and a pink golf shirt. When he spoke and pointed, the other three men stopped and listened motionlessly.

"El jefe," I said. I reached into the back seat, grabbed my DSLR camera, and adjusted the zoom lens. From a hundred yards, it would be unlikely for them to see me through the closed window. But I ducked low regardless and made quick work of it, snapping rapidly and lowering the camera between shots.

The four walked to the gate and the Maserati driver used a key to open it. They walked along the dock until they reached a sleek yacht that I estimated at ninety feet. There were oval windows low on the hull, then a row of larger spherical windows off the deck, and above that another trio of dark windows around the cockpit. As they approached the gangway, a man in shorts and a green shirt greeted them and offered his hand in assistance.

From my angle I could see only the starboard side, and that view was partially obstructed. But it didn't matter, because the men promptly disappeared into the cabin.

I watched for ten minutes. The man in the leather jacket appeared on deck, untied the mooring ropes, and signaled toward the pilot house. The boat slowly pulled away from the dock and headed toward the bay inlet. Just as it reached the end of the cove, I spotted Claudia, in a bikini bottom and heels, smoking a cigarette on the aft deck with the tall white man. She was topless, her brown nipples dark on her augmented breasts. A minute later the pilot hit the gas and the yacht grew smaller until it faded from view. When I lowered the binoculars, I saw Cody walking up with two Styrofoam containers in his hands.

"What's the haps?" he said.

"See those cars parked next to Claudia's?"

"I saw them."

"Four dudes pulled up, got on a yacht, and headed out to sea. I spotted Claudia onboard."

"What kind of yacht?" Cody asked, handing me a container.

"A big one. Maybe a hundred feet long. Here's some pictures." I handed him my camera and watched him scroll through the screen.

"Got to be worth millions," he said. "You think she's working as a party girl?"

"I don't know. I didn't see any other women aboard. But she was topless, so go figure."

Cody and I stood leaning against our car, eating hamburgers as the watery horizon lost its shine. The low clouds had turned red and the powder blue sky was darkening from above. "They'll probably be gone for hours," he said.

"Let's go take pictures of the license plates," I said, nodding toward the Maserati and Alpha Romeo.

"Then let's get a beer," Cody replied. "I have a few things to share with you."

• • •

The bar in the marina restaurant overlooked the pier and through the floor-to-ceiling windows I could see a number of boats on the water, their deck lights twinkling on the glassy surface of the bay. We sat drinking beer from ice-coated pint glasses. I took a long, slow swig and tried to immerse myself in the tranquility of the moment.

"I got a download from a P.I. in Denver I've been talking to," Cody said, interrupting my respite. "Get this: After Landers got his ass fired from SJPD, he moved back to Denver and got a P.I. license. He's been trying to buddy up to everybody or anybody at Denver PD, but they all think he's an asshole."

"Imagine that."

"So Landers hooked up with his old pal, Magnus Swett, whose career as a D.A. was on shaky ground, because, wait until you hear this, about a year ago someone in Denver PD found out that Malcom Swett, convicted rapist and murderer, is Magnus's younger brother. Within a week, everyone in Denver knew about it."

"How did Magnus react to that?"

"The issue wasn't how he reacted, but how everybody he worked with did. They're all looking at him, thinking, what fucked up gene pool did you come from? Seriously, a D.A. has to have a squeaky clean background. It was guilt by association. You got baggage like that, it's very difficult to do the job."

"So the city fired him? Or did he resign?"

"I'll get to that. So Swett is trying to keep his head down and weather the storm, but he could really use a high profile conviction to help his reputation. Then the perfect opportunity comes along. About six months ago an entire family is murdered in an otherwise quiet Denver suburb. Denver detectives can't figure out a motivation, and they're getting nowhere. So Landers hears about it and here he comes to the rescue. He claimed to have evidence that the hit was carried out by Denver's most notorious gang, the same gang Denver PD had been chasing for years. When asked why a middle-class family with two teenage children would be targeted by the gang, Landers pointed to a single misdemeanor possession charge on the 18-year-old son. The kid was out partying and got popped with a quarter gram of blow."

"Was anyone from the gang arrested?"

"Yeah, they did a raid and brought in eight members and held them without bail. But before the first trial was held, another family got waxed in the same suburb. But this time, the killer got sloppy and left DNA evidence. I mean, he shot up a whole family then made himself a freaking sandwich."

"A psycho case."

"No doubt. So within twenty-four hours they arrest the perp and the next day he confesses to both shootings. But this puts Swett in an awkward position, because he's already blabbed to the press about taking down the drug gang. So when his case went up in smoke, the press made him look like a jackass. There was no fixing it, and a month later he was gone, supposedly cut a deal for a couple months pay and left town."

"And then he lands in Lake Tahoe."

"Apparently your town has low standards."

"Our city officials aren't serious bureaucrats. They're mostly semi-retirees who moved to the Sierra for the scenery."

"That means they don't bother with due diligence?"

"It's not the first time," I said, thinking back to the corrupt Tahoe sheriff who caused me considerable grief a few years ago.

"I'd say the good people of South Lake Tahoe deserve to know a little more about their District Attorney, wouldn't you?" Cody smiled widely and clinked his beer mug against mine.

I tried to smile, but I didn't see how discrediting Swett would lessen the charges against me. It sounded like a long term strategy, and I doubted it would help my immediate problem. I drank the last of my beer and resisted the urge to share my thoughts with Cody. Instead, I said, "Thanks, buddy. Let's go back and wait for Claudia to return."

•   •   •

I thought we'd probably be sitting in the parking lot until eleven or midnight. So when I saw the yacht approaching the dock at a little past nine, I lowered the binoculars from my face and said, "That didn't take long."

"You don't take a big boat like that out for a quick trip," Cody said. "It's like a floating mansion."

We watched in silence as the yacht maneuvered into position against the pier. The man in the leather coat tended to the mooring while the other men gathered on the deck. Once the gangway was in place, they walked in line to the gate and then to their cars. Claudia Merchan was not with them.

"No Claudia," I said. "She must still be aboard."

"Why?" Cody said, his voice flat.

"I don't know," I said. "Maybe they left her behind to clean up."

The man in the leather coat opened the Alpha Romeo's passenger door, and the pink-shirted man climbed in. The tall, effeminate man and the man with the ugly expression got into the Maserati. That left the man in shorts and a green shirt who had been on the yacht when the other four arrived. He stuck a key into the door of Claudia's car and lowered himself into the driver's seat. Then they all drove toward the marina exit. As soon as they left the parking lot, I started my car and followed them, lights off.

"Still think Claudia's on the boat?" Cody asked.

"Not really."

"She's fish bait."

I drew in a breath. "We don't know that. Who you think we should follow if they split up?"

"Stay with Claudia's car. Let's see if we can have a private chat with the boat captain."

The three cars stayed together for the two minutes it took us to reach I-395. Then the Alpha Romeo took the freeway on-ramp, while the Maserati and Claudia's Honda continued north, then turned left, and then a mile later jogged right. The evening traffic was light and I was able to tail them easily, until they turned left onto a dark street on the eastern border of Allapattah.

We were in an industrial area, the buildings all single-story and closed for the day. I hoped they wouldn't go far, since we were the sole travelers of this road and I had turned off my headlights to avoid detection. So I was pleased when they quickly stopped in front of a white structure with a chain-link gate out front. I pulled to the curb a couple of hundred feet behind them. A moment later the gate slid back, and the Honda turned into a parking lot.

"Take the wheel," I said. "I want to run up there and get a better look."

I left the car, grimacing as the interior light came on. I closed the door as silently as I could and ran across the street. Then I was able to stay in the shadows as I darted up the sidewalk, until I was directly across from where the Maserati was parked.

Though the building was unlit, I could make out the lettering on the white stucco wall: *AZ Auto Body.* I stood behind a scraggly bush at the corner of a barbwire fence, and saw the Maserati driver's window lower. The fair-skinned man behind the wheel lit a cigarette. In less than a minute, the man who'd driven Claudia's Honda through the gate returned and got into the Maserati. I ran back to my car as they took off. As soon as I got in Cody bolted from the curb in pursuit.

"Chop shop," I said. "They're probably dismantling it now."

"By morning it will be as if it never existed." Cody turned right and we followed the Maserati north on 12th Avenue.

I cursed under my breath. "My only direct lead, probably dead. I can't fucking believe it."

"Sure you can," Cody said. "You assumed she was in bed with drug dealers. You know how cheap life is in that business. They'll beat you to death on the slightest suspicion."

"I know."

"They kill their own as often as they kill their enemies. To say they're psychopathic is an understatement. We should have braced Claudia first thing."

"That's easy to say, in hindsight."

"Hindsight's twenty-twenty, Dirt. But my foresight ain't far behind. And I say the best move is to front these douchebags tonight."

I watched the Maserati approach the 95 Freeway. "Shit, how hard can it be to identify one guy?"

Cody followed as the car took the northbound entrance. "Depends who the guy is."

"Let's see if we can isolate one of them," I said, reaching into the back-seat. "Better gear up."

12

The Maserati took us north for seven miles, then we exited the freeway and headed east toward the Intracoastal Waterway. We crossed the bay and a few minutes later entered a neighborhood of shoreline residences. The houses were all set back from the street, and most had elaborate gates blocking their driveways. We drove deeper into the neighborhood until the Maserati stopped in front of a home. From a few hundred feet back I watched a scrolled wrought-iron gate swing open. A man standing at the gate looked up and down the street.

"Security guard," I said, as the Maserati rolled through the gate and disappeared behind a hedgerow. Cody peered through my binoculars. "That son of a bitch has an Uzi under his coat."

We waited five minutes before driving forward. When we reached the house, the security guard was nowhere in sight, but we were the sole vehicle on the street, and stopping would make our presence obvious if anyone was watching. Cody drove past the house, which was a large, two-story hacienda-style estate. The roofs were Spanish tile, and the driveway was brick laid in a herringbone pattern. Six towering palm trees grew along a stone pathway leading to the front doors. When we reached the end of the street, Cody hung a U-turn, and we parked a hundred feet away from the house.

"What kind of money would it take to afford this joint?" I muttered.

"Millions, just like that luxury yacht," Cody said.

"Drug money."

"Excellent deduction, Doctor Watson. You think they're in for the night?"

I looked at my watch. "I doubt all three live here. I hope green shirt will split soon."

"That would be nice," Cody said, and I hoped he was thinking the same thing I was; confronting an armed guard would be a bad idea, and second, our chances of having a productive conversation were nil unless we caught one of them alone. Despite his inclinations, Cody surely understood that we needed to wait for the right opportunity. At least, I hoped he saw it that way. But when I looked at him, he was staring at the front gate with an intensity that made me pause.

"I wonder if we could get the guard to open the gate if we walked over there," he said.

"Seriously doubt it."

"I'm thinking, sucker-punch him and carry him back to our car."

"They got cameras on the gate. Look under the second story gutter."

Cody grunted. "Too far away to get a clear image."

"Even so, how would we convince him to open the gate?" I said.

"I don't know," Cody replied with a sigh. "I guess we wait."

·   ·   ·

We called it quits at three A.M. Apparently the three men who'd entered the fancy home were spending the night. I didn't know what conclusions to draw from that. Maybe they all lived there. Or maybe just one did, and the other two were guests. Maybe they were sitting around drinking and snorting blow and would be doing so until the sun came up. I smirked at the thought, but I felt a tension in my chest, as if my body was wrapped by coils that were slowly tightening.

I didn't realize how tired I was until I fell into bed in my hotel room. I slept solidly until I woke in the middle of a dream at ten in the morning. I blinked and stared at the ceiling and waited for the slumberous narrative to release its grip on my mind. The setting for the dream had begun at my home, then shifted to an inner city labyrinth of narrow streets and towering tenements. I was wandering in search of something nameless, but the deeper I traveled into the decaying maze, the more confused and frightened I became. Faceless men clawed at me, and I threw punches that hit nothing but air. And then I found myself in a dark hallway, the ceiling so low I had to duck. I opened a creaky door and heard Candi's voice, but I couldn't find her. I grew frantic and ended up on a window ledge hundreds of feet above a deserted boulevard. I woke just as the ledge began to crumble under my feet.

I sat on the edge of the bed and shaded my eyes from a blinding shaft of sunlight that had invaded through a gap in the curtains. I tried to yank the curtains closed, but only allowed more light to enter the room and spill over the desk, where a creased picture of Luis Alvarez lay unfolded, the grainy features like a ghostly taunt. I pushed it away and started making a cup of coffee, but my eyes kept falling back to the picture.

Maybe I'm going about this all wrong, I thought, plugging in the coffee maker. All I needed to do is simply identify one person. His fingerprints didn't pan out, but what about his DNA? A recent case in California used DNA to identify a serial killer from thirty years past. Ancestry websites provided the link, allowing cold case investigators to match DNA from old crime scenes to a younger family member, who, curious about his heritage, submitted DNA samples to a commercial genealogy site. The murder suspect, an ex-cop now in his seventies, was arrested and made a full confession.

I opened my computer and began researching the California investigation, which was conducted by Sacramento PD detectives. The articles I found didn't discuss how challenging it would be or how long it might take to locate and match DNA samples through ancestry websites. But they did comment on legal limitations and ambiguities in this emerging arena, mostly pertaining to privacy concerns. I then ran a search on Florida DNA law, assuming that if Luis Alvarez had any U.S. relatives, they'd most likely live in Florida. I found a few legal web pages claiming that a court order, probably in the form of a search warrant, would be necessary to compel any website that collected DNA samples to share data with the police.

Would Lake Tahoe PD be legally obligated to share Luis Alvarez's DNA profile with me? I knew that current discovery laws required the prosecution to share evidence that they intended to use at trial. But that wouldn't include a DNA sample, unless the prosecution had reason to use Luis Alvarez's DNA as evidence, and I couldn't imagine why they would.

I drank from my paper coffee cup, then drained the lukewarm contents. If I were to pursue the DNA angle, I'd need Marcus Grier's help in getting Luis Alvarez's DNA report. He should have access to the one or two-page document. But sharing it with me would probably be above and beyond the court's obligation, and Grier was ultimately a servant of the court. Regardless, I felt it was worth a try.

It was eight A.M. in California, and I imagined Grier was sitting at his kitchen table, dressed in his green sheriff's uniform, having breakfast. I imagined his wife and two daughters were with him, enjoying and taking for granted the familiarity of the moment. I also knew that Grier placed his family time above all else, and he hated being bothered at home. Plus, every time I asked him for help, he acted as if it was not only burdensome, but could put his job at risk. So instead I called my lawyer. Sam Ruby was still vacationing in Italy, where it was five P.M.

The phone rang ten times before he answered.

"Hello, Dan.

"Hi, Sam. How's Florence?"

"It's like something from a fairy tale. An escape from the real world."

"Must be nice. Look, I'm sorry to impose, but I'm still working on the identity of the man who tried to kill me. I'd like to get your take on tracking his DNA thru ancestry sites."

"You're talking about that case in the Central Valley."

"Right. What do you think?"

"There's not a lot of legal precedent with DNA tracking."

"Do you think you could make Magnus Swett provide the deceased's DNA profile?"

"You're assuming they've created a DNA profile. For the sake of argument, suppose they have. No way Swett would cooperate out of kindness, so I'd have to make a case to the South Lake Tahoe judge."

"I may need you to."

"I'll have my paralegal begin researching it."

"I see," I said after a moment.

"Listen, even if you had it today, I doubt any of those sites would cooperate. There's been a lot of scuttlebutt about Fourth Amendment privacy issues."

"But if the prosecution wanted cooperation, they could just get a warrant."

"That's right."

"So the defense is screwed."

"Dan, even if we could get the DNA and the full cooperation of every genealogy site out there, it could still take weeks, if not months, to conduct a search. And it's still a crap shoot if it would be productive regardless of how long it took."

"I'm just trying to think out of the box."

"You're one the best investigators I know. I have every faith in you."

"Thanks," I said absently. "Have a good rest of your vacation."

It was 11:30, and I was ready to call Cody when my phone chimed. It was an alert for the bugs I'd placed in Claudia's apartment. I initiated the download, then sat before my notebook and plugged in a set of earbuds. I waited for the download to finish, and it only took a minute, which meant the recorded content must have been brief. There was just a single conversation recorded, at two P.M. the previous day. Claudia's voice was easy to hear, while the male she spoke to came through with less clarity, obviously through a cell phone speaker. The conversation was in Spanish, and I selected an option to transcribe it in English.

Claudia: *Hello?*

Male voice: *How are you, my dear?*

Claudia: *Fine, I guess.*

Male voice: *Come join us tonight, on the boat.*

Claudia: (after a pause) *I'm sorry, I'm not feeling so well.*

Male voice: *I'm sure the fresh air will be good for you.*

Claudia: *Is this about Júnior?*

Male voice: *No, I already told you, there's nothing to worry about.*

Claudia: *Promise me, Rodrigo.*

Male voice: *Claudita, you have my word. We'll have fun, it'll be very nice. Be at the dock at six-thirty.*

Claudia: *If I must.*

Male voice: *Stop being like that. I'll see you tonight.*

I clicked the repeat function and listened to the conversation again. Then I read the transcript, staring hard at the two names, Júnior and Rodrigo. It seemed clear that Rodrigo was one of the men on the boat, and likely lured Claudia aboard with the intention of killing her. Although I had no hard evidence that Claudia was dead, I had to assume so.

But I was far more interested in Júnior. Why would Claudia be worried about him, and why did Rodrigo try to pacify her? Who was Júnior? Could he be Luis Alvarez? If so, was Claudia's life forfeit because of what happened in California?

I stood, opened the drapes, and squinted as sunlight poured into the room. In the back of my mind, I had clung to a hope that the bugs in Claudia's apartment would reveal the true identity of Luis Alvarez. Then all I'd need to do was access his criminal record, which hopefully was extensive enough to get me off the hook. In which case I would have booked the next flight home.

"Nice thought," I muttered. I called Cody's cell, and when he didn't answer, I went down the stairs to the hotel lobby, thinking about something to eat. The elevator door opened just as I reached the lobby, and I nearly ran into the woman who walked out. She wore a tight white dress and teetered on five-inch heels. It took me a second to recognize her. It was Aisha, the woman we'd met on our first night in Miami. The same one who asked Cody if he wanted to party.

"Hi, there," I said.

"*Buenos Dias*," she replied, then she stopped and laughed, her voice full of gusto. "You're the man from California."

"That's right."

"My friend likes you, if you're looking for company," she said easily. I could see the freckles glowing on her bronze cheeks, and her eyes looked radiant and almost exhilarant, as if she was basking in the afterglow of a grand indulgence.

I shook my head. "Thanks, anyway."

"So serious," she said, and made a clicking sound with her tongue.

"Yeah, that's me."

"Your big friend was asking me about the man you're looking for."

"Do you have any idea who he is?"

"Not really," she replied, then she waved with her fingers, her red nails flashing, and strutted out the front doors. I watched as she left, her long locks of black hair falling to just above her swinging ass.

"Christ," I mumbled, sitting at a table in the lobby. I saw her climb into a car that stopped at the curb. As the car pulled away, I called Marcus Grier's cell. He picked up after a single ring.

"You still in Miami?"

"Yes."

"The D.A. is tweaked about it. He's wondering if you're a flight risk."

"He can wonder all he wants."

"What's that supposed to mean?"

"It means I don't give a shit what he thinks. Besides, I'm making good progress here," I lied. "Can you help me with a couple license plates?"

"You know that's a direct violation of the rules."

"I've got a lot at stake, Marcus."

"So do I. Like my job."

Which you wouldn't have if it wasn't for me, I almost said, feeling a swell of anger rise in my throat. But I took a deep breath and instead replied, "At least they're not trying to throw you in prison for self-defense."

Grier grunted something unintelligible, then he said, "Read me the plates, make it quick."

I read him the license numbers from the Maserati and the Alpha Romeo. "As soon as you can, Marcus."

"I'll get to it when I get to it," he said, then hung up.

"Lucky me," I grunted, and tossed my phone onto the table. It rang while it was still clattering on the glass top. It was Cody.

"Get any sleep?" I asked.

"Yeah, why?"

"I saw your new love interest out in the lobby."

"Who?"

"Your hooker."

"Oh, Aisha. You're right, I might be in love. Goddamn, what a piece of ass."

"You ever hear of sexaholics?"

"Tell her, not me. She couldn't get enough, I swear. I should have asked her to pay *me.*"

"Yeah, right."

"Plus, she had a crazy idea about finding your man. Meet me in the lobby, I'll tell you about it over breakfast. I'm starving."

"It's noon."

"Breakfast, lunch, who cares? I'll be downstairs in five minutes."

I stood and paced around the lobby, then sat on a couch against the far wall and called Nate Esparza.

"Who's calling?" he answered.

"Nate, it's Dan Reno."

"Oh. I thought it might be another spam call."

"There ought to be a law."

"There is, but nobody pays attention to it."

"Listen," I said, "I've got something I think you'll find interesting."

"Go ahead."

"Last night, Cody and I caught up to Claudia Merchan. Her car was parked at the Miamarina wharf, and I saw her on a yacht with five men. They left the harbor and returned after a couple of hours. The five men got off the boat, but not Claudia. One of the five drove off in Claudia's car, straight to an auto body shop. Then I followed them to a fancy pad up in Bal Harbour. There was an armed guard at the gate. We waited until past three A.M., but no one left."

"So, you think they left Claudia on the yacht?"

"No, I think they killed her and dumped her into the ocean. Then they took her car to a chop shop."

"All right," Esparza said slowly. "Why would they kill her?"

"Whatever Luis Alvarez was up to, Claudia knew too much. She'd become a liability."

Esparza inhaled sharply. "Drugs is a dirty business. You got an address for the house?"

"Yeah."

"You trace it yet?"

"Haven't had time."

"Read me the address. I'll tell you who owns it."

I recited the address and listened to Esparza tap on his keyboard for a minute. Then he said, "Legal owner is Exportar Digital Limited. Probably a dummy corporation. You spend enough time peeling the layers, maybe you can find where the money came from."

"I'll see what I can do. Has Vasquez had any epiphany on Luis Alvarez yet?"

"No, but she's been busy. I'll let her know you called."

"Appreciate it."

When Cody showed up a moment later, his hair was wet, and he didn't break stride as he walked past me. "Let's go get a Cuban," he said.

"You burn a lot of calories last night?" I followed him outside.

"She gave me a workout, all right. Drive us back to that sandwich joint we went to yesterday, would you?"

As we walked to our rental car, the sun disappeared behind a swath of clouds that suddenly turned dark. The temperature didn't drop, but the air felt heavier. By the time we climbed in the car it was raining, the drops splatting heavily on the windshield. I turned on the windshield wipers and drove out to the thoroughfare.

"Dig this," Cody said. "You could put an ad in the newspaper. Plaster a picture of Luis Alvarez in the sports section and offer a reward for his identity."

"This was Aisha's idea?"

"Yeah. What a trip, huh?"

We stopped at a light. The rain was coming down in a torrent, wide streams of water running down the hood. I flipped the wipers to high speed, but found the manic pace annoying, so I turned the wipers off and just let the rain pelt the windshield.

"Have you ever run a newspaper ad in an investigation?" I asked.

"Nope, never even considered it. But you have a different kind of case here."

When I didn't reply, Cody said, "All it would take is one person to tell you who he is."

"You think we should drive over to the Miami Herald? Ask about rates?"

"If you want. Bet it's damn expensive, like five or ten grand. But you could probably get an ad published in a few days."

I turned the wipers on again, just in time for the light to turn green.

"Of course," Cody said, "we do have more expedient options."

"Such as?"

"We stop contemplating the nature of the universe and go after the dirtbags on the yacht. It's pretty obvious, Dirt. They're your direct link to Luis whoever-the-fuck-he-is."

I saw the restaurant at the last second and turned hard, skidding and splashing through a gutter puddle. We bounced into the parking lot and found a parking spot right in front of the El Tropico Cafeteria. As we walked into the joint, without any forewarning, an abrupt and peculiar shift took hold in my head, almost like I'd entered a time warp. And then, before I could understand what was happening, I was flooded with a sense of relief, as if I'd finally accepted an inevitable truth, and in doing so had acknowledged my true self. I could never recall having such a feeling. It felt both profound and euphoric.

We sat at the counter, and Cody was talking but I didn't hear him. Instead, my mind was occupied by the presence of my dead father. His spirit felt so real I almost tried to reach out and touch him. My hair stood on end, my face blasted by a thousand pins and needles. Images from my past played in my head, as if I were viewing my childhood on a screen. I saw my dad fighting an evil man in the driveway of our home and later prosecuting the man and sending him to prison. I heard him speak with mesmerizing force to captivated courtroom audiences. I smelled the scent of popcorn and hotdogs while we sat at the old Oakland Coliseum, watching the A's play the Red Sox. And then I felt his hand on my shoulder, heavy as lead, unshakable and resolute.

Richard Reno was a San Jose attorney when he was murdered by a deranged psychopath. The criminal had spent twelve years in prison due to my father's prosecutorial vehemence. As soon as he was released, the man ambushed my dad as he was leaving his office. One shot in the chest from a twelve-gauge shotgun, and Richard Reno died helplessly in a darkened parking lot.

My father had been a person of seemingly conflicting traits, eccentric and fun-loving, but principled and relentless. He believed that not all who committed crimes were true criminals, and to those he was merciful. But for those he deemed evil, he was their worst nightmare. He had grown up poor and had lived in an environment where the wicked routinely victimized the defenseless. Although he never spoke of it, I knew he felt it was both his calling and obligation to not only serve justice, but to punish those who preyed upon the weak. And he punished severely, sometimes doing everything he could to stretch the boundaries of prison sentences.

But as a child I only caught brief glimpses of that part of my dad, and it was only after his death that I realized the gravity of his convictions. My recollections of him are mostly of a zany and easygoing parent, whose love and affection was deep and unconditional.

My father has been dead for more than twenty years. I no longer think of him every day. Maybe he decided to pay a visit to remind me that some bonds never die, and I could not unshackle from my past. That was my last thought before I felt his presence lift and float weightlessly away. And then blood rushed to my face.

"Hey, man, you okay?" Cody said.

I looked at him in confusion. "Your face is beet red and your eyes are watery," he said. "You looked like you were in a trance."

"I think I just saw a ghost," I rasped.

"Seriously?"

I nodded. "Who?" he asked.

"My old man."

"What'd he say?"

I swallowed and rubbed the stubble on my jaw. "That the means justify the ends in all things noble."

"You read that in a book somewhere?"

"Nope."

"Is there some underlying meaning to it?"

"Beats me," I said, but Cody kept his eyes glued on mine until I looked away and said, "I called Grier earlier, and he's running the plates from the Maserati and Alpha Romeo. He said he'd call me, hopefully today."

"And?"

"I see no reason to waste time waiting for him. So let's eat up and head back to the big house in Bal Harbour."

"I guess that's pretty straight forward," Cody said, grinning broadly.

"Whatever it takes."

"You're always so much fun when you get mad."

"I'm not mad," I said.

"You know what I mean," Cody said, winking.

·   ·   ·

The midday traffic was light, and it only took fifteen minutes to reach the gated home north of Miami Beach. The rain had stopped and steam was rising from the pavement. The sky was now cloudless, except for a lone thunderhead looming over the sea. I parked three houses down the street, and Cody and I set out on foot. We both wore windbreakers to conceal our body armor and firearms. It was nearly ninety under the blazing sun, and I'm sure we looked conspicuous, but I wasn't worried about it.

When we reached the gate, the armed guard was nowhere in sight. The home was resplendent in the sun. Circular balconies enclosed by scrolled iron railings jutted from the second story and overlooked the front yard, where the tall palms were still wet and glistening. Pots of colorful flowers rested at the base of the peach-colored stucco, and the front door was deep in shadow at the end of a columned portico. To our right was a long drive-way leading behind the house.

· I could see video cameras mounted on the balconies, pointing down at us. "My, such a splendid abode," Cody said. He fit his huge paw on one of the gateposts and rattled it. "Anybody home?" he yelled, waving at the cameras.

Within a minute a man came out the front door. He wore a tan wind-breaker, and the presence of a machine pistol beneath his coat was obvious. He held his right arm awkwardly to prevent it from swinging as he walked.

"Hey, thanks for taking the time," I said, smiling and waving. He was the same guard we'd seen here the night before.

"What do you want?" he said.

"There's this guy I met, and I don't know his name. I owe him money, and I want to pay him."

The guard blinked and cocked his head. He was an average-sized fellow, a bit pudgy, not someone whose purpose was to intimidate. But when he looked at me I saw a certain deadness in his eyes, and I reminded myself that a man doesn't need to be physically imposing to be deadly. It doesn't take much strength to pull a trigger.

I unfolded a picture of Luis Alvarez and handed it to him, sticking my hand between the gate posts. He took it and looked down at the sheet.

"What is your name, *amigo*?" he said, raising his eyes.

"Charles Ulysses Farley. And I hate letting a debt go unpaid. I'm serious about that."

He looked hard at me. After a long moment, he said, "Wait here. Maybe someone inside knows him."

"Okay, thanks, buddy," I said. "Right on, man."

The man walked down the brick path and disappeared into the house.

"Turning on that old Chuck U. Farley charm, huh?" Cody said.

"He recognized the picture. Otherwise he would have told us to beat it." I stared into the dark shadows within the portico. "Maybe he'll come out in a minute and kindly tell us the identity of our man," I said.

"Now, that's thinking optimistically."

"Don't underestimate the power of positive thinking."

"Just to be safe, I'll keep my hand on my piece, if you don't mind."

There was no shade near where we stood at the gate. The sun seemed to shine with an added intensity, as if to make up for the rainy interlude. I felt a drop of sweat run beside my ear. A minute passed and Cody said, "Maybe they'll let us bake out here until we split."

"I don't think so," I said, as the front door opened. Walking toward us was the gate guard and a second man, who I immediately recognized as one who'd been on the yacht. He strode aggressively, his shoulders bulging against a white T-shirt, his gait bowlegged to accommodate his thick legs.

He glared at us with an ugly, undisguised hostility. As he got closer, I saw his knuckles were oversized and scarred.

"What do you want with this man?" he demanded, clutching the sheet of paper. His accent was thick and his teeth were chipped and stained.

"Like I said, I owe him money, and I'm just trying to learn his name. Can you help me?"

He stared at my face, his deep-set eyes dark and accusing. "Where are you from?" he asked.

"California," Cody said, moving right up to the gate. "How about you?"

The man paused and his thick lips pursed. "Have you met this man?" He held the picture of Luis Alvarez and shook it at us.

"That's what I've been trying to tell you, good buddy. I did some work for him and owe him a refund. Six hundred bucks. But I never got his name."

The knotted ridges over his eyes quivered as if his brain was working overtime. His eyes shot from me to Cody and back to me. "What's your name?"

"Like I told your man, I'm Chuck Farley. Look, it's getting hot out here. If you can't help me, I'll be on my way."

"I'm not done with you yet."

"Then, hell, invite us inside and serve up some drinks, because I'm sweating my ass off," Cody said.

"You're a big man with a big mouth."

"Yeah, people keep telling me that."

The man glowered at Cody for a tense moment, then turned to me. "Give me your phone number," he said.

"You gonna call me?"

"Give me your number and you'll find out."

"All right," I said, and watched while he punched my number into his mobile phone. Then he pivoted and began back toward the house.

"Hey, man, you got a name?" I said to his back. "So I know who it is when you call?"

He stopped for a long moment before replying. "Paco," he said, shooting a brief glare our way before he and the gate guard continued to the front door.

"Nice guy," I said, watching them disappear into the house. Cody and I turned and walked up the street to our car.

"Boatloads of charm."

"His knuckles have seen a lot of action."

"Paco's the hired muscle. Probably beats the hell out of poor bastards tied to a chair."

"I doubt that's his real name," I said.

"Who cares? He's just a thug."

"I wish Grier would call me back with the owners of those cars."

"He always comes through for you, doesn't he?"

"It depends."

We climbed into the car and I turned the AC to full blast. I pulled away from the curb and when we drove past the house I saw the gate guard standing with a pad and pen in hand, staring at us and scribbling.

"He got your license. They'll try to contact the rental car agency and get your name," Cody said.

"So what?"

"I'm sure Claudia told them your name. They'll know who you are. And they'll know you killed their comrade."

I steered onto the causeway and we began driving over a narrow section of Biscayne Bay. The water was blue and sparkling under the bright sun. "What do you think they'll do about it?"

"Maybe something. Maybe nothing," Cody replied, lighting a cigarette and opening the window to let in a rush of warm air.

"I still think our best chance is to get one of those pricks alone," I said.

"You might be in luck. We got a tail," Cody said, adjusting his side-view mirror. "Black Maserati."

"Who's driving?"

"The dude we just met. Señor Paco Sunshine."

I grimaced. "We're not gonna get anything out of him."

"You never know. Depends what he wants from you."

"I'll tell him whatever he wants, if he'll tell me the real identity of Luis Alvarez."

"Maybe he'll want you to answer for killing him."

We came off the bay, and I turned onto the street leading to the free-way. I glanced in my mirror. "Is he still following?"

Cody adjusted my mirror, then said, "Yeah, there he is, back a few cars."

"You think he wants to get into it, here and now?"

Cody kept his eyes on the mirror. "I don't think he's that stupid. He probably wants to find out where we're staying."

"Then let's take him to bumfuck Egypt."

"I'll find a nice little hotel for him," Cody said, working his phone. "The freeway's up ahead. Get on it and head north."

I took the ramp onto I-95 and drove in the middle lane, keeping my speed consistent. The Maserati stayed a car or two behind, moving from our lane to the right lane and back again. We cruised through the early afternoon traffic for twenty minutes, passed through Hollywood, and finally took the exit for the Fort Lauderdale Airport. We passed a few hotels until Cody pointed and said, "This one." I turned onto a side street leading to a Marriot business-class hotel and parked in the open lot near the front doors. We got out of the car quickly and walked inside without looking back. As soon as the door shut behind us, we turned and stared out the floor-to-ceiling windows, watching the Maserati take a lap around the lot. The car drove behind the building and reappeared after a minute. Then Paco backed into a shaded spot at the far end of the lot, as if planning to wait, but a few minutes later he pulled out and drove away.

"Let's go talk strategy in the bar," Cody said. We walked into an adjoining dining area, but there was no bartender on duty. "What's up with this place?" Cody groused.

"It's too early for their clientele, so you'll have to go thirsty."

"Ridiculous."

"Let's go sit by the window. That dude seemed indecisive. I want to see if he comes back."

We took a table at the front windows and sat looking out at the parking lot.

"Why don't you call Grier, see if he ran those plates?" Cody asked. I looked at my watch. It was a little before noon on the west coast.

"All right." I hit Grier's number, and he answered after a half dozen rings.

"Hey, Marcus."

"Let me guess, you're calling about the plates."

"Your intuition is spot on today."

"Yours isn't if you think I've got nothing better to do."

"Come on, Marcus."

"You got a pencil?"

"Yeah."

"I got the owner's names. Alpha Romeo is registered to Ivan Sanhueza, address listed as 74 Bal Bay Drive, Miami. Maserati is owned by Celso Santos, 1800 Brickell, number 1010, Miami.

"You didn't happen to check for criminal records, did you?"

"Nope."

"Well, if you have any spare time…"

"I'm sorry, I've got to go," he said.

"See you later," I said, as the line went dead.

"Fire up your notebook," Cody said, taking the sheet of paper from me and staring at the scrawled names. "Let's see what we can learn about these all-stars."

I pulled my PC from my backpack and logged onto the people finder site I subscribed to. It only took ten minutes to access the public records for Ivan Sanhueza and Celso Santos. While both were U.S. citizens, neither had records previous to 2010, which meant they probably hadn't lived in the U.S. until that time.

"Any indication what country they're from?" Cody asked.

"Yeah," I said, clicking away on my keyboard. I turned my screen so Cody could see it. "Ivan Sanhueza, age 51, was granted citizenship in 2010. He was a Colombian national." I continued typing, and what looked like a passport photo came up.

"The boss man," I said. "Recognize the face?"

"Yeah. What else on him?"

"No bankruptcies, liens, marriages, divorces. No real estate ownership."

"You think he's renting that big house?"

"If he owns it, it's not in his name."

"No criminal record?"

"Just a speeding ticket and a lapsed registration fine." I hit a few more keys. "There's also a court document."

"For what?"

"Let's see," I said, scrolling. "It looks like he was charged with money laundering in 2015. But the charges were dropped."

"It never went to trial?"

"Guess not."

"Any business licenses?"

"Nothing listed."

"So nothing to indicate his source of income."

"No, but I wouldn't expect there to be in his public profile."

"Hmm," Cody said. A cloud passed and a blast of sunlight fell across our table. Cody's face looked carved from granite, except for the shine of his narrowed eyes. "What about the other pud-puller?"

"Celso Santos, thirty-six years old. Also became a citizen in 2010. He was born in Cuba." I pulled up the picture from his naturalization file and said, "He was driving the Maserati at the boat dock."

Cody leaned over to look at my screen. "Ho, ho, homo," he said.

"Maybe so, but look at his record. He's been popped four times in ten years. A concealed firearm charge, assault and battery, and two murder raps. Only conviction was the concealed handgun. He skated on everything else."

"A fairy with a mean streak. Bet he's got a good, high-priced lawyer."

"I'm sure he does."

A man with a gold name tag on his chest appeared from a side door and walked behind the bar.

"Hey, Gunga Din, can we get a couple cold ones?" Cody called out.

"Sorry, we don't open until four."

Cody shook his head. "What's up with this place? A man could die of thirst."

I looked at my watch. "They open in fifteen minutes. I'm sure your liver can make it that long. Then let's head back to Bal Harbour and see if we can put a tail on one of them."

"You know what I'd like to do?" Cody said, tapping his fingers on the table top. "Make a friendly offer to the *jefe*. Like, tell us who Luis Alvarez is, and in exchange we won't put our good buddies at the IRS onto you."

"You got contacts at the IRS?"

"You know I do."

"Yeah, but that was a while ago."

"My buddy's still there, and he always appreciates a good tip."

"I thought you pissed him off and the relationship went south."

"It was a minor misunderstanding. It's all good now."

"Hmm. Could be promising."

"Damn right. Look, these guys are obviously mobbed up. And the one thing that scares the shit out of all mobsters is the taxman."

"All we got to do is figure out how to have a nice talk with *Señor* Sanhueza."

"I'm sure you can impress him with your Spanish accent. Maybe we can just call and make an appointment. He's a businessman, right?"

"Now that's positive thinking."

"Speaking of all things positive," Cody said, nodding toward the window, "Look who's back."

It was the Maserati, with Paco behind the wheel. He parked, got out of the car, and took a good look around before heading toward the hotel entrance.

"I imagine he'd like to chat," I said.

"I don't think he's the talkative type," Cody replied. He reached beneath his windbreaker and rested his hand near where his Glock was holstered.

A moment later we saw Paco in the lobby. "Over here," I said. He turned toward us in surprise, then he tried to smile, but it didn't fit his face. He stood watching us while his pained grin vanished and his features reverted to the ugly scowl that seemed natural to him. After a moment he walked to where we sat.

"I got somebody knows the guy you're looking for," he said. "You want to follow me, you can talk to him."

"To Bal Harbour?" I asked.

"No," he said, resting his hollow eyes on mine. "Somewhere else."

I exchanged looks with Cody, who then said, "Well, that's mighty good of you, buddy. I suppose we owe you a favor."

Paco smiled and this time it wasn't forced, but it still looked more like a sneer. "Let's go," he said.

We followed him outside, where the sun was now shining brightly and the palms swayed in the warm breeze. The air smelled like damp soil. We climbed into the rental car and waited for the Maserati to pull ahead. Then we drove behind it and within a minute we were heading east on I-595.

"Turn on your navigator," I said to Cody, as I braked for traffic. We were right on the Maserati's bumper, and I saw Paco watching us in his mirror. The traffic eased after a mile, and we drove at freeway speed for ten minutes, passing over the Florida Turnpike. Five minutes later we crossed the 869 interchange and Cody said, "He's taking us out of town, into the Everglades."

I saw a sign identifying the road as Alligator Alley, and a minute later we passed the 27 on-ramp and the road narrowed to two lanes. Thirty foot waterways ran on either side of the pavement and beyond that were flat, marshy grasslands.

"There's nothing for almost a hundred miles," Cody said. "Next city is all the way on the western coast of Florida." But as soon as he spoke, the Maserati's brake lights flashed, and it kept slowing until it turned onto the shoulder and took a sharp right leading across a narrow wooden bridge. We crossed over the water and onto a dirt road. I hit the brakes and stopped.

"What are you doing?" Cody said. "Go."

"Where do you think he's taking us?" I said.

"What are you worried about? We're armed."

"You got to be fucking kidding, Cody."

"This guy has the information you need, and you want to back off? Step on the gas, we're losing him."

I let off the brake. "I can't afford for this to go bad, goddammit," I said. "I'm already under indictment."

"Relax. Stay alert. Everything will be fine."

I accelerated and the grass grew taller, rising to three feet or so. We came around a bend and entered a wooded swampland, the road nothing more than a path atop a levee. Stands of mangroves grew from the water, their exposed roots like colonies of crouching spiders. The foliage became heavier, and then we saw a structure built at the back end of a turnabout. It was a small, wood-sided building, perhaps large enough for two or three rooms. My first thought was it could be a residence for a park ranger or a game warden, but the white paint was faded and peeling, and the tin roof was coated with dead leaves, the gutters sagging under the weight. As we got closer, I saw a black pickup truck parked to the side.

"Not good," I said, watching the Maserati stop behind the pickup.

"Turn around," Cody said. "Park facing toward the road."

Paco climbed out of the Maserati waved for us to join him. I executed a Y-turn, my gut buzzing, and looked at Cody.

"Showtime," he said, unbuckling his seatbelt.

We got out of the rental car and began toward the structure. Paco waited until we got within a few feet, then he said, "Come on, nothing to worry." He pulled on the rickety door, and it screeched in protest. A dim light from inside revealed moldy green walls but not much else.

Paco went through the doorway, Cody followed, and I brought up the rear. As soon as I stepped over the threshold, my nostrils were assailed by the odor of stale must and animal urine. The floor was concrete and the only furniture was a raw wooden table and two chairs in the center of the room. One of the chairs was empty. In the other, the gate guard from the big house in Bel Harbour sat behind the table.

"Hey, we meet again," Cody said. Paco moved to the single covered window in the room, and I stepped from behind Cody and stood watching the two men. The gate guard sat with his hands hidden beneath the table. In the next instant, without the slightest warning, his right hand came from below the table, holding a revolver. Without seeming to aim, he shot at Cody. The report was deafening in the small room.

The bullet hit Cody dead center in the chest, and its velocity threw him against the front wall, where he crumpled and lay face up. I stared at him in astonishment, blood pounding in my ears. When I looked back at the assailant, his pistol was pointed at me.

"Hands up," he said.

I raised my hands and moved toward the opposite wall, away from the single window. The gate guard kept his revolver aimed at my gut. I was about ten feet from the rear corner of the room.

"No more games," said Paco. "We know who you are."

"Don't shoot," I said, moving my raised hands in front of my face in a defensive gesture. I took a step toward the rear corner. "What do you want?"

"The Ford minibus. Where is it?"

"You mean the Ford Manuel Alvarez was in?"

"Don't play stupid," the gate guard said, but Paco said nothing. Instead, he responded by pulling a double-edged fighting knife from beneath his shirt.

"You'll answer my questions or I'll gut you here and now." He came at me in three quick steps and stuck the point of the blade under my chin. I moved back from him, now pressed up against the room's back corner, behind and to the right of where the gate guard sat at the table. I looked down at the ugly features of the man holding the knife. The gate guard had turned in his chair to face us, his pistol still in his hand but resting on the table.

"I know where the Ford minibus is," I said. "No problem." I kept my eyes on the man, resisting the temptation to look past him at where they assumed Cody lay dead.

In hindsight, the men who planned to interrogate and kill us were stupid and unprepared, and probably used to slaughtering adversaries who were both unarmed and caught by surprise. Maybe their foolish arrogance was the result of working for drug kingpins who, by virtue of their wealth, were effectively above the law. Whatever the case, they had not deemed it necessary to search either Cody or me. Either that, or they assumed that once they had the drop on us, we'd have no recourse, armed or not.

"Start talking," Paco said, and those were his last words, because Cody had silently pulled his Glock from the holster beneath his jacket. Arm outstretched, he fired a single shot into the back of Paco's head. The hollow point round flattened upon impact and Paco's eyes and forehead vanished in an explosion that showered my face with blood and gristle. Before his faceless body hit the ground, Cody fired two shots at the gate guard. Both shots were aimed low; the first splintered the table, and the second round ripped a trench through the man's forearm and exited near the elbow.

The gate guard tried to grasp his revolver with his good hand, but Cody fired once more, hitting the man's shoulder. That took the fight out of him.

By this time I'd pulled my Beretta, but it was hardly necessary, for one man was dead and the other in shock and incapacitated. I stepped over where Paco's corpse lay at my feet, trying to avoid the growing puddle of blood. Cody pushed himself upright with a groan, and we approached the gate guard, who sat in a bloody mess in his chair.

"I've got a first aid kit," I said. "Then we'll take you to the hospital." He looked up at me, a glimmer of hope showing through his agonized expression. "But first I need to know the name of the man whose picture I showed you."

He was shaking and blood spilled down his lips as he tried to speak. "Escobar," he moaned. "Please help me."

"What's his first name?"

"Luis." His head fell forward and he began to slip out of his chair. I grabbed him by the arm, soaking my hand in his blood. A small cry of pain escaped his lips.

"Tell me more," I said. "Where's he from?"

"I'm dying," he whispered.

"No, you're not. Come on, partner, I need more. Then we'll fix you up."

He managed to raise his head and his pleading eyes met mine. "He's the son of Escobar's whore," he said.

"What?" I said, but his body shuddered and his breath left him in a long wheeze. A second later he fell to the side, his sleeve ripping where I held it. His body collapsed to the dirty concrete floor, his belly soaked in blood, his sightless eyes staring at wherever death was taking him. Cody's first bullet must have pierced the man's gut from underneath the table, and the shot proved to be fatal. Cody and I stood looking down at him for a long moment, before Cody said, "That's what you get for shooting me, asshole."

"Let's get the hell out of here," I said.

"Check the bodies for phones," Cody said, reaching down and patting the gate guard's pockets. I did the same to Paco, but neither man was carrying a device. Instead I took Paco's keys, then we left the decrepit structure, leaving the two bodies to rot in their moldy tomb.

"Don't leave any prints," I said, as Cody shouldered the door open. I took a deep breath of the humid air, then unlocked the Maserati and saw Paco's phone in the center console. Cody opened the pickup truck's door and emerged a moment later with a phone. I stuck Paco's phone in my pocket and washed my hands and face in a muddy puddle near the building.

"Come on," Cody said, and a minute later we were driving along the levy and approaching the small bridge before the highway. "Stop," he said. "I need to dispose of my Glock. You owe me five hundred bucks." He ejected the cartridge and disassembled the gun, detaching the slide from the frame and removing the barrel. He got out of the car and heaved the frame a couple hundred feet into a swamp, then he threw the slide into the marsh on the opposite side of the levy. After looking around for a moment, he ran behind me and winged the barrel deep into a pond of stagnant black water.

"Hit it," he said, climbing back into the passenger seat. I steered over the bridge and turned onto the pavement. It was five o'clock and the sun had fallen behind a thunderhead on the horizon. A moment later the sun's rays burned through the cloud, sending streaks of light and shadow across the roadway. I drove into the surreal pattern, feeling numb and detached, as if I was somewhere else and had not participated in the events of the last hour.

"Those bodies will be gone by morning," Cody said, lighting a cigarette. "We don't have to worry about the cops. I'm sure Ivan Sanhueza will send a cleanup crew after his goons don't come home. No one will ever miss those two. I doubt they were even U.S. citizens."

"I gave Sanhueza a chance to work it out. I would have told him where the damn Ford is. Instead, he tries to kill us?"

"Maye he'll keep trying."

"If he's smart, he'll cut his losses," I said. "I don't plan on sticking around here much longer. Light me a fucking smoke, would you?"

"All right," Cody said, eyeing me. "But we need to think clearly here. Maybe best to relieve the stress with a drink or two. You always like to drink after killing someone, right?"

I exhaled loudly. "I didn't kill anybody."

"Oh yeah, it was all me, saving your ass."

I started to reply, but realized I didn't know what to say or think at that moment. I kept my eyes glued to the windshield and drove at exactly the speed limit. I had no idea if anyone might have heard the shots and alerted the police. All I knew was we needed to put distance between us and those bodies.

"Ease up, Dirt," Cody said after a minute. "The *Federales* ain't around the corner. And I never keep a hot piece. That's one of my rules."

I dragged deeply on the cigarette Cody had given to me. The smoke swirled in my face before vanishing into the slipstream, and I felt the tension in my chest start to ease. A minute later we reached a crossroad, and Cody said, "Hang a right. This road will take us all the way back to Miami." Then he reached over and tapped me on the arm. "You need to get rid of that shirt."

I looked down and saw a splatter of blood across my shoulder.

"Let's go straight to the hotel and check out," I said. "Our rooms are under my name. They may be able to trace it."

"Good thinking," Cody said, his face bunched in a grimace, his hand wedged under his vest near where the gate guard's bullet had been stopped by Kevlar armor.

"Hurt?" I asked.

"Like a bitch," he replied.

13

Sometimes, in a moment without warning, a weighted lump of guilt will take residence in my heart. This can occur shortly after a killing, or days later. To what degree the dead deserved their fate plays no part in my emotional equation. Nor does the role of self-defense. It's as if I subconsciously believe every person, regardless of their actions, has a basic right to live. Of course, this is an utterly foolish notion. In my career I've crossed paths with more ruthless criminals than I can remember. Some have tried to kill me, and none succeeded because I killed them first. Those who sought to end my life surrendered any potential for leniency. I can't think of a more rational way to put it.

There are those in the justice system who have viewed my involvement in violent incidents as overzealous and unnecessary. These individuals were never shot at, run off a road, nearly drowned to death, stabbed, drugged and kidnapped, or had their loved ones threatened. Their attempts to blame me for acting in self-defense always struck me as detached from reality. They lived their lives free of deadly threat, but I did not. Perhaps they felt that, when faced with death, I should simply concede?

It was twilight when we arrived at our hotel. The faces of the two cartel assassins Cody shot dead were still flickering in my head, as if they were calling to me from their journey to hell. I parked and looked at Cody. He had popped a couple pills, probably oxycodone, and seemed perfectly at peace with the world. Goddamn Cody. He'd never failed to be by my side when I needed him. Trouble was, there were times when I probably could take a less confrontational path to resolving a case, but that was rarely an option in Cody's book. I sighed and tried to push the images of the dead men out of my mind.

"Hey, man, you got the name you needed," Cody said. "Let's get our gear and boogie, find a joint with booze and wireless."

"I think I could use a drink or two."

"Right on, brother."

We went to our rooms, and I quickly showered and stuck my blood-stained shirt in a plastic bag. Within fifteen minutes we were back in our car, driving south. I avoided the clogged rush hour freeway and stayed on surface streets. We passed by the perimeter of the airport, and I turned left after a few more miles. I stopped when I saw a garbage bin in a restaurant parking lot. I knotted the plastic bag and tossed it in the container, then returned to the boulevard.

"You got somewhere in mind, or we just driving aimlessly?" Cody asked.

"There are lots of bars and restaurants in Little Havana. We should be getting close."

Cody tapped on his phone for a minute, then said, "The main drag is Eighth Street. Keep going and take a right on Seventeenth."

I was hoping to find a quiet neighborhood lounge, something dark and anonymous, but as soon as we turned onto *Calle Ocho*, Cody pointed at a neon cocktail sign beckoning from above the awning of the "World Famous Ball & Chain Bar & Lounge."

"Looks like a tourist trap," I said.

"Ain't that what we are?"

"I wish."

"Park there and let's go sample a few *Cuba Libres*."

"I was more in the mood for whiskey."

"When in Rome," Cody replied.

It wasn't quite six o'clock when we entered the Ball & Chain, and the place was only half full. It was a big, rectangular room with a large stage at one end and a bar at the other, and I would have bet that by ten P.M. the music would be thumping and the dance floor packed. We walked to the bar, a square unit faced with red, green, and white panels that looked like sections of old wooden doors. At each corner were baskets piled high with limes and lemons. A chandelier hanging from the wood beam ceiling provided dim lighting, aided by a number of surrounding light fixtures that looked like little bird cages. Cody grabbed a stool, but I pointed at a green wall and said, "Let's take a booth." The bartender poured us rum and colas, and I led us to a booth in the far corner.

"Remember when we were eighteen, and we used to pound rum and Cokes at Kay's Bar?" Cody asked, sliding behind the table.

"How could I forget?"

"I still remember Kay, that little oriental lady, eighty-sixing you."

"She did have a temper."

"I'm sure you brought it out of her. Do you remember why she kicked you out?"

I took a long pull from my highball. "No, not really."

"You were playing pool and hit the ball so hard it flew off the table and drilled some poor drunk in the hand. He dropped his beer, and the glass broke and made a big mess. That's what pissed her off."

"You still remember that?"

"Sure. You were nothing but trouble back then."

"And you weren't?"

Cody raised his glass and clinked it against mine. "Some things never change, Dirt." He downed the remainder of his drink, the ice cubes rattling against his teeth, and headed to the bar for a refill. I pushed my half-full glass to the side and took my computer from my backpack. By the time Cody returned, I'd already connected to my people finder website.

"How many Luis Escobars you think are out there?" I said.

"In the U.S.? I don't know. It sounds like a common name."

"I'll start with Florida."

"The guy said he was the son of Escobar's whore, whatever that means."

"Probably nothing," I said, tapping on my keyboard. "But I'd bet he lived within a ten mile radius of where we are."

"Anything come up yet?"

"The results are still downloading." I reached for my drink and said, "I should call Candi."

"Okay, Captain," Cody said, saluting me as if I was the commanding officer of a Navy shore patrol on a mission to get drunk and find willing women. For some reason, the gesture seemed both funny and sad. Before heading outside I stopped at the bar and guzzled a fresh *Cuba Libre*.

When I walked out to the sidewalk, the tropical air greeted me with a warm embrace. The twilight sky was streaked with orange wisps, and I could smell fresh pineapple and mango from a street vendor's cart. Next door, an elaborate sculpture of an ice cream cone rose from the adjoining building, and the scoops of chocolate and strawberry looked ready to topple onto the Ball & Chain's roof. A group of twenty or so people, mostly teenagers, were congregated in front of the ice cream parlor, laughing and horsing around. I walked away from them and found a quiet area across the street from where a five-foot-tall statue of a rooster stood outside of a restaurant. The rooster was painted in stars and stripes, as if it were wearing the American flag.

I took in the scene, relaxing as the quick drinks softened my mind's edges. I held my phone and thought how I would keep the conversation with Candi light and positive. I'd tell her about Miami, the pleasant weather, the Latin vibe, the picturesque waters. I'd tell her I was making good progress on my investigation and expected to be home in a few days with information that would surely exonerate me of the manslaughter charge. Then I'd steer the conversation to her, to how she was feeling and what was happening at home. I tapped my phone, looking forward to hearing her voice.

When she didn't answer after about ten rings, I was ready to hang up and text her. But then she answered, and before she spoke I heard other voices.

"Candi?"

"Yes. Hi," she replied after a moment.

"Where are you?"

"I'm at the hospital. I'm just leaving."

"The hospital?" I felt a tic of alarm in my gut. "What for?"

"Dan, I had a miscarriage this morning."

"A miscarriage?" I asked stupidly, as if I didn't know what the word meant.

"I woke up this morning with cramps and saw some bleeding. I called my doctor, and he told me to come in."

"Candi, are you okay?"

I heard her take a deep breath. "The doctor said I'm fine physically. Miscarriages are a common thing."

"Oh," I said. "I didn't know." I tried to formulate another sentence, but my mind was frozen. The silence grew awkward, then she said, "I'm sorry I lost our child."

"Sorry? No, don't be sorry, it's not your fault, I mean..."

"It was my baby. It was our baby." Her voice began to crack.

"But," I said haltingly, "Can you get pregnant again?"

"Yes," she said between sniffles. "But I feel like part of me died with the baby."

"No."

"The nurse told me it's a normal reaction. It will take me some time to recover."

I looked down and pressed my fist to my forehead. "I wish I was there with you," I said hoarsely.

"Me too."

We didn't speak for a long moment, then I said, "What causes miscarriages?"

"The doctor said the most common cause is chromosome abnormalities. But that doesn't mean either of us have anything wrong with our chromosomes. It just means something went wrong with the embryo."

"Okay," I said. "Man, I didn't expect this."

"Me neither."

"Could there have been any external causes?"

"No, nothing that would apply to me. I wasn't injured or anything."

"What about stress? Could that cause a miscarriage?"

"Some people think so, but it's never been proven."

I realized my face was clenched, my brow furrowed, my forehead knotted with pressure. I closed my eyes and blew out my breath. "Are you going home now?" I asked.

"Yes, in a few minutes. Look, my mother had miscarriages. It's very common, like twenty percent of pregnancies. I can get pregnant again, and there's no increased risk. I just need some time."

"It'll be okay, Candi," I said, the words sounding vapid and trite the moment they left my mouth.

"How is your case going?"

"I just found out the real name of the man I punched. Cody and I are getting his records. Once I get that to my lawyer, he'll be able to defend me. He'll shut this thing down."

"When do you think you'll be home?" she asked, suddenly weeping, as if the last reserves of her emotional strength had been drained.

"Two or three days, tops. It will take no longer than that. We'll put this behind us and you'll be pregnant again soon. I'll see to it." I was trying to cheer her up, but she was silent for a long moment. Then she said, "Please come back soon. I need you."

•   •   •

I don't remember walking back to the bar. I found myself ordering another drink and sitting across from Cody while he typed like a fiend on my keyboard. The computer looked tiny before his massive shoulders, and his fingers struck the keys with so much force I could feel the impact through the table.

"How's the old lady?" he said after a minute.

"Not so good. She had a miscarriage."

Cody raised his eyes from the screen, his big mug staring at me. "Sorry to hear that," he said. When I didn't reply, he said, "Does she know what caused it?"

"Not really."

"You think it has anything to do with the strain of your situation?"

"Who knows?" I took a long pull from my drink. "You find any matches for Luis Escobar?" I asked.

"No, I was looking into something else."

"Like what?"

"Denver," he replied, his expression flat. "It looks like your search for Escobar downloaded. Here." He pushed my notebook across the table.

I spent the next hour sorting through the search engine results. There were twenty Luis Escobars in Florida. Five were too old, and four too young. I looked carefully at the remaining eleven and eventually was able to locate photos of each. None were a match for the man I was looking for.

I closed my computer and pushed it aside. The bar was now nearly full, and a trio of musicians were setting up equipment on the stage. My alcohol buzz, which died after the call to Candi, had morphed into a pounding headache.

"Let's get out of here and get some food," I said, popping a couple aspirin and guzzling a glass of water. "The booze ain't working for me."

"Oh, my, that's not good," Cody said, as if all my other troubles were trivial in comparison.

We strode out to the gaily lit boulevard and headed down the street to the restaurant with the sculpted rooster out front. The hostess sat us at an outdoor table facing the sidewalk. I could hear Latin music from a cantina next door, the cowbells and timbales churning along in a pulsing rhythm. I ordered *Fajitas Estilo Habaneras,* a plate of chicken, shrimp, and fried plantains. Cody ordered a Cuban sandwich.

"You don't want to try anything different?" I asked.

"When I find something good, I stick with it," he proclaimed.

My order arrived, and I dosed it with hot sauce. As I ate, my head began to clear, as if the spices were relieving my mental congestion. The shock of Candi's miscarriage was subsiding, replaced with a confused mash of guilt, regret, and concern. I also felt a growing resentment, for I should have been at home taking care of her. Instead, I was three thousand miles away, trying to dig up the dirt on a man I'd been wrongly accused of killing. In addition, I'd already burned twenty grand on bail, and would probably owe my attorney many thousands more. Plus, I was putting not only myself, but also my best friend at risk by my actions in Miami. Two hitmen with my and Cody's name on them lay dead in a musty, decaying structure out in the everglades, their corpses not even old enough to stink.

"Let's go find a new hotel," I said. "I want to see what we can get from those thug's phones."

We left the restaurant and ten minutes later checked into the Regency Hotel on Le Jeune Road. It was right off the freeway bordering the airport, in an area clustered with hotels catering to business travelers. Affordable and anonymous.

Working from my room, Cody and I started searching through the phones we'd taken from the dead men's vehicles. Both were password protected, but both used passwords set up for convenience rather than security. It only took a few minutes to find that Paco's password was 9999 and the gate guard's was 1234. Once the passwords were cracked, we had full access to phone, text, and email records.

I worked Paco's phone while Cody tapped away on the gate guard's. The first thing I searched for was contact information for Luis Escobar. I looked through Paco's contact list and came up empty, then checked his emails and text messages without success.

"Ditto," Cody said, sitting on the edge of the bed. "No Luis Escobar in contacts, and nothing when I searched the name in emails. But I did find Claudia Merchan."

"Maybe we should call her, for the hell of it," I said, picking up the landline. I dialed her number, and it rang once and disconnected.

"It's probably on the bottom of the sea with her," I said. I handed Cody a small pad of hotel stationary. "Let's go through all their dialed numbers. There's got to be something."

For the next hour we logged each call made in the past ninety days, listing the number and the receiving party. Most of the numbers were in the phone's contact lists, and most were Miami numbers. Some were to local restaurants, and others to individuals who may or may not have been criminal associates. I rubbed my forehead. If I had no better option, I could track down these individuals and question them about Luis Escobar. But I was hoping to find a more direct link. And something in Paco's phone piqued my interest; there were six calls to an area code I didn't recognize.

"You ever hear of area code 829?" I asked Cody.

"No, why?"

"Paco called an 829 number three times back in February, twice more in March, and again in early April. It's not in his contacts."

"So?"

I turned to my PC and pulled up an area code directory, and a minute later I said, "There's an 830 in Texas and an 828 in North Carolina. There's no 829 in the U.S."

"Try an international area code directory."

"You see any 829 numbers in the gate guard's phone?" I said, typing away.

"Nope."

I quickly found a site that provided international area codes, but it required that I know the country before providing the code. "Screw it," I mumbled, picking up the landline and dialing the number. It was nine P.M.

It rang eight times before a prerecorded message in Spanish said: *Thank you for calling Trinidad Transport, your Dominican water taxi company serving the Caribbean Sea. We are open nine to six P.M. daily. Please leave a message and we'll return your call during business hours.*

The phone beeped, and I hung up. "Hey," I said.

"What?"

"Did you bring your passport?"

"Yeah, why?"

"Remember the residence you found for Manuel Alvarez?"

"It was a company address," Cody said as I stood. "In the Dominican Republic."

"That's right. Trinidad Transport. You found their website."

"I remember," Cody said. I looked at him, then banged on my keyboard.

"Here it is," I said. "On the beach in Santo Domingo." I scrolled down to where two names were listed: *Hugo Trinidad, President, Manuel Alvarez, pilot.*

"Our boy Paco called Trinidad Transport six times since February. I'm thinking Hugo's involved."

"Maybe Paco just called to talk to Manuel."

"No," I said walking to the window and looking out over the parking lot. "I think Manuel was a bit player, a driver, a mule. He wasn't a decision maker."

"What do you think was in that minibus?"

"Coke, meth, pills, take your choice."

"Must be worth enough to kill for."

"The people we're dealing with would slit your throat for five hundred bucks. I'll get us on the next plane to Santo Domingo. Pack your bag."

•   •   •

189

After Cody left for his room, I began searching for flights. I found a departure at noon the next day, but before booking it, I backed away from my computer. Then I checked my watch and called Nate Esparza. It was a little before ten P.M.

"Hello?"

"Nate, Dan Reno. Got a minute?"

"Yeah, why not."

"Thanks. I was told the man I'm trying to identify is named Luis Escobar. But I ran a people search in Miami and came up empty. You ever hear of anyone by that name?"

The line went silent, then he said, "No, not specifically."

"I was also told he was the son of Escobar's whore. Does that mean anything to you?"

"Really?" he replied. "Who told you that?"

I paused, then said, "Someone who works for Ivan Sanhueza."

"Oh shit, sounds like you've been busy."

"You know Sanhueza?"

"Yeah, he's one of our local movers and shakers. He keeps a low profile for the most part, but I'm sure he's moving a lot of goods. He's paid off the right cops."

"I'm sure he has. But what about this son of a whore thing?"

He cleared his throat, and I heard a door close and the flick of his lighter. He exhaled, then said, "There was this rumor going around years ago, almost like an urban legend. When Pablo Escobar was at his peak, he had a number of whores at his call, despite being happily married. There was one in particular, a Dominican woman named Valentina who he was fond of. It was said she had a son by him, but no one ever knew what became of her."

"That's it?"

"No. It was said that this son grew up and wanted to follow in his father's footsteps, even though I doubt he'd ever met Pablo Escobar. The rumor was that he wanted to build his own narco empire, but there's no evidence that ever happened. But there have been ongoing suggestions that this man is involved in the drug trade, both as a trafficker and a hitman."

"In Miami?"

"Not so much. The stories are usually from the islands. The Dominican, Puerto Rico, the Bahamas."

"And this man is named Luis Escobar?"

"If he really exists, yeah. But I can tell you, there's no record of him in the U.S."

"Hmm. When Mrs. Vasquez looked at his picture, she said she might recognize him. Maybe he reminded her of Pablo Escobar?"

"I'll ask her," Nate said.

"All right. Listen, I've got another name for you. A Dominican named Hugo Trinidad. Ring any bells?"

"Trinidad? Maybe. Hang on and I'll check my database."

I waited for a couple of minutes until Nate said, "Yeah, Hugo Trinidad from Santo Domingo. A couple years ago he was popped in the Miami airport with a couple kilos of coke strapped to his body. He made bail and vanished. There's still a warrant for him."

"Any link to him and Luis Escobar?"

"Nothing I can see. But there's another thing about Trinidad. A Miami man was found dead in Santo Domingo last year. Tied to a chair and lit on fire. Burned to death. Hugo Trinidad was considered a person of interest."

"But he wasn't arrested?"

"It's tricky since the crime didn't occur here. The Dominican is supposed to be cooperative with U.S. law enforcement, but their justice system is extremely corrupt."

When I didn't reply, Nate said, "I hope this is helpful."

"Yeah, it is."

"Keep me updated. That's our deal."

"Right," I said, my foot tapping the carpet rapidly.

14

Cody and I didn't converse much the next morning as we made our way to the airport. We were both unhappy knowing we'd have to leave our firearms behind. If we tried to check them onto the flight, even if they made it onto the plane they'd likely be confiscated by the Dominican authorities, and we'd have a lot of explaining to do.

"We could probably bribe them," I said, as we left the hotel.

"Not worth the risk," Cody replied, his face grim.

Although our hotel was so close to the airport we could feel the skies rumble as the planes took off, it still took us almost half an hour to navigate through the morning traffic and drop off our rental car. Then we walked for another fifteen minutes to the security checkpoint. Cody and I both carried day packs with a single change of clothes. I wasn't planning on spending more than a night in Santo Domingo. If things went well, maybe we could even get a late flight back to Miami.

When I said as much to Cody, he said, "I'll need to stop in Denver on the way back to Cal."

"I'll go with you."

"No need, I'll take care of it. Besides, you should get home to your woman."

An hour later, our noon flight to Santo Domingo thundered down the runway and lifted off into cloudy skies. By the time we reached 10,000 feet, we were already over the ocean and heading southeast. The clouds soon disappeared, and from our cruising altitude I had a clear view down to the Caribbean Sea, the blue waters stretching to the curve of the horizon.

I turned to Cody, but he was dozing. For a moment I felt a pang of affection for my old buddy. The dichotomy of his life was something I understood better than anyone, but elements of him would forever be beyond me. He lived on the outskirts of convention, bending and breaking the law with regularity, but always for the right reasons, and always within his innate ability to know what he could get away with. Money-wise, he seemed to spend carelessly, but had invested successfully in financial fields I knew nothing about and was certainly far wealthier than I would ever be. As for his interpersonal relationships, he couldn't bring himself to commit to a woman, but whenever I was in trouble, Cody showed up without asking and never hesitated to put himself at great risk. He basked in his wanton lifestyle, but at times I could sense the weight of regret on his shoulders, as if he wondered if he would ever change. But most of the time, Cody was happy as a pig in shit, and this was doubly true when he faced imminent conflict. Putting the cleats to the bad guys was something that brought him immense satisfaction. That much I knew for sure.

A half an hour later Cody stretched and said, "Are we there yet?"

"Hey, man," I said. "When we get back, we'll go hit South Beach. Live it up, wherever you want."

Cody smiled serenely and gave me a fist bump. "It's all good, brother."

· · ·

I spent the remainder of the flight reading a web page on the Dominican Republic. My knowledge of the Caribbean islands was nil. Except for Mexico, I'd never been to a country where Spanish was the primary language. Fortunately my Spanish was decent, although my accent could never pass for a native speaker's.

Santo Domingo is the capital of the Dominican Republic, and it's the largest city in the Caribbean. With about a million residents, it's nearly the size of San Jose, my former stomping grounds. The population in Santo Domingo is primarily mestizo, a term referring to people of combined European and indigenous American descent. Aided by foreign investment, the city has become significantly modernized since the 1990s, and has developed a growing middle-class. But slum conditions dot the city like a bad case of acne, and with poverty comes desperation and crime.

As we began our descent, I gazed down at the ocean and a few minutes later saw a cluster of high-rise buildings near the coast. We flew over the city as the plane dropped, then a runway appeared beneath us. We hit the pavement with a screeching jolt.

Ten minutes later we were waiting in a customs line of at least a hundred people. It was nearly noon, and the line was moving slowly. There seemed to be a bottleneck near a single booth where a uniformed man was checking passports. After fifteen minutes and little movement, it became clear that unless another agent or two came on duty, we'd be waiting for at least an hour.

"You've been to a lot of other countries, right?" I said to Cody.

"A few. I went to Spain and Italy a couple years ago when Heidi Ho and I were getting along."

"Are the customs lines always like this?"

"No. They go pretty quick for the most part."

I sighed and checked my phone to make sure the international wireless program I'd purchased was working. We crawled forward and thirty minutes later, when only a few people were ahead of us, a second customs agent appeared.

"He must have been on his lunch break," I said.

"Well, I'd hate for him to go hungry while we all sit here twiddling our thumbs."

When we reached the agent, he looked at us with doleful eyes, as if the situation called for sorrow and despair.

"What is the reason for your visit here?" he said.

"We want do some sightseeing in Santo Domingo before heading to Punta Cana," I replied.

He glanced at me and his lower lip moved to one side. "You two are vacationing together?"

"That's right," Cody said, lisping, his voice soft. He put his hand daintily on my shoulder.

The agent stared at us for a long moment, then the suspicion on his face was replaced with a look of pronounced disgust. He stamped our passports and pointed with his thumb. "Go," he said, as if he couldn't wait to be rid of us. We hurried away, and once we were out of earshot Cody said, "I guess he didn't think we made a cute couple."

"Nice work with the gay impersonation. You even had me convinced."

"Latinos tend to be homophobic."

"And you're not?"

"Hey, I was ready to give you a big kiss if I had to."

"Glad it didn't come to that," I said.

"The sacrifices I make."

"Don't worry, I won't tell anyone."

"I'm starving," Cody said, looking ahead at a cluster of eateries. "Is the food safe here?"

"I hope so. But I wouldn't drink the water."

"Not even the ice cubes? I was kind of in the mood for a highball."

"I'll buy you one when we get back to Miami. Look, there's a Burger King. Probably a safe bet."

We ordered and ate our fast food in the open-air arrivals hall. "This airport is one hell of a lot smaller than San Jose's," Cody said, his hamburger tiny in his oversized paw. "I thought you said Santo Domingo has a million people."

"I guess they're not the traveling type. At least not on planes."

"Probably not much international business here."

"Not the legal kind," I said, looking across the expanse to where I could see cars picking up passengers. There were a couple of yellow Ford sedans with taxi emblems waiting at the curbside.

"Let's go catch a cab to Trinidad Transport," I said, balling my paper bag and tossing it in a trash can.

"Pick an address a block or two away. Let's scope out the area first."

"Sounds like a plan." We walked to the curb and got into a car with a *Taxi Turistico* identification affixed to the window.

"Take us to *Playa de Guibia,*" I said to the driver.

"Any address?"

"No, we just want to walk around the beach."

The cab pulled away, and a minute later we were heading south along a four-lane highway named after an ex-Dominican president. It was a muggy, sun bleached afternoon, the clouds sparse. The highway was bordered by a fence built in a manner unlike anything I'd seen in the U.S. It consisted of wire strung along and nailed to rows of trees. The trees varied in diameter and height, but all served equally as fence posts. Beyond the fencing were tangles of thick tropical growth, a virtual no-man's land, impassable without sickle or machete.

A few miles from the airport, I began noticing activity on the road's shoulder. First a single motorbike, and then dozens more emerged, most putting along at twenty to thirty miles per hour, none powerful enough to achieve freeway speed. Many looked like little more than minibikes, and some appeared to be contraptions pieced together from available parts; a frame from a 1960s Husqvarna, a Suzuki or Yamaha 2-stroke motor from the seventies, tires and spoked rims from who knows where, a homemade seat, and a rear rack large enough to carry a passenger or a cardboard box containing whatever the rider deemed worth moving. None of the cyclists wore helmets, a few were shirtless, and on one bike a woman sitting behind the throttle man held an infant in her arms.

After five miles or so, we entered a densely developed area. We drove through apartment neighborhoods, past schools, gas stations, vacant lots filled with chunks of broken concrete, and shanty roadside storefronts offering pre-paid cellular cards, diapers, used furniture, car stereos, ice cold *cerveza,* and meat stew with plantain mash. We hit a stop light next to a large cemetery, the headstones veined with moss. After that came sections of nameless warehouses with incredible jumbles of electrical wires overhead, the snarls lurching from one metal hanging pole to the next.

The taxi continued south, and we skirted the downtown area, where modern office buildings rose above statues of men on horseback in old plazas lined with sidewalk cafes. The cab jerked from stop signs to signal lights, narrowly missing pedestrians that crossed the streets as if oblivious to the traffic. We continued until we reached where the road ended in a T. The cabbie pulled to the curb. *"Playa de Guibia,"* he said, pointing at a row of palm trees along a boulevard running parallel to the shoreline.

I paid the driver in American dollars and we stepped out onto Av. George Washington. From where we stood I could see waves breaking gently on a stretch of beach. We waited for traffic, then crossed the street onto the promenade.

"Why the hell would the Dominican Republic name a street after a U.S. president?" Cody said.

"Maybe they ran out of their own presidents."

"Whatever. Trinidad Transport is this way?" Cody pointed to our right.

"Yeah, should be a few blocks." I checked my watch. It was four P.M. "They should be open until six."

We walked down a long section paved in square brick. The beach narrowed until a concrete retaining wall dropped into a bed of jagged rocks near a single-story blue and white building. When we reached the structure we slowed. A small sign next to a glass door read *Policia Municipal.* Sitting on a metal chair out front was a uniformed officer smoking a cigarette.

"Keep walking," I said.

A minute later the beach widened, and we stopped at a beachside restaurant next to a perfectly groomed volleyball court on the sand.

"What the hell is *pizzarelli*?" Cody said, eyeing the restaurant's sign suspiciously.

"Probably pizza would be my deduction."

"Thanks for figuring that out."

We continued along the promenade, past rows of streetlights, restaurants with colorful paint schemes, and groups of kids running about under the watchful eyes of adults chatting and eating ice cream cones. Then we came to a metal fence and a short bridge over a culvert, marking the end of the boardwalk. We crossed the bridge and followed the path back toward Av. George Washington until we stopped where the beach was broken by rocky outcroppings interspersed with a pair of jetties. Partially hidden among clusters of trees and sitting on a broad dirt plot between the road and the beach were five or six low buildings with rusting tin roofs.

"It should be one of those," I said, looking at my navigator.

"Let's go scope it out."

Rather than climb down a craggy bank of rock, we continued up to the street. On our right automobile traffic flowed, and the sun reflected in bursts off the windows of the tall buildings a few hundred yards from the thoroughfare. To the left of the sidewalk, groves of trees grew on a plot leading to the beach. We reached an unpaved trail leading into the trees, wide enough for a car, but not by much. From where we stood we couldn't see where it led.

Cody followed me down the trail, which was scored with tire tread marks. The path forked at a small clearing that served as a parking lot. Two motorcycles leaned on kickstands in the shade. They appeared new, but I didn't recognize the make, and the vertical rear shocks and chrome fenders seemed from a different era. Next to the bikes were a white Ford pickup truck and a police squad car.

"Wonder what the *Federales* are doing here," Cody said. We stopped and eyed the vehicle warily. Beyond the clearing the path split in two directions. "Let's try this way," I said, and began down a narrow path to our left. The dirt was hard, but I could smell the sea and hear the waves breaking on the shore. After a minute, we came to a large fenced yard, the wood slats broken and missing, the metal links corroded. In the yard were outboard motors, propellers, an upside down twenty-foot boat with a partially painted hull, and other marine equipment I couldn't identify. At the end of the lot was a metal door leading into a concrete block building.

We continued to the front of the building, where a wooden section had been added. A red painted sign above the covered porch identified it as Trinidad Transport. I glanced through the sliding glass door and saw a uniformed policeman talking to a man behind a counter. We continued down the pathway, into a stand of trees fifty feet from the beach. From there we could watch the building without being obvious.

"What's the plan?" Cody said, lighting a cigarette.

"I wish it was dark."

"Why?"

"Because I'd feel more comfortable questioning Hugo Trinidad after hours."

"You think that's him in there talking to that cop?"

"Yup."

"You think they have an unholy alliance?"

"I think Trinidad knows the story behind Manuel Alvarez and Luis Escobar. I think Trinidad is up to his eyeballs in this case."

Cody knelt and peered at the building from behind a tree. "That cop is probably just there to collect a payoff. Hopefully he'll split soon."

"I want to do some quick recon. Hang here for a few minutes."

I walked through the trees to the right until I came to a foot trail leading to the beach. I followed the trail in the opposite direction and soon reached a shack adjacent to Trinidad Transport. The sign out front advertised souvenirs and trinkets, but the interior was dark. I walked behind the building and came to the rear corner of Trinidad's yard. There was a plastic canopy built over a pair of sawhorses and what looked like an ancient drill press. A row of gas cans sat near a disassembled motor lying in an oily mess on a square of cardboard. I walked along the fence, looking for a gate. I crept all the way back to the front of the building, spotting no alternative exit, and seeing no people about. Satisfied that the sole exit was from the front of the building, I retraced my footsteps, but instead of heading back to where Cody waited, I followed the trail out onto the sand.

The late afternoon sun was still bright over the sea, but was low enough to make me shade my eyes. The surf broke on rocky sections and advanced and retreated lazily over the sand. A solitary fishing boat moored at the end of a jetty swayed with the roll of the waters. I looked left to the activity on *Playa de Guibia,* where people still sat at picnic tables and threw Frisbees, and then right to where the beach was deserted. A few palm trees rose from the sand, and the only structure I could see from my vantage was a TGI Fridays restaurant a few hundred yards off, its black windows looking over the ocean.

I returned into the trees. Cody had found a stump of sorts and was sitting, his eyes trained on Trinidad Transport's front porch.

"That's the only way out," I said. "No rear exits."

Before Cody could reply the sliding door opened, and the cop walked out and headed toward where we'd seen his car. We waited five minutes, then I walked out to the parking area and saw the last of his tail lights as he turned onto Av. George Washington. When I returned to Cody, it was nearing 5:30.

"They're supposed to close at six," I said.

"I doubt he'll get more customers today."

I stared at the porch for a long moment, then said, "Let's do it."

We walked out of the trees and up the single step onto the porch. I smiled and turned to Cody. "Look happy," I said. Then I pushed open the slider, and we entered the interior. But there was no one at the counter.

"Hola?" I said.

"Un momento," a voice replied from a back room.

I leaned on the front counter, watching an open doorway on the left. A minute later, a slim man with a pocked face and straight black hair came before me. He wore a white shirt open at the chest and a gold medallion rested below his throat. When our eyes met, his were half-lidded, as if he was disinterested, but his stare was very still, and I knew he was calculating what my presence meant.

"Hugo Trinidad?" I said.

"And you are?"

I started to reply, but before I could, Cody darted around the counter. "Your worst nightmare," he said, and Trinidad's hand moved to his pocket, but Cody was too quick, and a second later had him in a bear-hold. "Get back here and search him," Cody said, but I'd already planted my hand on the countertop and was scissor-kicking over it. When I landed, I patted Trinidad's pockets while he struggled and swore in Spanish. I pulled out a black-handled switchblade, pushed the button, and a five inch shank flicked free. "I'll keep this as a souvenir," I said, pocketing the weapon. Then I jumped back over the counter and locked the sliding door. "Take him to the back," I said. Cody walked Trinidad before him, and I followed them behind the wall. We entered a room about fifteen feet square, with a couch against one wood-paneled wall and a round table and chairs in the center. Cody pushed Trinidad into one of the chairs, and I zip-tied his wrists behind him. He fought, but I discouraged him by digging my thumb into a pressure point on his neck. Then I tied each of his ankles to the chair legs.

"I'm sorry for being less than courteous, but we kind of got off to a bad start here," I said.

"What do you want?" Trinidad asked in English. If he was concerned about his situation, neither his expression nor his voice conveyed it.

"Just information," I said. The room was lit by a single lamp hanging from the ceiling, and Trinidad's face was shiny in the glare. "This can be very easy or very difficult. But I think you're a pretty smart guy."

"I don't think you know anything."

"Wrong," Cody said. "We know a few things." Then Cody stepped forward and fit his right hand around Trinidad's throat and lifted him and the chair off the ground. Even though Trinidad was not a heavy man, I still considered it an impressive show of arm strength, because Cody held him for a full five seconds before dropping him to the cheap carpet. Trinidad coughed as if trying to remove a block from his wind tunnel, and I caught him before his chair toppled over. His eyes were now threaded with red veins that looked like electrical current.

"So let's get started," I said.

"If you touch me again, you'll die," he said, glowering at Cody.

"I know Manuel Alvarez worked for you," I said. "I know you were involved with his trip to Reno. And I also know you know who this is." I pulled a picture of Luis Escobar from my back pocket and held it in front of Trinidad. He didn't reply.

"To start, I want you to tell me everything you know about Luis Escobar."

Trinidad spat on the photo. "*Chinga tu madre.*"

I lowered myself to eye level with Trinidad and smiled. "I speak Spanish, so I understand you. And that is a very rude thing to say."

Trinidad inhaled deeply, then spat full in my face. I recoiled, then before I could stop myself, I backhanded him hard. The blow snapped his head back and bloodied his lip. "If you want to keep your face intact, I recommend you seriously consider the next thing that comes out of your mouth," I said, looking around for something to wipe the saliva off my face. When I didn't see anything, I ripped the shirt off Trinidad's torso and used it as a towel. Then I threw it at him and said, "I have all night, my friend, but I'd rather get out of this shithole sooner. So let's try this again. Tell me about Luis Escobar."

"You think I'm scared of you, *coño?*"

"If you're not, you're about to learn a hard lesson." I drew my fist back.

"Dan, hold up!" Cody said, grabbing my wrist and pulling me back. "Look, Hugo, my partner here, he can't control his temper, so he'd probably put you out of your misery with a single punch." Cody released my wrist and stepped in front of me. "But I'm different. I'll hurt you in ways you never imagined, and when I'm done you'll be alive, but the rest of your life will seriously suck. I guarantee it."

"Do what you want to do, you think you're so bad. I got nothing to say to you *putas.*"

Cody lifted his knee and slammed his heel down on Trinidad's soft canvas shoe. I heard the crunch of bones, and Trinidad hissed and his face bunched in agony. But I also felt my face contort as gall rose in my throat. And at that instant Trinidad looked at me. "You don't have what it takes for this, do you?" he said.

I turned away and stared at the wall. Torturing a bound man for information was not beyond my experience, but the only time I'd done it was when two men broke into my home with the intention of kidnaping Candi. When I discovered what they planned for her, I inflicted some serious pain, and to this day I don't regret their suffering. But the situation with Trinidad was different. He had done nothing to directly antagonize me. My reason for accosting him was solely based on my suspicion that he was linked to Luis Escobar and played a role in Manuel Alvarez's ill-fated trip west.

For a moment a wave of weakness and regret struck me. Maybe Trinidad was right; maybe I didn't have what it takes to make him talk.

I squeezed my eyes shut, and an image of Candi sitting alone on our couch, her face downcast and tear-stained, flashed before me. Then it was replaced by a vision of my father, a man I'll forever remember as fearless and always in control. And then I pictured myself in prison, losing everything I had, my life wasting away as the years passed. My mouth went dry, and I blinked hard, before the voices in my head suddenly stopped, and were replaced with a startling clarity that felt almost drug induced. The muggy air in the room seemed to lighten and become cool.

When I turned back to Hugo Trinidad, I had no doubt he was a man who had tortured and killed without mercy. His bare chest was covered in tattoos, some that looked like jailhouse scrawl. Despite the injury to his toes, he looked at me with a defiant, cocksure scowl.

"I'll make you a one-time offer," he said. "Leave here now, and I'll let you leave this country alive. I'm expecting visitors soon, and they'll be armed."

"Yeah, right," Cody said, but I was staring at the metal door leading out to the yard. "I'll be right back," I said. I walked to the door and stepped outside. It was still full daylight, but the sun was dropping quickly. To my right I spotted the engine parts and red fuel cans I'd seen earlier. I jogged to the cans and picked up the first one. It was large enough to hold a gallon, but it was empty. I lifted the second one and the third, and both were also empty. But the fourth was heavy, and I could feel the gasoline slosh when I tilted it.

I went back inside, and Cody was hovering over Trinidad, speaking rapidly. "You might want to leave for this," I said.

"Huh?" Cody looked up, his eyes round. "Why?"

"I heard you were involved in burning a man to death," I said, unscrewing the lid of the petrol can. Before Trinidad could reply I poured gas over his head, the fluid running down his face and torso and onto the crotch of his pants. Then I shook the can and splashed him full in the face.

"Let me take an educated guess here, Hugo," I said. "When that man burned, you watched and listened to his screams, and it really turned you on. You probably still get a hard-on thinking about it. Am I on the right track?"

"You get away from me," he said.

I poured the fuel onto the white shirt laying in his lap, then I tied it around his neck. Next I drained the remainder onto his pants. The scent of gasoline was thick in the air.

"I'm done negotiating, my friend," I said. "Cody, toss me your lighter, would you?"

"You never, you never would," Trinidad sputtered. He blinked rapidly, trying to relieve the burn in his eyes.

"If you don't talk, I'm fucked, Hugo. I'll admit it. I seriously got nothing to lose here." I caught Cody's lighter and flicked it. The flame burst to life for a second before I let it die.

"Stop that!" Trinidad yelled.

I leaned in close to him. "You answer my questions, or I'll light you up, asshole. And I mean now." I tapped him on the nose with the butt of the lighter.

His eyes darted and the cords in his neck stood out as he flexed his arms against the restraints.

"I'm running out of patience," I said, flicking the lighter again.

"Okay, okay! What do you want to know?" His jaw had dropped, and he was breathing in quick, short rasps. One of his eyes was squeezed shut, but the other was wide and the pupil looked like a black marble.

"Everything you know about Luis Escobar. If I think you're lying or holding back, you'll burn, motherfucker."

When Trinidad began speaking, the words came in staccato bursts, each word clearly enunciated. "He wanted to follow his father's footsteps, but the timing was all wrong, and he didn't have a head for business. So he became an enforcer, a killer for hire, for whoever paid the most. Killing is what he does best."

"How many has he killed?"

"I don't know. Dozens. He was convicted once, but only did six months."

"Who did he work for?"

"A variety of cartel bosses. Like I said, whoever paid him."

"Who in Miami?"

Trinidad hesitated, and I held the lighter beneath his nose. "Don't test me, goddammit."

"Most recently, Ivan Sanhueza."

I looked over to where Cody was standing next to the couch, arms crossed. "Is he really the son of Pablo Escobar?"

"Yes, I believe so. He claimed to be, and I knew his mother, the whore Valentina."

"Where is she?"

"I don't know. I don't know if she's still alive."

"Here's the moment of truth, Hugo. You need to prove you're not lying to me. That's the only way to save yourself."

"Sanhueza hired Escobar to find a missing load of cocaine heading for California. It's the truth."

Cody came forward at that moment and said, "Listen, creep, you've been lying all your life, so your word don't mean shit. But there is one way you can get out of this. Call your buddies at the local police and tell them to bring over a copy of Luis Escobar's criminal record file. I mean the full fucking report, with pictures and everything. I'm sure they have a thick file on him."

Trinidad was silent for a moment, then he said, "I can get it. But it will be expensive."

"How much cash you got in this dump?"

"Only what's in my pocket. It's not enough."

I wedged my hand in Trinidad's back pocket, removed his billfold, and counted the purple notes. "Three thousand pesos," I said.

"What's that worth?" Cody asked.

"About sixty bucks."

"You better hope the cops you pay off will accept it," Cody said, glowering at Trinidad.

"They won't. It will cost at least five hundred American dollars."

"Bullshit," Cody said.

I checked my wallet and found four hundred in cash. "Where's your cell phone?" I said to Trinidad.

"Should be under the front counter."

I walked around to the front and spotted the cell phone. When I grabbed it I also noticed a set of keys, which I put in my pocket. I glanced out the front glass and the low sun had broken through the trees and cast a shifting patina of shadows on the dirt. Other than that there was no activity or motion outside.

I went back to where Trinidad sat in a puddle of gasoline. "Here's how we do this," I said. "You give me the number, and I'll put it on speaker.

Then you tell your man to bring the file to the TGI Fridays over there. You tell him what I look like and tell him I have three thousand pesos plus four hundred American dollars. And tell him to make it quick."

"Hey," Cody said. "Let me do it. You stay here and babysit this tough guy. It's your party."

"All right," I said, then added, "Just don't think about going inside to the bar," but Cody's face was all business. "Make the call," he said.

"Don't forget," I said to Trinidad in Spanish, "I'll understand everything you're saying. So no tricks."

"Si, Comprendo."

Trinidad told me where on his cell to find the contact for Octavio Delgado. "Who is he?" I said, scanning his contacts.

"He's a patrolman."

"You know anyone else on the police force?"

"Delgado's who I know best."

I found Delgado's number and took a deep breath. Then I pushed the call button and held the phone near Trinidad's mouth.

"Que pasa, Hugo?" the voice answered.

"I've got some easy money for you. Four hundred sixty American dollars," Trinidad said in Spanish.

"For what?"

"I need the police file on Luis Escobar. I need it right now."

"What for?"

"I'll explain later. How soon can you get it to me?"

"Twenty minutes or so, if I want."

"Do you want the money or not?"

"Sure, but more money would be better."

"All I have is four-sixty. If that's not enough, I know other people who will gladly take it."

The line went silent, then Octavio Delgado said, "All right, I'll do it."

"Good. Bring it to the TGI Fridays near my business. A man with the money will meet you there. Big man, *Americano*, red-blond hair. Big like an American football player."

"*Americano?* Who is he?"

"It doesn't matter, Octavio. He'll give you the money and we'll never see him again."

"Is everything okay, Hugo?"

"Everything is fine."

"Then I'll be there in twenty, thirty minutes."

"Make it twenty."

"Tell the *Americano* to be patient. *Adios.*" I looked at the screen and saw the call disconnect.

I turned to Cody. "What do you think?" I said.

"I don't know, Hugo," Cody said. "Is your man legit?"

"He wants the money. He'll be there."

"He better, for your sake," I said. I flipped the lighter into the air and watched it fall back to my palm.

"I'm gonna head over to Fridays, check it out," Cody said. "Give me the cash."

I handed Cody the bills, and he said, "If I'm not back in exactly thirty minutes, come find me."

"All right," I said. "Call me if anything looks wrong."

Cody shoved the money into his pocket. "I'm sure you two can have a nice chat while I'm gone," he said.

· · ·

I walked out to the front counter with Cody and whispered, "We need to get out of here, I mean on a plane tonight." I tapped my watch and Cody nodded and said, "See you in a few." I watched him leave out the front slider, then I re-locked it and returned to Trinidad.

"Next subject, Hugo. You're gonna talk about Manuel Alvarez and what he was involved in. Keep in mind, I already know certain things, so if you lie, I'll know it. You tell me everything I need to know, I walk out of here and it's like tonight never happened. But you fuck me around, you'll go up in a blaze of glory. It's your choice."

For a moment Trinidad's eyes glimmered in defiance. "Maybe time for you to cut your losses," he said. "The police will be here soon. Then you'll be fucked."

"Wrong answer," I said. I knelt at Trinidad's feet and lit his canvas shoe afire. The flames quickly rose from his shoe to his pants leg.

"Put it out!" Trinidad screamed. "I'll talk!"

I smothered the flames with a large rag I'd placed behind Trinidad's chair. I saw a heat blister on his shin, and I tore his burnt pant leg aside so I could get a better look at it. "If you make it through this, you should see a doctor for that. It could get infected."

Trinidad swore under his breath, and then he began talking. The words fell from his lips at a steady pace, and soon he was telling me about Manuel Alvarez as if he was glad to relieve himself of the burden. He spoke for five minutes without pausing. He started from the time the teenager had asked for a job, then described how he helped arrange for Manuel to be arrested and jailed. This was part of a plan to terrorize and motivate Manuel to become a willing and cooperative mule for a load of cocaine Ivan Sanhueza needed to move to the west coast.

"Why didn't you just offer to pay him?" I asked.

"This way was cheaper. And Manuel never knew he was transporting drugs. He was only told to deliver the vehicle to a contact in Reno, and his troubles in the Dominican Republic would be over."

"What about the other people in the minibus?"

"They all came from our jail. The women were whores and thieves. The other man was a rapist. We thought that two couples traveling together would be less suspicious than one or two men."

"And who stabbed the man?"

"I don't know. Maybe one of the whores. Maybe Manuel."

"But Manuel was neither violent nor a criminal, right?"

DAVE STANTON

"Yes, that's true. One of the women could have done it. Maybe he wanted something she didn't want to give."

"Have you heard from Manuel or either of the women?"

"No."

"So, Ivan Sanhueza hired Luis Escobar to find Manuel and the mini-bus? What about the two prostitutes?"

"They were meaningless. But Manuel had mistakenly seen Ivan Sanhueza and his men. That was a problem. Sanhueza wanted Escobar to recover the merchandise and tie up loose ends."

"Escobar would have killed Manuel?"

Trinidad nodded affirmatively. "Manuel was a loose end."

"What about Escobar's woman, Claudia Merchan?"

"She was one of Sanhueza's girls. Sanhueza told her to have sex with Escobar. Apparently Luis liked it, but the main reason she came on the trip was she was an American citizen with an American driver license. She was useful for car rental and hotel reservations. Escobar never liked booking anything under his name."

I looked up at the ceiling. The plaster was water-stained and insects crawled from a crack in a shadowy spot.

"Are we done?" Trinidad asked.

I glanced at my watch. Nearly twenty minutes had passed since Cody left. "One more question," I said. "How much blow was in the mini-bus?"

"I don't know exactly," Trinidad replied. "A hundred kilos. Maybe more."

I grabbed the rag I'd used previously and tore free a long strip.

"What now?" Trinidad asked.

"You're done talking," I said. I tied the strip tightly on his mouth, forcing his jaw open, then I flipped the light off and left the darkened building.

The skies were dim with the last of the day's light as I set off for the TGI Fridays restaurant that sat on a rise and overlooked the beach. When I walked out of the trees and onto the sand, I looked up and was surprised to see the restaurant was unlit. I saw no sign of Cody, but from my vantage I could only see a portion of the building.

I hurried off the sand and onto a trail that led uphill through a mishmash of rocks, foliage, and palm trees. It took three minutes to reach the edge of the restaurant's parking lot. And then I saw a squad car parked on the far side, away from the street and hidden in an area that couldn't be seen from the street or the beach. The car was the only one in the lot, but parked next to it was a motorcycle. The restaurant was either closed or out of business.

When I stepped from the trail up onto the pavement, I saw Cody's head, and as I walked forward, three more figures came into view. Cody and three uniformed cops were standing behind the white and blue patrol car. I paused for an instant, and one of the policemen turned his head toward me.

I swallowed a curse and instead smiled, waved, and continued forward. As I neared them, I tried to read Cody's expression. His lips were downturned, and he met my stare then shifted his eyes to the shortest of the men, a stocky, older cop who stood with his hand resting on the butt of his holstered pistol.

"*Que pasa, amigos?*" I said, trying to maintain my smile.

The two taller uniforms stepped to the car's rear bumper. One was a fellow with narrow shoulders and a spare tire around his midsection. The other was about my size and wore boots and gloves.

"What do you want?" the one with the spare tire said in broken English.

"I'm with him," I said, nodding at Cody. "Did you bring the file?"

"Yes, we have it. But your friend doesn't have enough money."

"Hugo said four hundred-sixty."

"It's four hundred-sixty *each*," spare tire replied, pointing to his partners.

"Oh," I said, widening my eyes. "There must be a misunderstanding. But if the file is complete, I can pay it."

"What do you mean, complete?" the older cop said. He was still standing with Cody on the opposite side of the car.

"You know, photos, fingerprints, all that good stuff."

"It's all there."

"Great, let me see it, then I'll go to my ATM and get the money. There should be an ATM nearby, right?"

The cops exchanged glances, then the older one nodded and said, "*Miguel, Dale el reporte.*"

Spare tire reached through the car's open window and pulled a gray folder from the interior. He opened it so I could see the pages. "No touch," he said.

On the first page was a color photo of Luis Escobar from the waist up. It was a mug shot, but the expression on Escobar's face was one of amusement. I motioned to see the next page, which showed a set of fingerprints, followed by a DNA report. The following pages were a jumble of hand and typewritten reports.

I looked over at Cody, then said, "Looks good." I brought my left hand up and raised my thumb in the universal positive signal while moving closer to the cop in the boots and gloves. Then I snapped a hard left into his chin, driving the jawbone back and jarring the brain. A well-thrown blow to the jaw will knock out all but those with the hardest head. That's why one of the first things they teach in boxing is to always tuck your chin behind your shoulder.

The cop collapsed as if his bones had been liquefied. Before he hit the ground, I hit spare tire with a right jab flush in the mouth. His eyes rolled and I snatched the report from his hand before he crumpled on top of the first cop.

This happened so quickly that Cody hadn't had time to react, but the older cop did by drawing his semi-automatic from its holster. But Cody grabbed the man's wrist before he could raise the weapon, then hit him with a massive uppercut to the gut. With his size and strength, Cody didn't need perfect technique. His punches were like blows from a sledgehammer, and in this case the force was enough to propel the cop onto the hood of the car, where Cody took the gun from his hand and cracked him across the skull with the barrel.

"Down there," I said, grabbing the larger cop's ankles. I dragged him over a curb and down into where thick scrub grew on the downward slope. I stopped at the base of a large palm and removed the officer's handcuffs from his belt. A moment later Cody joined me, dumping the stocky cop onto the ground. Then he ran up the hill for the third cop.

I handcuffed the policemen together by their wrists, and when Cody brought the third unconscious body, I took the cuffs from his belt and cuffed him to one of the other cops. Then I pulled them around the tree trunk and cuffed them together, linking them in a circle around the stout trunk.

"They'll shout," Cody said, breathing hard.

"Gag them with their socks," I said, yanking off one's shoe. We gagged all three, working rapidly, then I found their handcuff keys and threw them down the bluff. "Same for their pieces," Cody said, emptying the older cop's pistol and winging it deep into the foliage. I did the same with the other cops guns, then we ran back to the trail and hightailed through the twilight, running toward Trinidad's building.

"How do we get to the airport?" Cody asked, puffing behind me.

"We're going to the dirt parking lot. I've got Trinidad's keys. I think the white truck is his."

"Let's hope," Cody said.

It was still just light enough to see, and that was fortunate, because we were running full out. We reached the grove of trees and followed a fork back toward the dirt turnaround where I'd seen a few vehicles parked before we found Trinidad Transport.

When we reached the clearing, the police car and two motorcycles I'd seen before were gone. The only remaining vehicle was a Ford truck model F-150. It was a late model two-seat version, the white paint decent except for the scratched and rusted bed. I took Trinidad's keys from my pocket. "Keep your fingers crossed," I said, and pushed the unlock button on the key fob. I heard a click from the truck door.

"Bingo," Cody said. "I'll drive, you navigate."

We got into the cab, and Cody jammed the seat back as far as it would go while I typed the airport into my navigation app. "Thirty minutes, all city streets," I said. "Drive at the speed limit, we can't get pulled over."

"No shit, huh?" Cody started the engine and steered us down the dirt road. There was no traffic when we reached Av. George Washington. The lights from the row of nearby high-rise buildings were bright against the darkened skies. I was still holding the gray folder, which I wedged carefully into the daypack that lay between my feet. "Turn here and go straight for the next four miles," I said. "We're going through downtown."

"Check on flights," Cody said.

I found a travel site and began searching for flights departing Santo Domingo. It was 7:15, and I was hoping to find a nine P.M. flight to Miami. But it soon became evident that not only were there no evening flights to Miami, there didn't seem to be available flights to any U.S. city.

"We might not be able to get a plane tonight," I said.

"To anywhere?"

"I'll keep looking. Turn right in three blocks."

I continued working my smartphone, but without specifying a destination, I couldn't find a way to determine if there were any more outgoing flights before tomorrow morning.

"We may need a Plan B," I said. "Take this right and it should be a straight shot, five miles to the airport."

"You mean spend the night?"

"We might have no choice."

Cody didn't respond. His face looked carved from rock, the crow's feet etched deeply beside his eyes. I could tell he was considering our options and weighing the risks. We both knew the clock was ticking before the handcuffed policemen were found. In a best-case scenario, they might have to wait until the morning before rescue. But all it would take is a random evening passerby, and they would be freed and plenty pissed off. The logical move would then be to issue an all-points bulletin for two *Americanos*. Airport security would probably be alerted immediately.

"Maybe we could hire a boat," I said.

"To where?"

"Puerto Rico. It's the nearest island. It's a U.S. territory."

"You really think we could get a boat out of here tonight?"

"I don't know."

Cody glanced at me. "Check how long it would take to drive to Haiti."

"Haiti? It's the poorest country in the Western Hemisphere."

"Yeah? No wonder Trump called it a shithole. But they got an airport, right?"

"I guess," I said, working my phone. "About five hours. Highway 2 takes us all the way to the border."

"You think the *Federales* would notify the border?"

"I doubt it, not tonight anyway. We could be there by a little after midnight."

"The airport's coming up. Let's go inside and see if there's any way to get a plane tonight."

As we drove the final few minutes to the airport, I pulled the gray folder from my pack and skimmed Luis Escobar's arrest history. The violent charges were numerous, but before I could read the details, we arrived at the outdoor parking lot in front of the single terminal. We hustled inside, and there were a number of people milling about, which gave me reason for optimism. But the American Airlines, United, and Delta ticket counters were deserted. The only attendant I saw was a young woman at the Copa Airlines counter.

"Excuse me, miss," Cody said. "We'd like to catch a flight to Florida tonight. Do you have anything?"

"I'm sorry, the only outgoing flight we have left is to Panama City, and they just closed the doors."

"Is there a departures board we could look at?" I asked.

"Yes, over there near the Spirit Airlines check in."

"Thank you, dear," Cody said. We strode to the digital sign and studied the listings. It only took a minute. "There's nothing," I said. "Unless we want to go to Brazil."

"A million people here, and not a single flight to the U.S.A.?"

"The flights are all in the morning or early afternoon."

"Let's get sandwiches and coffee and get out of here."

• • •

I studied my navigator as we made our way back to Trinidad's truck. I imagined he was still trying to free himself, but the chair I'd secured him to was stout, as were the plastic ties. But even if he got free, what could he do? Call his cop buddies and report I stole his truck?

"Hey, man, you got a quarter?" I said when we reached the Ford pickup.

"Yeah, why?"

"Let's swap plates with one of these cars."

"Here," Cody said, tossing me a coin. I used it to unscrew the plate from the sedan in the next spot while Cody stood lookout. It took less than two minutes to complete the job, and then we hopped in the truck and pulled away.

The route to Haiti would take us west across the length of Hispaniola, the island Haiti shared with the Dominican Republic. As for the drive, I had no idea whether to expect winding mountain roads or straight flats, or potholes, flooded sections, speed traps, unpaved conditions, or wild herds crossing the highway. I also didn't know what type of border control we'd run into. All things considered, I wasn't thrilled with the prospect of a long, unfamiliar drive in the dead of night. But our risk of arrest increased with every minute we remained in the Dominican.

When we left the airport it was full dark. Cody drove while I took screen shots from my navigator in case we lost connectivity during the trip, which was probably a given. We drove south, skirting Santo Domingo and through a town called San Cristobal, and then we were on the open road, heading southwest on a straight, rolling stretch of highway.

"The good news is Hugo left us with a full tank," I said.

"Hey, maybe he's not such a bad guy after all."

"No, he's a world-class asshole."

"You didn't light him up, did you?"

"Just enough to make him talk."

"He's still alive?"

"What, you think I'd kill him just for the hell of it?"

"Well, accidents happen… as you know."

"No turns for twenty miles," I said, ignoring his comment.

"You should scan and email that police report to your attorney."

"Speak up if you see any copy shops."

"Use your cell. Take a picture of each page and send it. Do it before we lose signal."

"Good idea," I muttered. "I should have already done that."

"I'll cut you some slack, you've had a busy day."

It only took a few minutes to take twenty pictures and email them to my lawyer. After receiving confirmation that the email was successfully transmitted, I set my phone down, sighed deeply, and squeezed my eyes shut.

"What's in Luis Escobar's jacket?" Cody asked.

I opened the police report and read through the individual arrest reports. "The Dominican police arrested Luis Escobar twice for murder and convicted him once. It says he was paroled after six months."

"I bet he bought himself early release. That's how it works in the third world."

"He also has three arrests for assault with a deadly weapon, including two stabbings. Plus arrests for intimidating a witness, domestic violence, and possession."

"And that's just in the Dominican? This guy's a real all-star."

"You think Magnus Swett will drop the charges when he sees this?"

"Hell, yes. If he doesn't, your attorney ain't worth minimum wage."

"I hope you're right."

"Of course I'm right, one way or another. Relax, man," Cody said. "I mean, that was a nice piece of investigative work, getting a police report from crooked cops in a foreign country. And I even kept your four hundo. Tell you what, we roll into Port-au-Prince, let's get a hotel near the airport, hopefully one with an open bar. I'd say we deserve a few pops."

"I need to call Candi."

"Get us a flight back to Miami first, would you?"

I tapped on my phone and found a flight from the Port-au-Prince airport to Miami at nine A.M. the next morning. But before I could buy tickets, I lost connectivity.

"We'll have to wait," I said. Cody grunted and drove on. We started gaining elevation, and the road became curvy. The truck's headlights flashed over fields of tropical scrub and occasional tin shacks built on hillsides. Then we descended and passed through a couple of small towns that looked dismal in the darkness. I stopped trying to connect to the internet.

"Hugo Trinidad filled me in on Manuel Alvarez," I said. "He came to work for Trinidad as an orphaned teenager. When Trinidad needed a mule to boat a shipment of coke to Miami, he chose Manuel. But first he had him arrested, to make sure Manuel knew what would happen if he didn't fully cooperate. When the boat made it safely to Miami, Manuel was then put on the minibus to Reno, as part of a four-person team."

"Was Trinidad working for Sanhueza?"

"Yeah, he was Sanhueza's man in the Dominican."

"Why didn't they just hire mules?"

"Part of it was they didn't want to pay anyone. But they also felt the best motivator was the threat of a long sentence in Dominican jail. If you end up there without money, it's a slow death."

"What about the other three people in the minibus?"

"Two prostitutes and a rapist. They were promised their freedom as long as they got the shipment delivered."

"One of the hookers probably stabbed the rapist, huh?"

"That would be my guess."

"And the magical mystery bus journey ended there, in Fernley, Nevada."

"Right. But Sanhueza didn't know that. I bet he put trackers on the vehicle, but they failed."

We were now driving through farm land, the road straight and flat and surrounded by rice paddy fields, the standing water illuminated by the moon. Then the paddies were replaced by three-foot tall sugar cane stalks. "Did you ask Trinidad how much flake was in the bus?" Cody said.

"He said at least a hundred kilos."

We passed a sign advertising molasses and a driveway to a white farmhouse. "That's worth about two million wholesale," Cody said. "No wonder they sent their chief fixer."

"We're coming up to a decent sized city. I'll try to connect and book our flight."

.   .   .

The miles fell behind us as we bore through the night. I made our flight reservations, but by the time I was done the cellular signal wasn't strong enough to complete a call, so I sent Candi a text telling her all was fine and I hoped to fly home tomorrow or the next day. An hour east of the Haitian border I took the wheel and navigated over a surprisingly steep pass, then dropped down beside a large lake. "Twenty miles to the border," Cody said.

It was nearly midnight and the two-lane road was deserted. I slowed as we passed through a small farming town, then accelerated. We were passing more rice fields when the red and blue lights came on behind us.

"What the hell?" I said.

"The border's five miles ahead. Keep driving."

"I wasn't speeding."

"Small town cops, probably looking for a bribe."

"Or maybe they're on to us."

"Anything's possible. Fuck 'em. Don't stop."

I kept my speed at sixty miles per hour. The cop car came right up on my bumper. When I didn't slow, the siren came on.

"No shit, huh?" I said.

"Four minutes to freedom, Dirt."

"What about the border crossing?"

"My bet is they don't have much border control. This ain't Tijuana and San Diego."

The cop stayed right on my tail and a minute later he swung into the opposite lane and tried to get alongside me. I jammed the accelerator and the V-8 howled in response. We launched forward, and I straddled the lanes, keeping the patrol car behind us.

"Nice move," Cody said. "Whatever you do, don't let him pass."

We were going eighty on a long straightaway. I brought it up to ninety, the siren loud in the cab.

"Two miles," Cody said.

Then the road widened to add a passing lane. The police car swung to the left and used the extra room to gain ground. I could see his front bumper nearing my door. At ninety miles per hour, he was gaining rapidly.

"All right, buddy," I said, and jerked the wheel, cutting him off. But he didn't brake quickly enough and his fender crunched into my door. His headlight burst, followed by a bang almost as loud as a gunshot. The sedan skidded to the left, the front tire flat and shredding, and screeched off the road into the rice paddies. I saw water shoot up from beneath the chassis as the front end cratered with a loud clang. The suspension bottomed and rebounded rapidly as the car bounced over the troughs. "He's done," Cody said, looking behind me. The wail of the siren faded as we roared away.

A minute later we entered the border town of Jimaní. The road was rough and unpaved in spots. I drove carefully past makeshift shelters with tarp roofs supported by tree limbs, crumbling concrete buildings, and shacks with corrugated tin walls and plywood roofs held in place by large rocks. The streets were strewn with rubbish of every sort. We came to the border crossing, which was a dirt road blocked by an iron gate attended by a black man in desert camo fatigues. A single spotlight attached to a tall pole illuminated the gate. I rolled to a stop and lowered my window. The man looked down at me and said something in a language I didn't recognize.

"Speak English?" I asked.

"Yes," he said. "Passports, please."

I handed him our passports. He glanced over them and said, "Why are you coming to Haiti?"

"We work for an American charity," I said. "Our president is a wealthy businessman and is considering large donations to Haiti. We've been assigned to visit and provide a report."

He said nothing in reply and his face was impassive. He continued studying our passports, then he bent down and peered into the cab. For a long moment I wondered if he bought my story or not. Then he handed the passports to me. "This is not the United States. Be careful with your belongings." With that he swung the gate open.

"It may not be America the beautiful," Cody muttered as we drove into Haiti, "but I'm damn glad to be here."

. . .

The airport in Port-au-Prince was only 32 miles into Haiti, but the drive took an hour and a half. The issue wasn't traffic or stop lights, but frequent pot holes big enough to bend an axle. After bouncing over a few, I slowed to thirty and weaved my way around them.

Most of the drive took us through heavily populated areas rather than open country. I had never witnessed such wretched and sustained squalor. Although I've seen poverty as bad in Mexico, and even in homeless encampments in California, it's offset by middle-class neighborhoods. In Haiti, I saw no sign of a middle-class. The destitution was so uniform and unrelenting that it seemed otherworldly. It wasn't until we reached the Toussaint

Louverture International Airport in Port-au-Prince that the landscape displayed a modest level of prosperity.

The nearest hotel was the Servotel, a ten-minute walk from the airport. It looked similar to an American business-class hotel. When Cody and I walked into the lobby, it was 1:30 A.M., and there was no attendant at the counter.

Cody banged his palm on the chrome desk bell, and a young man promptly came from the back.

"We need a couple rooms and some food and drink, my good man," Cody said.

"Of course, sir," the attendant replied in halting English. "Rooms, yes, but our dining closed at ten o'clock. But we have items for sale here." He pointed to an alcove on the left where candy bars and potato chips were displayed.

"No beer?" Cody asked.

The man shook his head. "I am sorry."

We got our room keys and trudged up a flight of stairs. "Meet me in the lobby at six A.M.," I said. "They got a free breakfast, then we'll hoof it to the airport."

Cody looked at his watch. "See you in four hours," he said.

When I went into my room, I made sure my phone was charged and alarm set, then I fell onto the bed. I was exhausted and hoped for quick, deep slumber, but my mind was jittery with images and recriminations, and sleep would not come. I tried to push my thoughts aside, and the last thing I remember before finally falling asleep was Hugo Trinidad's face, his black eyes depthless and almost subhuman.

• • •

I was dreaming when my alarm jolted me awake at 5:15. For a moment, I didn't know where I was. The room was hot, and I was sticky with sweat. I sat on the edge of the bed, my hands gripping my knees, and stared at the wall. In my dream I was condemned by an assemblage of men, all bald and clad in long robes, as if they belonged to a clandestine government cult. My crimes were unspoken, but I'd been declared guilty by these nameless arbiters of justice, who rendered verdicts by codes they alone determined. And then I was sitting on my couch with Candi, listening to the police pound on our front door. I sat staring at the door, frozen as if paralyzed. I felt worse than powerless; I felt like I was literally coming apart.

"Jesus Christ," I wheezed. "I need coffee." I brewed a pot in the small percolator in the room, then took the paper cup into the shower and let cold water pound on my head. Fifteen minutes later I was dressed and checking my phone to make sure the flight was on time. Then I went down the stairwell and saw Cody chatting with a young woman in the dining area. She wore a shin-length pattern dress and had a scarf tied on her hair. She stared up at Cody, her eyes big against skin so dark it was almost purplish. They were the only ones in the room.

"I'm serious," he said as I walked up. "I want you to have it. It runs very well, I promise. The only problem is a little dent in the driver's door. Drive it home when you get off." Cody took her hand and placed Trinidad's keys in her palm. She looked at the keys, then back at Cody. Her eyes narrowed, but she still looked hopeful. "Is this a joke or something?" she said.

"Nope. But don't tell anybody until you get home. Okay?"

"Why you want to give it to me?"

"Because I live on the other side of the world, and I can't bring it home."

A small smile began on her face, as if the situation was beginning to make sense. She dropped the keys into her apron pocket, then smiled bigger, her teeth wide spaced. "Okay, sir. I'll take care of it for you. When you coming back for it?"

"Not in this lifetime."

Her face turned quizzical again. "So it is for me?"

"Yes, but only if you bring coffee."

She paused, no doubt contemplating what motivation her unusual visitor might have, and what price might ultimately be attached to the offer.

Then she tilted her head and her face brightened. "Two coffees?" she said, looking at me.

"Yes, ma'am," Cody replied, turning to the buffet. He grabbed a plate and began piling it with scrambled eggs and ham.

"Don't forget the plantains," I said, joining him.

"All for you, dig in."

We sat and ate. The woman brought coffee, then left us alone. After a minute I looked at my watch and said, "Let's walk. I want to get there early. I don't want to risk missing the plane."

"We got plenty of time. Let me get another plate."

"I almost missed a flight from Mexico once because they had some bogus customs paperwork. I had to bribe a guy forty bucks to stamp my form, or I'd still be there."

"All right, all right. Give me two minutes."

I waited for Cody, then we walked out the front doors and into the humid morning. I led us down the street, striding vigorously. It took less than ten minutes to reach the airport, and it was two and a half hours before our departure time. But as soon as we entered the terminal, I was glad we'd hurried. The place was a swarming, chaotic mess of people, mostly locals I assumed, for we were the only white faces in the building. It took twenty minutes to get our boarding passes, then nearly an hour and a half to clear security and customs screening. I was worried we might be pulled aside for further questioning when an armed official studied our passports and tickets for what seemed like a long time, but he let us pass, and we finally boarded the plane.

The cabin was almost full, but we had an aisle to ourselves. I closed my eyes and tried to relax as we took off, but my nerves were like a tangle of razor blades. I could feel the weight of a frown on my jaw. I blew out my breath and tried to force a smile, but the frown returned.

"Hey," Cody said, as we reached cruising altitude over the sea, "What's up with the black cloud over your head?"

"I got a lot on my mind."

"Ease up, man, we're in the clear."

"I think I need some more sleep," I said. My eyes felt bloodshot and dry. "I also need to make some phone calls."

"Do it when we land," Cody said. "Hey, you know what? I forgot to congratulate you on taking out the son of one of the most ruthless killers in history. I don't think the apple fell far from the tree with Pablo and Luis Escobar, eh? I mean, seriously, you're a freaking hero." Cody was smiling broadly. "Actually, you're *my* hero!" Cody's eyes were round with mirth, and then for no reason I could fathom, I felt a great release in my head, and I started laughing. Cody reached over from his aisle seat and patted me on the shoulder. "My freaking hero," he said. And I began laughing harder, and then I was seriously losing it, my eyes watering and shoulders shaking. I tried to control myself, but I was laughing so hard I was nearly crying.

"I'm serious, I'm gonna make you a trophy," Cody said.

"Stop," I said, hiding my face in the window as the stewardess approached.

"Is everything okay here?" she asked.

"Just peachy, miss," Cody said.

"What's so funny, if you don't mind me asking?"

"Life in the fast lane."

She shook her head and walked away. When my spasms subsided, I closed my eyes again, and this time I fell into a deep, dreamless sleep. I didn't wake until Cody jostled me. "Look, I think that's Miami Beach," he said, leaning over me, his big mug looking out the window.

15

We took a cab to the Holiday Inn, where we were still checked in and had left our luggage and firearms. We went to our rooms, and I sat down and called Sam Ruby. He answered promptly.

"Are you back from Italy yet?" I asked.

"Yes, we flew home yesterday. Got in late."

"Did you get the email I sent you?"

"I saw it, but haven't opened it."

I looked at my watch. It was a little before nine A.M. in California. "Are you in front of your computer?"

"Give me a minute, please."

I set my phone down and opened the drapes. The sun was hidden behind clouds and it looked like it might rain. I plugged in my notebook, turned it on, and waited for my email to sync.

"Okay, I'm looking at the file you sent. This is definitely the deceased?"

"Yes. His fingerprints are there. So is his DNA. Luis Escobar is his true name, not Luis Alvarez."

"I see. This is from the Dominican Republic?"

"That's right. Luis Escobar was a Dominican citizen."

"Interesting. You don't by chance have a hard copy, do you?"

"Yeah, I do."

"How in the world did you get it?"

"Does it matter?"

"Probably not," he said.

"You think you can get the charges dropped?"

"I'd have to say so. Unless the D.A. wants to waste the taxpayer's money on a case he'll probably lose."

"Probably?"

"Look, prosecutors are graded based on conviction rates. No D.A. wants to waste time on a case unless they feel a conviction or a plea is likely."

"All right," I said slowly. "Something else you should know, Sam. Luis Escobar is the biological son of Pablo Escobar."

"The Colombian drug lord?"

"That's right. The same man responsible for over five thousand murders."

"You're sure about the relationship?"

"You should be able to get Pablo Escobar's DNA report from Colombian officials, right? And then compare the two. They are father and son."

"My, that is amazing. But what about the eyewitness, the woman?"

"Claudia Merchan. I don't think she'll surface."

"Why not?"

"I think she was killed earlier this week by the cartel Luis Escobar worked for. Apparently they didn't want her around. She knew too much."

"She probably wouldn't have been a cooperative witness, anyway."

"If anything, she would have lied, said I killed without provocation."

"Are you back in South Lake Tahoe?"

"No, still in Miami. But I'll be booking a flight back today."

"Let me know your schedule. Then we can go meet with Magnus Swett."

"I'll be in touch," I said. As soon as we disconnected I called Candi, thinking I'd catch her before her ten A.M. class started.

"Are you at the college?" I said.

"Yes, but I'm just grading some projects. Where are you?"

"I just got back to Miami. I've been in the Dominican Republic."

"Why would you go there?"

"Because the John Doe was a Dominican citizen. I got his police report. He was a criminal and a murderer. I sent it all to Sam Ruby and just spoke to him. He thinks the D.A. will drop the charges."

"Oh, Dan," she said.

"Listen, I've got to book a flight home. I'll call you when it's done."

"Okay. Let me know and I'll pick you up from the airport."

I began checking flights and found a United three o'clock departure to Reno with a layover in Houston. I could be home by eleven P.M. I booked the flight, cringing at the cost, then called Cody.

"I need to head back to the airport pretty soon," I said. "Got a three o'clock flight."

"The best I can get is an eight P.M. direct flight."

"To San Jose?"

"No, Denver."

"You're not thinking of meeting up with Russ Landers?"

"Why would I want to talk to that shitbag?"

"So why go?"

"Take a guess."

"Magnus Swett?"

"Yeah. There's a few more people I want to talk to. Hey, before I forget, forward me Escobar's rap sheet, would you?"

"All right, I'll shoot it over. I talked with my lawyer, and he looked at it and thinks Swett will probably drop the charges."

"That's good," Cody said absently. "Let's go get some lunch, huh?"

·　　·　　·

I left Cody at a nearby restaurant where a buxom waitress was clearly fixated on him. An Uber driver took me to the airport, and I went straight through the uncrowded security check point. I had time to kill and found an empty stool at an airport bar. I nursed a beer and tried to convince myself my troubles were behind me. Despite the lingering uncertainties, by the time I'd boarded the plane, I'd done a decent job of it. I kept turning over the issues and couldn't find a logical reason to worry. Two beers and a double bourbon no doubt aided my conclusions. As the jet took off, I started thinking about a secondary set of challenges, namely my significantly depleted savings, but more importantly, whether I could continue working in South Lake Tahoe.

I still considered Marcus Grier a friend, but it was clear his support was waning. While he'd helped me somewhat, he hadn't done so readily, despite what I had at stake. Every time we spoke he made it clear he was not thrilled, which was akin to not giving a shit. Of course I didn't expect him to stick his neck out too far on my behalf, and I couldn't blame him for not wanting to risk his position at South Lake PD, but this was my hour of need. I sighed and tried to swallow my disappointment. It seemed Grier had forgotten that I'd nearly died uncovering the crimes of the sheriff who fired him, and if not for my efforts, Grier wouldn't have his job. Not only this, but I'd never done anything to run afoul of Grier. He'd always looked at me as an ally, or at least as one of the good guys.

I ordered a whiskey when the flight attendant came by, and stared at the ice cubes melting in the amber liquid. Maybe I was to blame. Maybe I'd pushed the envelope and would need to change my ways. Maybe I needed to walk away from violent situations instead of engaging them head on. Or maybe the best idea was to get into a different line of work.

But what had I done wrong? Early in my investigation, I'd punched a man in Nevada who was attacking a police officer. Without my intervention, the officer would likely have been shot. And then I'd punched a man who attacked me with a knife. This man was trying to kill me, and my defensive strike was with a lesser weapon. I'd hit him with nothing more than my fist, and my right cross was meant to disable, not kill him. Couldn't Grier see that? Did he not trust my account?

As the plane flew over the Gulf of Mexico, I sat with my jaw rested on my hand and looked down at the pale sea. I wondered what Magnus

Swett might have said to Grier about my case. It was possible that Swett had motivations beyond normal prosecutorial vehemence. If so, could I have been set up? It seemed unlikely, but Cody said Swett went way back with Russ Landers, the ex-cop who hated Cody and who once arrested me on a bogus charge.

The plane hit some rough air, and I gripped my drink tightly to keep it from spilling. When Landers threw me in jail, I shut him down with evidence of his misdeeds, including drug and prostitution kickbacks. It ultimately cost him his job. I'm sure if Landers could find a convenient way, he'd pay me back. Maybe when Swett left Denver for Tahoe, Landers told him to screw me over if he could. In that case, the death of Luis Escobar would have been the perfect opportunity.

Of course, I'm sure Swett harbored a serious direct grudge against Cody, who coerced a murder confession out of Swett's brother, resulting in a life sentence. Maybe Landers convinced Swett that Cody and I were partners in crime, and he could hurt Cody through me.

Beyond that, I didn't know what to think. All I knew was I had the key to my innocence secured in my pack, and a smart, savvy defense attorney. I looked forward to meeting with Swett and seeing the look on his face when his case went up in smoke.

·　　·　　·

As the plane descended, I could see the snow-covered peaks of the Sierra grow larger in the moonlight. Then we were over the city, the brightly lit casinos looming ahead. The wing tipped and the pilot executed a sweeping turn. Five minutes later we touched down in Reno.

I left the plane and made my way to baggage claim. I had expected Candi to be waiting in her car at the curb, but she was standing at the luggage carousel. She wore heels, jeans that hugged her hips, and a tight-fitting shirt I bought her when we first met. Her hair was down, her face made up. I hadn't seen her like this since she'd become pregnant. She smiled as I approached.

"My man," she said, as I took her in my arms. We embraced for a long time, silently holding each other. "You look tired," she said when we parted.

"Been a busy trip."

"But you got what you need."

"That's right."

"When do we get to celebrate?"

"The next step is for Ruby and me to meet with Magnus Swett. Once he sees the details on Luis Escobar, he'll drop the charges."

"For sure?"

"Unless he's a fool or a masochist. And I don't think he's either."

"Well, we're celebrating tonight." She ran her fingernails up my thigh.

"Done deal, babe."

. . .

When I woke the next morning, it was not yet light outside, and the house was cold. I lit the stove, then put on my coat and boots and went outside. Wisps of vapor streamed from my mouth as I stood on the deck watching the dawn come. Once the sky lightened, I walked to my back gate and started down the trail to the stream. I hiked through the thick, brown grass, ice cracking beneath my feet. Dirty patches of snow spotted the meadow and clung to the deadfall. Just as I came to the river bank, I heard a rustling sound, and two raccoons scampered away through the brush.

I stood by the water for a time, looking at the icy flow and then out over the meadow and the pine-studded ridges that rose from the forest surrounding Lake Tahoe. I waited for the particular sense of tranquility I often felt when alone in the meadow. I tried to force all thoughts from my head and be at one with the natural elements. After a while, I gave up and returned home.

When Candi woke, I made her breakfast, then busied myself with household chores. But there wasn't much that needed to be done, and at ten A.M. I found myself sitting and staring at the newspaper without reading. My trial was scheduled to begin in exactly seven days.

"Maybe I'll head over to Zeke's and help with the lunch rush," I said to Candi.

"It's Monday. Probably be pretty slow," she replied.

"Yeah." I stood and stretched. "I'm going to the gym, then." I started to our room to change clothes, but stopped when my phone buzzed with a text alert. It was from Sam Ruby: *Meeting with Swett tomorrow 11am. Call me please.*

"It's my lawyer," I said, pressing the call back function. Ruby answered and told me he'd booked a dawn flight the next day from San Jose arriving at 7:30 A.M. in Reno. If I wanted to save expense money, I could pick him up from the airport.

"I'll be waiting at the curb outside baggage claim," I said.

•   •   •

When I drove from my house the next morning, I had to force myself to not speed through the dawn. I'd spent three hours the previous afternoon researching legal precedents and California case law. There was simply too much complexity and gray area to draw any conclusions, and I finally accepted that my fate lay in the hands of my attorney. I was anxious to hear Ruby's strategies for our meeting with Swett.

Spooner Pass looked like a moonscape in the gray dawn. Then, as I steered through a long bend, a sliver of blinding sun rose from behind a hillside. I began to see orange and purple flowers sprouting among the sagebrush, until I ascended into snow fields near the summit. After that came more sweeping turns, the hills increasingly barren as I approached the high desert floor in Carson City. Then all that remained was a straight shot, half an hour blasting through the desolate badlands to Reno. I drove automatically, my mind shut down as if I'd worn a groove in a record and there was no song left to play.

I arrived at the airport early and took a few laps around the terminal before I spotted my lawyer and pulled to the curb. Sam Ruby was tall and had a peculiar gait, his knees bending in an exaggerated fashion, his shoulders rolling and arms swinging. It almost looked like he was ready to break into dance. He smiled while he walked to where I waited, as if each step brought him pleasure. His gray suit jacket was unbuttoned, and with every stride his red necktie swayed from side to side and his briefcase swung recklessly and looked like it might fly open at any moment. He had wide-set brown eyes, a prominent nose, lips that were a little too full, a jolly smile, and a big chin.

I stepped out to greet him. "Good morning, Dan," he said, grinning.

We shook hands, and I tried to return his smile. "You want to get breakfast or coffee somewhere?" I asked.

He looked at his watch. "About an hour to South Lake Tahoe?"

"An hour and fifteen."

"We've got plenty of time. Let's go find a diner and talk."

I drove back north to Carson City and found a cinder block restaurant near the capitol building. We took a booth in the back, and Ruby set a yellow paper pad on the table.

"I need a full accounting of the altercation, plus all the events leading to it, and everything you did afterward."

"Everything? I've already told you most of it."

"Let's do it again. I don't want to be caught unaware if the D.A. has an angle."

I looked down for a long moment. "Some of what I tell you could implicate me in unrelated things."

"You don't need to worry about that. Keep in mind, the majority of people commit crimes every day without ever knowing it. Our state and federal laws are so dense that it's virtually impossible to avoid breaking the law."

"Yeah, but the nature of my work puts me at heightened risk. And I'm not talking about jaywalking."

A waitress approached and we both ordered coffee. When she left, Ruby said, "I'm your defense attorney. Everything you say is protected by attorney-client privilege. Nothing you say to me can ever be used against you."

"I know," I said. "All right, here goes."

I spoke for an hour, often pausing so Ruby could finish taking notes. I started with the initial phone call from a man who claimed to be Luis Alvarez and described our meeting at Zeke's Pit. I detailed my search for Manuel Alvarez and eventual doubts about Luis Alvarez's identity and motivations. I then recounted the meeting with Luis and Claudia Merchan at the Hotel Becket and the ensuing altercation.

After a few questions, Ruby said, "Okay, now tell me everything that happened after you posted bail."

"Well, my partner Cody Gibbons rolled into town to help me out."

"Your old buddy," Ruby said, smiling.

"That's right," I said. Then I described everything that happened in Miami, the Dominican Republic, and Haiti. When I was done, Ruby put down his pencil. "Man, you live on the edge."

I turned my palms upward. "What can I say? I'm just trying to survive."

"You ever consider a tamer approach?"

"Yeah, I have."

"But?"

"My actions are always in self-defense. It goes with the territory when dealing with the scumbags. I don't know how else to put it."

"I got to hand it to you," Ruby said, shaking his head.

"What?"

"You and Gibbons are hell on the bad guys."

I shrugged. "So what about my case?"

"Given what you uncovered on Luis Escobar, no jury would convict you. Keep in mind, a conviction must be unanimous; all twelve jurors must agree. Even one hold out, it's a hung jury."

"Here's Luis Escobar's official police record from the Dominican," I said, sliding the gray folder across the table. Ruby spent a minute flipping through the pages.

"It's admissible, right?"

"The inadmissibility of prior bad acts is designed to protect the accused. But there's nothing in the code that prevents its admissibility in this situation. Luis Escobar is not the defendant; you are."

"I hope it's that easy," I said.

.   .   .

We arrived at the South Lake Tahoe Government Center a few minutes before eleven. We drove past the police station to the courthouse where Magnus Swett's office was located. Ruby spoke with a receptionist and we sat on a bench in the lobby. The minutes ticked by and my stomach began to churn. Finally, at 11:15, the receptionist brought us to the same interview room where I'd first met Swett.

"Hello, Mr. Swett," Ruby said, extending his hand. For a moment I wasn't sure if Swett would shake it, but then he did, albeit briefly and without looking up.

"I've got a lot on my plate today, so let's make this quick, please," Swett said. His jacket was draped over a chair, and the sleeves of his white shirt were rolled on his forearms. He wore suspenders on his thick, bullet-shaped torso. There were open chairs, but Swett remained standing and didn't invite us to sit.

"I'll be as concise as I can," Ruby replied, smiling easily. "We have the identity of the deceased John Doe. He was a citizen of the Dominican Republic with an extensive criminal record, including stabbings and a conviction for murder. I have his complete police record here."

Swett's nostrils flared as if assailed by a rotten stench. Ruby held out the gray folder and said, "If you have a copy machine, I'll print you a copy."

"Let me see that," Swett said, taking the gray folder from Ruby's hand. The prosecutor sat and looked through the pages for less than a minute.

"This is from a small, foreign country. How can you prove it's not a fake?"

"The fingerprints are there, Mr. Swett, and so is a DNA report. The report is indeed legitimate and I can have it validated by the Dominican authorities."

"It's meaningless, anyway. Prior bad acts are not admissible."

"The issue of inadmissibility exists to protect defendants from unfair prosecution, as you surely know, Mr. Swett. In this case, this document serves to both identify the John Doe and to establish his predisposition to violence. The two knife offenses in the report constitute similarity of occurrences, as defined in People versus Thompson. If you were using this arrest record to prosecute a defendant for a knife attack, it would be admissible. It is likewise admissible to establish that a knife attack by the deceased was not abnormal, but directly similar to his previous acts."

"Where did you go to law school, Mr. Rubenstein?"

"It's Ruby. I went to Stanford, sir."

"Then you should know that People versus Thompson is highly subjective and open to interpretation."

"I'd be happy to take this before a judge and let him decide," Ruby said. "But there's one more thing you should know. The deceased's name is Luis Escobar, and we believe he is the biological son of Pablo Escobar, the Colombian drug kingpin responsible for thousands of brutal murders. We'll have a DNA match shortly. How do you think that will play in front of a jury?"

"It's irrelevant," Swett said, but his voice had turned gravelly and I could see the blood rise in his face.

"You have accused Mr. Reno of manslaughter when he was acting solely in self-defense. California has very liberal self-defense interpretations. There is no chance a jury will convict, and you know it. Continuing this prosecution would be a waste of taxpayer money. If you insist on proceeding with this charade, after Mr. Reno is acquitted, I will file suit for wrongful prosecution."

"Do you think you can come in here and threaten me?" Swett said, the words clipped and his face growing redder.

"I wouldn't dream of it. I'm simply requesting you drop the case and am telling you how I'll respond if you do not. You can factor that into your decisions as you see fit."

Swett turned away and put his hands on his hips for a moment, and when he turned back to us, his voice was calm. "There's something you're unaware of, counselor," he said. "I have located an eyewitness who will testify that there was no knife involved in the altercation."

"You're bluffing," I said.

"No, Mr. Reno, I am not, and you are about to learn a hard lesson. I offered you a plea, and I'm willing to keep it on the table for another minute. Take it or I'll see you in court on Monday."

"Give us a moment, please," Ruby said. We stepped into the hallway and closed the door.

"The only possible witness was Claudia Merchan," I said, "and even if she's not dead, she's not credible, right?"

"What are the chances she's alive?"

"One in twenty."

"How about the possibility of any other witness?"

"It was dark and there were no lit windows, and no one came by when the police arrived. And even if there was someone who saw what happened, they would validate my story."

Ruby was silent in thought. "Sam, I'm not taking a plea, so don't even think about it."

"I'm not," he said.

We went back into the room. Swett was seated, his face drained of color, his eyes small. "When will you provide us the name of the witness and their statement?" Ruby said.

"By Wednesday," Swett replied. "My plea offer will be long gone by then."

"I will not plead to a crime I didn't commit," I said.

"Then we're done here," Swett said.

.   .   .

The morning was still brisk in the shadows of the tall pines, but the cloudless blue sky promised a fine spring afternoon. But I didn't feel any of that mojo as Ruby and I walked back to my truck.

"Drive me to the Hotel Becket," Ruby said. "I want to see where this all took place."

I steered out of the parking lot, drove to Highway 50, and turned right toward the state line. A few minutes later we arrived at the hotel. I parked in the same spot I'd occupied on the night in question.

"This is exactly where it happened. I was parked right here."

We stood at my front bumper and I went over every detail of Escobar's attack. We walked to the hotel's rear door and back again, retracing the steps Claudia and Escobar would have taken. There were no street lights, nor were there any lights mounted to the hotel's back wall.

"How about these businesses over here?" Ruby said, pointing across the street.

"They were all closed and unlit."

"And you didn't see anyone at all who could have been a witness?"

"No. It was dark and no one was around. And even if someone saw something, it happened very quickly and it would have been too dark to see any details."

We stood there in a sunny spot, shading our eyes and looking around, until Ruby said, "Something's not right about Swett."

"Like what?"

"I don't know, but I think we're going to find out. I'll need a room for a night or two."

.   .   .

I drove home after Ruby checked into the Hotel Becket. Candi was working, and the house was empty. It was past noon, but I wasn't hungry. I tried to busy myself with chores, but kept forgetting what I was doing. Eventually

I went outside, the vacuum cleaner still plugged in and sitting in the middle of the family room. I pulled my picnic table out of the shade of the big pine tree, then sat and let the sun warm my arms. I wanted nothing more than to exit my head and think about nothing.

I was nearly dozing when the ring from my cell startled me. It was Cody.

"Please tell me you have some good news," I said.

"Why, what's up?"

"Sam Ruby and I just met with Magnus Swett. Ruby showed him Luis Escobar's rap sheet and asked him to drop the charges. Swett said no way. He also said he has an eyewitness against me."

"Well, not to worry, kemosabe, because I saved your ass again."

"What?"

"Make sure you're sitting down for this, all right?"

"Talk to me."

"So, yesterday I met with the Denver P.I. who originally told me about how Magnus Swett was shit-canned out of Denver. As it turns out, this private dick was hired by a group of Denver cops who wanted Swett gone after they found out about his brother, Malcom."

"Malcom's still in prison, right?"

"Hell, yes. He's rotting away in Pelican Bay supermax."

"And?"

"The P.I. offered to sell me his entire case file for a grand. I said, let me see it first. And not only does it include recorded conversations with Russ Landers, it comes complete with a video of Magnus Swett in a room, smoking crack with a topless sixteen-year-old hooker."

"Come on."

"I shit you not, Dirt. It's the real McCoy."

"Was the video ever shown to the Denver authorities?"

"No. Swett screwed the pooch on his own by falsely arresting those gangbangers for the murder of a family, remember? That's ultimately what got him fired."

"So no one's ever seen the video?"

"Nope. Not until this morning."

"Where are you?"

"I just had a sit-down with the El Dorado County District Attorney. The elected attorney, who's up for reelection in six months."

"You're in Placerville?"

"Yeah, I flew into Sacto last night, then drove here first thing this morning."

"How did you get a meeting with the head D.A.?"

"I called his office and told his secretary I have information that has serious implications for his reelection. I said I'd be willing to share it with him today, but if he's too busy, I'll take it to the press and the candidate running against him. An hour later I was in his office. Keep in mind, this is Magnus Swett's boss."

"And you played the video for him?"

"Indeed, I did. And I said, how can you hire a perverted asswipe like this, who was fired from Denver for unethical behavior, and who also has an ongoing relationship with a former San Jose police captain who was fired for taking dirty money?"

"What'd he say?" I was pacing around my backyard.

"You should have seen it, he was walking on his lips, a buh, a buh, a buh. And then I told him that, at a minimum, he needs to make sure the bogus charges against you are dropped. I explained your situation and showed him Escobar's rap sheet. I told him Swett doesn't care that you're innocent, he just wants to break your balls. By the time I left, we had a deal."

"Which was?"

"The charges will be dropped by tomorrow, in return for me handing over the P.I.'s file and keeping my mouth shut."

"You're serious?"

"What, you think I'd make this up? You're soon to be free and clear, brother. Hold on a sec, someone's calling me."

The line went silent, and I stood staring at my phone, stunned and disbelieving. Of all the crazy things I'd seen Cody pull off, this had to be near the top. He'd basically blackmailed the El Dorado County D.A. It was an incredibly risky gambit, and I wondered if it could backfire. But Cody's ability to gauge how far he could lean over the cliff without plunging downward was uncanny.

I returned to the picnic bench and thought about how Swett would react when his boss ordered him to drop the charges. Hell, I wondered if he could keep his job. Nothing would make me happier than to see him get fired and leave town with his tail between his legs.

My phone rang, alerting me Cody had returned. "Dirt, you're not gonna believe this."

"Believe what?"

"It was Magnus Swett calling."

"You're joking"

"No, it was really him."

I blinked and tilted my head. "Did his boss already talk to him?"

"No. He called because he wants to meet with me, face to face, today."

"What the hell for?"

"He said I'm the only one that has a chance of keeping you out of prison."

"Huh?"

"I don't get it either. But he wants something from me."

"He didn't tell you what?"

"Nope."

"Obviously he doesn't know he'll be ordered to drop the charges," I said.

"He still thinks he has a hand to play, but he's drawing dead."

"You're not gonna meet with him, are you?"

"He wants to meet behind an office building in Nevada, over off Kingsbury. I said I'm in San Jose, and the earliest I could be there is five o'clock. He said to come alone, said he'd search me for a wire."

"Why bother? Screw him."

"No, I think he deserves an audience."

"What do you expect to get out of this?"

"I think Swett's fixing to bury himself. And given everything he's put you through, why should we deny him?"

"I have to admit, he's not exactly the sunshine of my life."

"I'm getting in my truck. I'll see you in an hour or so."

·   ·   ·

It was two o'clock when I saw Cody's Dodge truck turn into Zeke's Pit. I got up from the table near the front window and walked out into the sunshine. The rattle of the diesel engine was loud as Cody jerked to a stop, his front tires bumping against the parking curb. He wore jeans and a black polo shirt that seemed to fit well, except the short sleeves clung to his biceps. His backpack dangled from his right hand.

"I never had lunch," he said. "You got any Texas brisket made?"

We went inside and sat at the table on the stage overlooking the parking lot. Except for a young local couple nursing drinks at the end of the bar, the room was empty. I went to the taps and poured a pitcher of Budweiser, then walked into the kitchen and asked the cook to prepare a couple of plates. When I returned, Cody was chatting with Liz, who'd just arrived for her shift.

"Hi Dan," she said. "Haven't seen you in a while."

"Been traveling," I said.

"He's an international man. You know, like James Bond." Cody winked.

"Yeah, right. James Bond drinks martinis, not domestic draught beer," she said, and walked behind the bar. I filled our mugs as Cody reached down to his pack and set a couple of items on the table.

"Here's how I see it," he said. "Whatever Swett has to say, he doesn't want anyone to know. So let's record him." On the table were two recording bugs, each about the size of a dime, plus a receiving unit that looked like a black tennis ball with legs.

"Here's what I'm thinking." Cody pushed his thatch-like hair up above his ear. "I'll shave a spot to stick the bug to my skin. My hair will cover it. Swett will never know."

"What about the receiver?"

"Let's drive over there and scout a place to put it."

The cook brought our lunch from the kitchen, and we ate quickly, then hopped in my truck. We drove to the state line, crossed into Nevada, and took a right on Kingsbury Grade. We passed a gas station, a bar and grill, a small strip mall, and a modest office complex. A quarter-mile later we turned right, where a newly constructed building was set back from the road. I parked on the street and we walked to the entrance. The doors were locked. It was all dirt surrounding the building, no grass or shrubs.

We walked behind the building and stopped where an overhang covered a half-dozen empty parking spots beneath the second floor. Sixty or seventy feet behind us was a backhoe parked on a dirt hill. Behind that, a rocky section of forest, scattered with pines, rose a few hundred feet.

"Looks like they just finished construction," I said. "No tenants yet."

"Swett wanted to pick somewhere discreet."

"He said to meet right here?"

"Yeah. He just said in back."

We were standing in one of the parking stalls. I looked around, searching for a suitable spot for the receiver. The parking area, aside from a loose coat of dirt, was bare; just the pavement and stucco walls. We walked from beneath the overhang and I spotted a half-filled bag of mortar sitting at the base of a tree. "How about this?" I said.

"Bring it over here," Cody said. I lugged it to the corner of the building. Cody placed the receiver in the bag, and I folded it shut.

"It should pick up the signal fine," Cody said.

"As long as you stay in this area."

"I don't plan on getting in his car."

"Come here," I said, walking toward the backhoe. It was a big, full-sized Caterpillar tractor, about twenty feet long. Our feet sank in the sandy dirt as we climbed up the hill.

"I'll hide here," I said, finding a spot behind the enclosed cab. The plastic windows would obscure me if Swett looked. Cody nodded and began back toward the building.

"One other thing," I said. "I'm gonna call Grier and tell him to join me."

"You sure he'll agree? He hasn't exactly been eager to help."

"His D.A. is dirty, and he needs to see it firsthand. It's time he got some skin in the game."

"Tell him he needs to grow a pair."

"I'll tell him you said so."

·   ·   ·

I called Grier's cell as we drove back into California. When he didn't answer, I parked at Harrah's and Cody and I headed inside and walked to the sports book. Unless there was a major sporting event going on, casino sports books were a good place to work. Individual seats with tabletops, relatively quiet, and usually uncrowded. We sat in the back row and stared up at the numerous big screens. There were a couple of baseball games and a horse race in progress. Almost every seat was empty.

I hit Grier's cell number again. This time he answered.

"Are you still in Miami?" Grier asked.

"No, I'm back in town."

"Good."

"Why?"

"Because our D.A. was concerned you might skip."

"No shit, huh? Did Magnus Swett talk to you about it?"

"He asked if I thought you were a flight risk."

"What did you tell him?"

"I said I would consider anyone facing a long prison sentence to be a flight risk."

"Did it ever occur to you I'm innocent of the charges, Marcus?"

The line went silent. Then Grier said, "Of course. Everyone is innocent until proven guilty."

I took a deep breath and fought back a surge of heat rising in my chest. "Let me give you an update," I said, trying to keep my voice quiet. "I got the dirt on the man who tried to stab me. He's got a long rap sheet, including a murder conviction in the Dominican Republic and two knife attacks. Plus, as a gold star bonus, he's the fucking son of Pablo Escobar."

"The Medellín Cartel Pablo Escobar?"

"That's right. And my attorney and I met with Magnus Swett this morning and shared it all with him. The evidence in my favor is overwhelming. No jury would ever find me guilty. But Swett was still trying to ram a plea down my throat."

"So he still intends to go to trial?"

"Yeah, but that's not all. He called Cody Gibbons and wants a secret meeting. It's happening in ninety minutes."

"Gibbons? Where's that crazy son of a bitch?"

"Right next to me."

"Oh."

"There's something else you should know. Not only is Swett the brother of a convicted rapist and murderer, but he was fired for incompetence and ethical issues in Denver."

"I have a hard time believing that."

"Really? Why don't you meet us here at Harrah's and I'll share all the details with you?"

"What kind of proof do you have?"

"Recordings, video, police reports, you name it."

I heard Grier exhale. "All right, where are you?"

"The sports book. And after we talk, I want you to come with me to Cody's meeting with Swett."

"I thought it was a secret meeting."

"That's why it's so suspicious. I want you there as a witness. Because nobody around here seems to trust my word anymore."

"What, you think Swett will do something illegal?"

"I'd bet on it."

.   .   .

I knew Swett would arrive at the meeting site early and have a good look around. I predicted he would show up half an hour in advance, at the most. So I wanted to get there at least 45 minutes before five o'clock to make sure we were situated. By the time Grier showed up at Harrah's, time was getting tight.

"We got ten minutes, Marcus," I said. He was in uniform, his .38 revolver tight against the gold stripe on his pants.

He nodded and said, "Mr. Gibbons."

"Hello, Sheriff. Have a seat." Cody opened the file from the Denver P.I., and we shared it all with Grier, detailing Swett's history. Then I showed him the Dominican police report on Luis Escobar. Grier listened silently, his expression blank.

"Is that it?" he said.

"You want to watch the video of him with the teenage girl and the crack pipe?"

Grier shook his head slowly. I tried to read his face, but couldn't tell if he was doubtful, weary, or just unhappy. "Sorry to be the bearer of bad news," I said.

"I don't need to hear anything else," he said. "Let's go."

We went to Cody's truck and piled into the cab. Five minutes later we arrived at the newly-built office structure. Cody dropped us off in front. "I'll be back at five," he said. Grier and I hiked to the back and climbed up the loose dirt to the backhoe. "I'm betting Swett won't climb up here," I said. We stood behind the big tractor and looked down at the covered parking stalls. We were about seventy feet away.

"I doubt we can hear them from this far," Grier said.

"Cody's wearing a bug. It will all be recorded."

"So what am I doing here?"

"I want you to witness that the meeting occurred. I want you to witness anything that Swett might say or do to incriminate himself."

Grier lifted his cap and wiped his forehead with his handkerchief. "Make sure your cell ringer is turned off," I said. Then we settled in to wait.

·   ·   ·

Swett arrived at exactly 4:30. From our vantage we saw him park and walk to the rear of the building. He was wearing black sweat pants, running shoes, and a matching windbreaker. He also wore sunglasses and a blue baseball cap, which I assumed were meant to obscure his identity. Grier and I bent low behind the backhoe, and watched Swett pace around the building, obviously looking for any sign that his meeting site was less than secure. He ignored the bag of mortar which held the receiver unit. For a moment I almost felt sorry for him. Clearly, he had no experience in this type of operation. But then he fixed his eyes on the backhoe and walked toward us.

Grier and I hunkered down, peeking from behind the dirty plastic windows enclosing the tractor's cab. Swett started up the hill, his shoes sinking deep into the sandy soil. He made it three steps in our direction, then frowned, lifted a foot, and kicked a few times. After a moment he turned around and returned to the parking stalls, where he leaned against a wall, removed his sneakers, and shook the dirt out. Scowling, he wiped his socks clean, jammed his feet back into his shoes, and resumed scouting the lower area.

I heard Cody's truck before it came into view. He parked next to Swett's Audi sedan and walked to the back of the building. When Swett saw him, he emerged from a shadowed stall and stood waiting, light glinting off his sunglasses.

The two faced each other, not shaking hands. Swett began speaking, and Cody put his hands against the building and let Swett pat him down. Swett again spoke, but we couldn't make out the words. Cody listened, arms crossed, then he shrugged his shoulders and raised his palms upward. Swett pointed at him, jabbing with his finger. Cody shook his head and said something in reply.

Swett moved back into the shade of the covered parking spots, and Cody followed him. The district attorney pulled a folded sheet of paper from his pocket and handed it to Cody, who stared down at it for thirty seconds. Then I could see Cody roll his eyes and smile. He held the paper for Swett to take back. But instead, Swett's hand emerged from his jacket pocket holding a small semi-automatic pistol, probably a .25 cal.

Cody raised his hands over his head and backed out into the sun. Swett followed, his gun aimed at Cody's gut. They exchanged a few more sentences, then Swett removed his sunglasses and extended his arm, now pointing the gun at Cody's chest.

I grabbed Grier's shoulder and rose to my feet behind the yellow shovel arm. "Drop the gun, Swett!" I yelled.

Swett whirled in my direction, his eyes round with surprise. He pointed his weapon at me, and I was exposed from the shoulders up. Without taking careful aim, it would be a difficult shot, especially with a short barrel pistol. For a flashing moment, I saw Swett's face change, as if he was stunned by the realization that he'd shoved all his chips into the pot and now must live with the outcome. Then he fired.

I ducked as the errant round split the plastic cab windows three feet to my left. The slug hit the bill of Grier's sheriff's cap and sent it twirling behind him. Swett shot again, the bullet pinging off the iron shovel arm. Then Grier barreled into me, knocking me aside and taking my position. He was holding his .38 revolver. Both hands on the weapon, arms outstretched, Grier shut one eye and pulled the trigger.

A burst of blood appeared on Swett's chest, and he staggered forward. Dropping to his knees, he looked at Grier and me with an expression that

I'll always remember as that of an evil man who wished for a last chance to explain himself and beg forgiveness. But if that's what he wanted, he'd have to do it from the grave, because he raised his cap as if bidding us farewell, then tipped forward. His forehead hit the pavement, and he remained in that position, like he was bowed in prayer.

"Call nine-one-one," I said to Grier, who was staring open-mouthed. I ran down the hill and stood looking down at Swett. Cody held out the sheet of paper Swett had given him.

"He wanted me to sign this," Cody said.

"Put it away," I said, as Grier came down the hill. I knelt and checked Swett's neck for a pulse. His body fell over, his sightless blue eyes dead in the glare of the sun.

When Grier looked at Swett's face, he holstered his revolver. "I, I can't believe this," he stammered.

"Thanks, Sheriff," Cody said. "Nice shooting."

"I never shot at a man," Grier said.

"You did so in self-defense," I said. "Cody and I will attest to it. Right, Cody?"

"Hell, yes," Cody said, patting Grier's beefy shoulder.

Grier squeezed his eyes shut, and when he opened them they were wet.

"It will take a little time, but you'll get over it," I said.

"You know what Dan always does after a shooting, Sheriff?"

"What?" Grier mumbled.

"Plows down cocktails until he's gonzo drunk."

"That's an exaggeration," I said.

"Maybe so," Cody said, "but booze helps, I guarantee it."

· · ·

A moment later we heard the sirens, and within five minutes we were surrounded by California and Nevada patrolmen and detectives. They stomped around in confusion and argued about who had jurisdiction over the crime scene, because of course they all believed a crime had been committed.

Their remarks escalated from sarcastic to accusatory, and then from out of nowhere, Bolo Jones, the South Lake Tahoe detective who was the first to interview me when I was arrested, appeared on the scene. He walked to where Grier, Cody, and I stood talking to a Nevada detective.

"You got to be kidding me," Jones said.

I ignored him and continued answering a question from the Nevada cop, who Jones shoved aside to reach me. He pulled a pair of cuffs from his belt, grabbed my arm, and tried to spin me around so my back was facing him.

"Jones, what the hell do you think you're doing?" Grier said

"Magnus Swett is dead, and you need to ask?"

"*I* shot him, you incredible jackass," Grier said. He'd recovered his hat, which had a neat hole through the bill.

"You? But what is Reno doing here?"

"Go away, detective. I need to finish with Douglas County."

"Hey, Bolo," I said, yanking my arm from his grip. "I hear you used to work for Denver PD."

"Who told you that?"

"I did," Cody said.

"So what? It's public knowledge."

"Swett brought his past with him to Lake Tahoe," I said. "And you're part of it."

"Are you accusing me of something, Reno? I find that hard to stomach, coming from someone out on bail for manslaughter."

"That bullshit charge died with Magnus Swett. What's coming next is an investigation of anyone linked to Swett. I'd say you're first on the list. Welcome to the jungle, prick."

Bolo Jones's face went blank for a moment, then his features bunched up as if he'd stepped from a warm room into the howling winds of a blizzard. "I don't have to listen to this shit," he said. He turned and walked back to his car, dirt spitting from his shoes with every step. When he drove off, he stomped the gas and laid rubber, the tires shrieking and producing a plume of white smoke. Everyone stopped and stared, except for the paramedics, who were working to fit Swett's corpse into a body bag.

It took an hour for the police on either side of the border to finish with their questioning. A Nevada detective who arrived late was insistent that Grier be arrested. I stood off to the side, watching the detective and two of his underlings interrogate Grier. Cody and I were free to go, and it would have been easy to do so. I could have simply spun on my heel and walked with Cody to his truck, leaving Grier to deal with whatever grief the Nevada justice system imposed on him. Maybe he'd end up spending the night in the Douglas County pen, and maybe he'd be charged with manslaughter. Then he could drain his bank account to post bail and pay thousands to an attorney to defend him against a crime he didn't commit.

I stood watching for a long moment before I said, "Come on, let's go throw in our two cents."

"Yeah, Grier looks like he's ready to projectile vomit." I followed Cody to where Grier stood trying to answer questions designed to make him look guilty regardless of his response. Grier's face looked drained of blood, and he indeed appeared nauseous. "Let me do the talking," Cody said.

"Detectives, excuse me, Cody Gibbons, here, along with my partner Dan Reno." The three plainclothesmen stopped in mid-sentence and glared at us, their expressions ranging from annoyed to openly hostile.

"We were eyewitnesses to the shooting. As an ex-cop, I can tell you that it was a cut-and-dried case of self-defense. The deceased held me at gun-point, then fired twice at Sheriff Grier and Mr. Reno. The sheriff returned fire in self-defense, and almost certainly saved my life as well as Mr. Reno's, since we were unarmed."

"Are you trying to tell us how to do our job?" a younger detective said.

"Nope," Cody said. "I'm just telling you what happened and how we'll testify if need be. And one more thing." Cody reached above his ear and pried the recording bug from his scalp, then he took a couple steps to the bag of mortar where we'd stashed the receiver.

"What's that?" the detective asked.

"We recorded the entire thing," Cody said.

We stepped back and allowed the detectives to continue questioning Grier. But apparently Cody's comments took the wind out of their sails, because a minute later the detectives returned to their cars and left the scene, following the last remaining squad car out to the road. Grier, Cody, and I were the only ones left. We stood in the ebb of the day's light, watching the sky turn purple as the sun fell behind a white ridge.

"They were ready to arrest me for murder," Grier said. He'd regained his color but still looked shaken.

"It ain't exactly a great feeling, is it?" I said.

"No," he said, then he paused. "I guess you've been there."

"You're goddamn right I have. And no one gave me the benefit of the doubt."

"That's how the system works," Grier said.

"It's not about the system, Marcus. It's about people."

"Well, I…I'll keep that in mind."

"All righty, then," Cody said. "I'm sure we can discuss this over a few much-needed beers. What do you say, men? How about we head over to Zeke's?"

· · ·

We drove back to Harrah's so Grier could pick up his car. Once he climbed out of Cody's truck, I said, "What did Swett try to make you sign?"

Cody swung a wide U-turn and headed toward the parking exit. "He wanted me to admit that I'd illegally obtained his brother's confession. He wanted to take it back to San Jose and get Malcom Swett's conviction overturned. He said if I cooperated he'd drop the charges against you."

I hit my forehead with the meat of my fist. "So that's what this was all about?"

"That's why he wanted to meet me."

"What did you say to him?"

"I told him his brother got off light, all things considered. I said the evil piece of shit deserved a worse fate than the women he'd tormented, and maybe that's just what he was getting at Pelican Bay. That's when Swett pulled his piece."

"You think that's why Swett arrested me? As a means to get to you?"

"I don't know. I didn't ask him."

"I wonder if Swett came to work here with that agenda."

"I doubt it. But I'm sure he was always butt-sore about his brother going down and hoped to find a way to spring him loose. When he figured out you and I were buddies, he saw his opportunity."

I stared out the window as we crossed into California, shaking my head. "Of all the screwy things," I muttered.

A few minutes later we parked in front of Zeke's and climbed up the weather-beaten stairs to the saloon doors. We sat at the table overlooking the lot and watched Grier turn in from Highway 50 and park his squad car. I excused myself and went out to the beer garden to call Candi.

"The charges will be dropped by tomorrow morning," I said. "This will all soon be behind us."

"Why are they dropping the charges?" Candi said.

"Because of Cody. He knew people in Denver that had dirt on Swett."

"What kind of dirt?"

"The kind that results from knowing the wrong people and doing the wrong things."

"Oh. What's going to happen to him?"

"Uh, he's no longer in the picture."

"Huh?"

"We met with Swett and he pulled a gun. Marcus Grier shot him."

"He's dead?"

"Yeah."

"Oh my god."

"Listen, Marcus is pretty shook up, and Cody and I are gonna have a few drinks with him over at Zekes. You know, help him decompress. You can swing by if you like."

"It's tempting, but I better leave you guys to your bro-mance."

"I'll be home late, babe. We'll celebrate tomorrow, all right?"

"Don't get too drunk."

.   .   .

My recollections of that night are fuzzy and some parts seem almost dream-like. We started with beers at Zeke's, and after three or four Grier snapped out of his funk. I don't know if this was because of or in spite of Cody's frequent pronouncements, such as, "Boys, we all know the world is better off when a scuzball gets his dick permanently knocked in the dirt," or, "Sending a douchebag to the next dimension is the highest form of public service."

"Good thing Swett couldn't shoot straight," I added.

"What do you mean, he put a hole through my cap!"

"He was shooting at me. You should have ducked."

"Not Marcus," Cody said, raising his mug. "He's got elephant balls."

Grier's wife came to pick him up around eight o'clock, after we'd annihilated a platter of chicken, ribs, cornbread, and home fries, all washed down with frequently refilled mugs of beer. When Grier staggered out of Zeke's, he smiled at his wife and patted his belly, as if he was at peace with the world. It was no doubt a temporary respite, but at least we'd gotten him past the initial shock that comes with being on the surviving end of a gun battle.

Next we headed to Whiskey Dick's, to swill whiskey and party with the local music crowd. The live entertainment was advertised as a blues band, but the group that took the stage was a punk rock act. The few middle-aged regulars at the bar fled once the music started, leaving the place to a hodge-podge of tattoo-covered skinheads with bones through their noses, longhairs who looked unwashed and ready to fight, and a group of ski bros wearing beanies and snow boots.

We decided the music wasn't good enough to risk hearing damage and left after two women got in a fight on the dance floor. I don't remember exactly how, but we ended up at the Midnight Tavern. A half-dozen women out for a girl's night were at a table near the bar. Cody spotted them as soon as we walked in, his face lit with alcoholic charisma and energy. They soon surrounded him as if he were the last man on earth and they were on a mission to repopulate the planet. Cody held court like a celebrity, hugging a woman in each arm, then grabbing a can of whipped cream from the bar and squirting it into their mouths.

It was a little before midnight when an Uber driver dropped us off at the Ho-Down on Highway 89. The dirt parking lot out front was lined with Harleys.

"I'd say a nightcap at the local knife and gun club is in order, Captain," Cody said, as we walked into the joint. South Lake Tahoe's ramshackle biker bar was packed. A Metallica song blared from the jukebox and the wooden floor planks rumbled underfoot. We ignored a few suspicious looks and made our way to the bar. The bartender and owner was a man who could have been mistaken for country-western singer Willie Nelson.

"A couple whiskey Cokes, Jed," I yelled over the music.

"You ain't lookin' for trouble, right, Reno?"

"No trouble, Jed. Just celebrating."

"What's the occasion?"

"The South Lake Tahoe district attorney got blown away," Cody said.

"The district attorney? Say what?"

"He got killed," I said.

"You shot him dead?"

"No," I said, but I saw Cody nodding yes, a drunken grin on his face.

"You ole son of a bitch!" Jed said, then he turned around and started ringing the hell out of a bell on the back bar. "Hey, all you soulless mother-fuckers," he shouted. "My man Reno here shot dead the local D.A.!"

Only a few people close to the bar heard him, and they barraged me with backslaps and fist pumps, and then someone turned down the jukebox

255

and the word quickly spread. My efforts to correct the story were futile, and in a second I was surrounded by bikers offering to shake my hand or buy me a drink. From out of nowhere a blonde lady lifted her tube top and flashed her breasts at me. "You're a fuckin' rock star," Cody shouted in my ear, as a simian biker in full colors grabbed my wrist and raised my arm as if I'd won a boxing match. The jukebox came on again, playing Lynyrd Skynyrd's *Sweet Home Alabama* at full volume. Inexplicably, a conga line formed, and I was forced into the line behind the woman, who swung her ass provocatively. We became a circle of revelers, dancing and hooting, jubilant in the drunken belief that true justice had been served. Eventually everyone in the joint joined the line, even Jed the bartender. "What a life!" Cody exclaimed, his hands heavy on my shoulders.

16

I woke late the next morning, my head heavy and numb. I brushed my teeth, guzzled water, and shuffled out to the kitchen. Candi was sitting at the table. It was ten A.M.

"You look like you could use some black coffee," she said. Smokey sat on her lap and meowed his agreement. I poured myself a cup and sat across from her, knowing I'd be useless for a few hours. A shaft of sunlight beaming in from the big window fell over me, and I closed my eyes. I was still a little drunk, my thoughts slow and blissfully muted. Then my phone rang, the loud chime interrupting my daze.

"Hello?" I croaked.

"Is this Dan Reno?"

"Yeah."

"This is Marilyn Bertrand from El Dorado County Superior Court. I'm calling to tell you the charges against you have been dropped. There is no further action required on your part."

"Have you contacted my attorney?"

"I'll call him next."

"Thanks," I said. I set my phone down and looked at Candi. "That's it," I said. "I'm a free man."

"No apologies or anything from anyone?"

"That's not the way it works."

"Maybe you should sue them."

I sipped from my cup. "That's something to think about," I said. "It's Friday, right?"

"Yes. There's no class today."

"How about I take you to lunch at that restaurant over in Camp Richardson?"

"The one with the deck on the lake?"

"Yeah."

"Let's go take a shower together first."

"Okay, babe."

· · ·

Six weeks passed, and I worked two small cases. The first involved a craps dealer in Reno who was in league with a pair of scam artists who had fleeced Harvey's for $200,000. The dealer vanished, but was arrested in Los Angeles two days after I was hired. The second case only took a day to resolve. I was called by a newly divorced businessman who wanted to track down a woman he'd had a fling with years before. He couldn't find her because she'd married and moved out of state. Once I discovered her new name, I found her Facebook profile and shared it with my client.

"For Christ's sake, she looks like she's gained fifty pounds!" he exclaimed. "What a waste of time."

Spring turned to summer, and I stopped calling attorneys to look for investigation gigs.

Instead, I took a night shift tending bar at Zeke's. The tourist traffic had picked up, and the bar was busy. I fell into a five-to-midnight routine, pouring drinks, cleaning glasses, wiping down the bar, mopping the floor at closing. It wasn't a career move, but at least it was a regular paycheck.

It was early June when Cody called.

"Hey, man," he said. I heard car horns blaring in the background.

"Where are you?" I asked.

"Stuck in traffic in Sacramento."

"Where you headed?"

"To Zeke's for dinner. How's the latest batch of brisket?"

"As good as ever."

"Can you meet me at six?"

"You're driving up here just for the food?"

"No, I've got an update you'll be interested in."

"Like what?"

"Keep your pants on. I'll tell you when I get there."

. . .

I was waiting outside the restaurant when Cody bounced into the lot, his diesel truck billowing a plume of road dust. He hopped to the ground and met me at the steps. He was wearing jeans and a western-cut plaid shirt with snaps on the pockets. His beard had returned, or at least a trimmer version of it.

You're not gonna believe this," he said. "Let's go sit down."

We went inside to the half full barroom, where a group of folks were seated at my favorite spot on the raised platform facing the front window. "Over here," I said. Cody followed me to a small table tucked in the corner between the stove and the end of the bar.

"So, you remember the grief I was going through with the Lopez brothers, right?" Cody said. He was sitting under the television, deep in shadow. I nodded and leaned close so he could keep his voice down.

"A couple weeks ago, Fatty showed up at my house, and he starts spouting off about how he's connected with the Mexican Mafia. He says, I'm either his friend or his enemy, take a pick. Meaning, if I pick the wrong answer, it has implications." Cody paused when Liz set a pitcher and two mugs on the table. He poured himself a mug and took a long swig.

"It so happens that a week earlier, I was following up on a Nevada state online auction. And guess what I see available for sale?"

"I don't know," I said automatically, then my head jerked. "The Ford minibus?"

"Very good, doctor. You ever buy anything from a government auction?"

"No."

"You might want to look into it. There's some good money-making opportunities out there. Anyway, the bidding started at three grand. Some hick is bidding against me, probably a high-desert dirt farmer, so I ended up buying it for forty-five hundred."

I stared slack-jawed at Cody. "Where is it?"

"I drove it home last Monday. Then I put it on jack stands in my garage and commenced to wrenching. And guess what? That shitbag Trinidad was telling the truth."

"What did you find?"

"A hundred keys of high-grade Colombian flake. It was everywhere. Sewn into the seats, in an auxiliary gas tank, in the rocker panels. The bags were all custom-fitted for the vehicle. I even pulled a few kilos out of the headliner."

I gripped my empty mug and rocked it on the table. "What the hell did you do with it?"

"Back to Fatty Lopez. When he originally gave me his little ultimatum, I told him I'm not going to threaten his brother's victim, a poor woman he raped, so go pound salt. But I met him a few days ago with a counterproposal. I offered to buy him off with a special deal. I mean, a deal so good that Fatty can truly become a big man on campus. I offered to sell him twenty keys at five grand a pop. That's half the best wholesale price a big-time dealer can pay in California. And Fatty knows it, so his eyes light up like a Christmas tree."

"Where is Fatty Lopez going to get a hundred grand?"

"He said he was connected with *La Eme*. He wasn't lying."

"So you sold him the coke?"

"Yeah, we met in an old parking structure in San Jose, just him and me. I'd staked it out to make sure we were alone, and there were no security cameras. He hands over a hundred large and I give him a duffel bag with twenty kilos. Then we go our separate ways." Cody smiled and filled my mug.

I looked at him warily. "So that's it?"

"Well, not exactly. See, Fatty ran into a bit of bad luck, because he was pulled over before he made it to the freeway. And then he resisted arrest and tried to run over a patrolman. The police weren't too happy with that."

"You dropped the dime on him?"

"Somebody had to do it," Cody said, his eyes twinkling. "Anyway, Fatty has now joined his twin brother, and they'll live happily ever after in the state pen."

"Assuming the Mexican Mafia doesn't kill him. They financed the deal, right?"

"Yeah, and of course Fatty told them I was the source. So they reached out to me with a few serious questions. We reached a settlement."

"What kind of settlement?"

"The kind that eighty keys can buy."

"You gave it all to them?"

"You think I'm running a charity? We cut a deal."

I blew out my breath. "That's a lot of blow on the streets."

"Really? Hell, this month alone the Feds intercepted over eighteen thousand kilos in Philly and Baltimore. A hundred keys is chicken shit."

"If you say so."

"I do, and I also have something else to say. Here." He took a large envelope from his pocket and handed it to me.

"What's this?"

"For your bail and attorney's fees. And expenses for Miami. And a little extra to put away."

"I don't know if I can take this, Cody."

"Bullshit. You earned it. And besides, this money's not dirty. It's attached to drugs that ended up in police custody."

"That's one way of looking at it."

"It's the right way to look at it."

I sat silently, the envelope sitting in my palm like an iron weight.

"Hey," Cody said. "Before you get too deep into your ethical contemplations, let me remind you, there's a fair chance that these twenty keys, currently sitting in an evidence locker, will magically find their way onto the street. And some asshole cop will slither away with enough money to live the high life for a couple of years. You know exactly what I'm talking about."

"So I'm supposed to measure myself against corrupt cops?"

"Dirt, this money falls in the gray area. If you don't give yourself the benefit of the doubt, no one else will, believe me."

I sipped from my beer, then I tilted the mug back and finished it. I didn't want to admit it, but Cody was right. He was the ultimate pragmatist. He knew our justice system was created and run by people, which meant it was vastly imperfect. He knew that even the best of cops, prosecutors, and judges have biases and personal grudges. And as for the worst, many are corrupt or just plain evil.

Cody's vision of the world may have been jaded and cynical, but I couldn't argue with his logic. The difference between us was I still clung to the idea that there was a higher moral ground to be had. And sometimes I was right, but not in this case. Not unless I chose to believe I could claim moral superiority by declining the spoils of a war I'd been unjustly forced to fight.

"Well," I said, jamming the thick envelope into my jeans pocket, "I struggle with my philosophy sometimes."

"Glad I could help straighten you out," Cody said, filling my mug.

"Thanks for everything, old buddy."

"Yeah, you owe me as usual."

A moment later Liz set plates of brisket, barbeque beans, baked potatoes, and green salads on our table.

"Tell you what, I'll buy dinner," I said.

"And drinks?" Cody asked.

"You got it."

"Excellent! I consider us even."

. . .

I took Candi to the Canadian Rockies for vacation that July. We stayed in a hotel in Banff that was a United Nations World Heritage Site and looked like a European castle. The weather was clear, the mountain peaks etched sharply against the cloudless skies. We explored the quaint town in the valley and then hiked into the back country to gaze at majestic waterfalls, lakes, and granite cliffs. The events surrounding the case of Manuel Alvarez seemed like they happened in a different lifetime.

On the day before we were to return to Lake Tahoe, I was in our hotel room when my phone rang with a 305 number. It was Nate Esparza from the Miami Herald. I waited for a number of rings before finally answering.

"I was hoping to hear from you," he said. "How'd everything work out?"

I lowered myself into a chair. "The charges against me were dropped. It's all good."

"Why were the charges dropped?"

"My lawyer got me off. It had nothing to do with anything that happened in Miami."

"Really? Well, maybe you can help me fill in some blanks."

"Like what?"

"To start, Vasquez has become very interested in Luis Escobar. She's convinced the picture you have is him, and she believes he is really the son of Pablo Escobar."

"I think she's right."

"Why?"

"Because I went to Santo Domingo and got his police report. He's got a long record in the Dominican. It includes his fingerprints and DNA profile."

"You have his police report?"

"That's what I said. I'll send it to you if you like. I have no more use for it."

"That'd be fantastic," he said. "How did you get it?"

"Don't ask."

"All right, I won't, but there's something else you should know. The cartel activity has been heating up here in the last few weeks. It all started when two of Ivan Sanhueza's bodyguards were found floating in a swamp, shot dead. Apparently a rival gang smelled blood, because just yesterday Sanhueza and his partner, Celso Santos, were gunned down in a Bal Harbour mansion. It was a real old-school Miami gangland style execution, bullets flying, the place shot to shit. It was done by a team of hitters."

"That's a shame."

"You have any further perspective? I know you were involved with Sanhueza."

"Involved? He was a person of interest in my investigation, nothing more."

"Was there a link between Escobar and Sanhueza?"

"Escobar was a thug for hire. My understanding is he had worked for Sanhueza recently. Other than that, I don't know."

"Come on, help me out here. This is a big story."

"That's all I got, Nate. I'll Fed Ex you Escobar's file. You just make damn sure to leave my name out of it."

"You got it. Please send it ASAP. Vasquez has already started writing."

•   •   •

The summers are a busy time in South Lake Tahoe. Tourists stream into town on the weekends, partying, littering, making noise, and creating gridlock on Highway 50. The locals complain like crazy, but most rely on tourism for their income. I had become part of that crowd, because I was still working full time at Zeke's. My investigative work had slowed to a sporadic trickle, and now my biggest headaches were dealing with families with unruly kids, or young dudes that ran out on their bar bill, or husbands who couldn't hold their liquor. And I was okay with that, because my safe deposit box was flush, and I was certain Candi would be pregnant again soon.

And that's how things played out for me in the summer of 2019. I didn't know if those quiet months would prove to be a brief interlude in my life, or something more permanent. All I know is that when I wake in the morning, I never forget to remind myself how lucky I am. I remind myself when I hike across grassy knolls and rest in the shade of the huge granite slabs scattered below the waterfalls that feed Lake Tahoe. I remind myself in peaceful moments at home with Candi, where our casual familiarity is at the surface of a deep, spiritual bond rooted in common childhood experience. And I remind myself how fortunate I am when I walk through my house, paid for by money I risked my life to earn, and then transformed into our home when Candi moved in.

I remind myself often, because I know that when my phone rings again with work, I won't decline. A more idealistic person might claim they cannot resist their higher calling. But not me; I just need to make a living.

ABOUT THE AUTHOR

Born in Detroit, Michigan, in 1960, Dave Stanton moved to Northern California in 1961. He attended San Jose State University and received a BA in journalism in 1983. Over the years, he worked as a bartender, newspaper advertising salesman, furniture mover, debt collector, and technology salesman. He has two children, Austin and Haley. He and his wife, Heidi, live in San Jose, California.

Stanton is the author of seven novels, all featuring private investigator Dan Reno and his ex-cop buddy, Cody Gibbons.

To learn more, visit the author's website at:

http://danrenonovels.com/

If you enjoyed right cross, please don't hesitate to leave a review at:

Amazon US: http://bit.ly/RightCrossreview

To contact Dave Stanton or subscribe to his newsletter, go to:

http://danrenonovels.com/contact/

More Dan Reno Novels:

STATELINE

Cancel the wedding–the groom is dead.

When a tycoon's son is murdered the night before his wedding, the enraged and grief-stricken father offers investigator Dan Reno (that's *Reno,* as in *no problemo)*, a life-changing bounty to find the killer. Reno, nearly broke, figures he's finally landed in the right place at the right time. It's a nice thought, but when a band of crooked cops get involved, Reno finds himself not only earning every penny of his paycheck, but also fighting for his life.

Who committed the murder, and why? And what of the dark sexual deviations that keep surfacing? Haunted by his murdered father and a violent, hard drinking past, Reno wants no more blood on his hands. But a man's got to make a living, and backing off is not in his DNA. Traversing the snowy alpine winter in the Sierras and the lonely deserts of Nevada, Reno must revert to his old ways to survive. Because the fat bounty won't do him much good if he's dead…

Available on Amazon.com US: http://bit.ly/Stateline-Amazon

DYING FOR THE HIGHLIFE

Jimmy Homestead's glory days as a high school stud were a distant memory. His adulthood had amounted to little more than temporary jobs, petty crime, and discount whiskey. But he always felt he was special, and winning the Lotto proved it.

Flush with millions, everything is great for Jimmy—until people from his past start coming out of the woodwork, seeking payback over transgressions Jimmy thought were long forgotten.

Caught in the middle are private detective Dan Reno and his good buddy Cody Gibbons, two guys just trying to make an honest paycheck. Reno, fighting to save his home from foreclosure, thinks that's his biggest problem. But his priorities change when he's drawn into a hard-boiled mess that leaves dead bodies scattered all over northern Nevada.

Available on Amazon.com US: http://bit.ly/TheHighlife

SPEED METAL BLUES

Bounty hunter Dan Reno never thought he'd be the prey.

It's a two-for-one deal when a pair of accused rapists from a New Jersey-based gang surface in South Lake Tahoe. The first is easy to catch, but the second, a Satanist suspected of a string of murders, is an adversary unlike any Reno has faced. After escaping Reno's clutches in the desert outside of Carson City, the target vanishes. That is, until he makes it clear he intends to settle the score.

To make matters worse, the criminal takes an interest in a teenage boy and his talented sister, both friends of Reno's. Wading through a drug-dealing turf war and a deadly feud between mobsters running a local casino, Reno can't figure out how his target fits in with the new outlaws in town. He only knows he's hunting for a ghost-like adversary calling all the shots.

The more Reno learns about his target, the more he's convinced that mayhem is inevitable unless he can capture him quickly. He'd prefer to do it clean, without further bloodshed. But sometimes that ain't in the cards, especially when Reno's partner Cody Gibbons decides it's time for payback.

Available on Amazon.com US: http://bit.ly/SpeedMetalBlues

DARK ICE

Two murdered girls, and no motive…

While skiing deep in Lake Tahoe's backcountry, Private Eye Dan Reno finds the first naked body, buried under fresh snow. Reno's contacted by the grieving father, who wants to know who murdered his daughter, and why? And how could the body end up in such a remote, mountainous location? The questions become murkier when a second body is found. Is there a serial killer stalking promiscuous young women in South Lake Tahoe? Or are the murders linked to a different criminal agenda?

Searching for answers, Reno is accosted by a gang of racist bikers with a score to settle. He also must deal with his pal, Cody Gibbons, who the police consider a suspect. The clues lead to the owner of a strip club and a womanizing police captain, but is either the killer?

The bikers up the ante, but are unaware that Cody Gibbons has Reno's back at any cost. Meanwhile, the police won't tolerate Reno's continued involvement in the case. But Reno knows he's getting close. And the most critical clue comes from the last person he'd suspect…

Available on Amazon.com US: http://bit.ly/DarkIce

HARD PREJUDICE

The DNA evidence should have made the rape a slam dunk case.

But after the evidence disappeared from a police locker, the black man accused of brutally raping a popular actor's daughter walked free. Hired by the actor, private detective Dan Reno's job seemed simple enough: discover who took the DNA, and why. Problem is, from the beginning of the investigation, neither Reno, the South Lake Tahoe police, nor anyone else have any idea what the motivation could be to see ghetto thug Duante Tucker get away with the crime. Not even Reno's best friend, fellow investigator Cody Gibbons, has a clue.

When Reno and Gibbons tail Tucker, they learn the rapist is linked to various criminals and even a deserter from the U.S. Marine Corps. But they still can't tell who would want him set free, and for what reason?

The clues continue to build until Reno and Cody find themselves targeted for death. That tells Reno he's getting close, so he and Gibbons put the pedal to the metal. The forces of evil are running out of time, and the action reaches a boiling point before an explosive conclusion that reveals a sinister plot and motivations that Reno never imagined.

Available on Amazon.com US: http://bit.ly/hardprejudice

THE DOOMSDAY GIRL

Melanie Jordan's life seemed perfect.

Until masked intruders arrive at her house, demanding gold she doesn't have. A savage blow to the head puts her in a coma for four weeks.

When Melanie regains consciousness, she learns her husband has been murdered and her ten-year-old daughter is missing.

Private Eye Dan Reno begins investigating, but nothing about the case makes sense. Was there gold at the house or wasn't there? Was Melanie's husband hiding something? And what happened to Melanie's daughter?

To complicate things, the case leads to Las Vegas, where Reno's loose-cannon buddy, Cody Gibbons, is trying to repair his relationship with his college-aged daughter, an intern with Las Vegas P.D.

When clues implicate Russian mobsters and a mysterious African illegal, Reno tries to stay in the shadows, but once the crooks feel the noose tightening, they raise the stakes to a deadly level.

And then, as they say in Vegas, all bets are off.

Available on Amazon.com US: http://bit.ly/TheDoomsdayGirl

Made in the USA
Las Vegas, NV
20 November 2020